Death Makes the Cut

Also by Janice Hamrick

Death on Tour

Death Makes the Cut

JANICE
HAMRICK

Minotaur Books New York

This is a work of fiction. All of the characters, organizations, and events portrayed in this novel are either products of the author's imagination or are used fictitiously.

 For information, address St. Martin's Press, 175 Fifth Avenue, New York, N.Y. 10010.

Design by Omar Chapa

www.minotaurbooks.com

Library of Congress Cataloging-in-Publication Data

Hamrick, Janice.
Death makes the cut / Janice Hamrick. — 1st ed.
p. cm.
ISBN 978-1-250-00554-0 (hardcover)
ISBN 978-1-4668-0031-1 (e-book)
1. Women teachers—Fiction. 2. Murder—Investigation—Fiction.
I. Title.
PS3608.A69655D27 2012
813'.6—dc23
2012005487

First Edition: July 2012

10 9 8 7 6 5 4 3 2 1

To my parents
James and Joyrene Pope
and to my daughters
Jennifer and Jacqueline Hamrick
with all my love

Acknowledgments

I am deeply indebted to the many people who made this book possible. My heartfelt thanks go to my editor, Matt Martz, not only for his precision editing, but also for his guidance, encouragement, and enthusiasm, to my agent, David Hale Smith, for his ongoing support and advice, to Anna Chang for her amazing copyediting skills, and to artist Ben Perini and designer David Baldeosingh Rotstein for another brilliant cover that made me laugh out loud. I am more grateful than I can express to author Stefanie Pintoff for her generous and much-needed words of wisdom. I would like to thank the many others who have made my first year in the business so much fun: Sarah Ann Robertson, Scott Montgomery, John Kwiatkowski, Anne Kimbol, Barbara Peters, Frank Campbell, Hopeton Hay, and Kaye George. I am also grateful to my friends at Get Up 'n Go Toastmasters who taught me to breathe and who make me look forward to Monday mornings. And finally, my thanks go to Cindy Marszal for reading my first drafts and introducing me to the 'burgh (FTC).

Death Makes the Cut

Chapter 1

FIGHTS AND FINES

The shouting started just after lunch, angry and loud enough to make me spring down from the chair that I'd been standing on to hang posters and race for the door of my classroom. I burst into the hallway, then stopped confused. Farther down the corridor, a couple of teachers peered out of their rooms like meerkats on alert, ready to scatter at the first hint of danger. Otherwise, the hall was empty.

A furious male voice boomed through the air, echoing along gray concrete floors and walls, coming from everywhere and nowhere. In the open building, sounds carried from the first floor to the second and from one corridor to the next without hindrance. When two thousand kids were on the move, the sound of feet on stairs, the talking, giggling, shouting, and the clang of lockers became an indescribable din. On this day, the last day of summer vacation, the school was all but deserted, and, until a moment ago, the halls had been silent.

White-knuckled, I grasped the railing of the stairwell and leaned out ever so slightly, trying to see movement on the first floor far below without really looking. I loathed heights. Even behind a firm rail, the drop made me feel a little queasy. A second shout made me turn. This time I had it. The argument was coming from the classroom directly across the hall. Fred Argus's room. Dashing around the intervening stairwell, I threw open the door with a bang.

Two men turned startled faces in my direction. Fred Argus, my fellow history teacher, stood behind his desk as though poised to flee, open hands raised to his adversary as though in supplication. The other guy was a stranger, a big man with the thick neck of a fighter, black-eyed and red-faced. He turned a malevolent gaze on me, and I felt an unexpected stab of fear. An aura of rage, barely contained and menacing, flowed from him. Alarmed, I stood a little straighter.

"What's going on, Fred?" I asked, trying to keep my tone light but not taking my eyes off the newcomer.

"Nothing that concerns you," the stranger answered for him. His was the voice that had been doing the shouting, a deep bullhorn of a voice, the kind that could carry across a crowded room or shout down a mob.

I ignored him. "Fred?"

Fred gave me a look of mingled fear and hope, like a beaten dog receiving a pat from his master. He didn't quite come out from behind the shelter of his desk, but he did straighten a little from his crouching position.

"Mr. Richards has concerns about the tennis team," he said, shooting a nervous look at the stranger.

"The tennis team?" I repeated blankly.

Of course I knew that Fred was the tennis coach, something I'd always found a little ironic, considering he was on the wrong side of sixty and smoked at least two packs of cigarettes a day. The sight of the white toothpicks that he called legs flashing from beneath a pair of spandex shorts had been known to cause convulsions in even the strongest of women. I also knew that our tennis team, although possibly the worst in the league, was one of the few high school teams which every kid, regardless of experience, was welcome to join. What I didn't know was why anyone would need to raise his eyebrows, much less his voice, for anything remotely related to the Bonham Breakpoints.

Mr. Richards took a step toward me, and again I felt a small flash of fear, so out of place in a bright classroom on an August afternoon. I knew from Fred's return to full flight-or-fight stance that he felt it too—this man was very close to violence.

"Is your child thinking of joining the team, Mr. Richards?" I asked quickly, trying to keep him talking so that he would focus on something, anything other than his anger. He reminded me of a bull at a rodeo. He'd thrown his cowboy and was now waiting for the clown to get a little closer.

His eyes narrowed, and he shot a glance at Fred that could have stripped paint from a wall.

"My son IS the team. The only real player you've got. And this old son of a . . ."

I cut him off. "Did you know Coach Fred started the tennis program here at Bonham, Mr. Richards?"

This distracted him for an instant. He looked at me like I was crazy. I went on in the most cheerful voice I could manage.

"Yes indeed, Coach Fred is the reason we have a tennis team at all. He was the one who lobbied to get the courts built. And he did all the paperwork and lobbying to get us into the league. We wouldn't have tennis at this school if it weren't for him."

I could have gone on like this forever. I was watching Mr. Richards's face, hoping to see the redness vanish or at least fade, but he drew in a deep breath in preparation for another tirade. Where in the world were those other teachers?

"Get out!" he shouted in a voice that practically blew my hair back from my face. He took another step toward me, and I felt a chill run down my spine.

"No." I stood my ground, holding his gaze with one of my own. My best teacher look, in fact, complete with the all-powerful lifted eyebrow. It was a look that could quell thirty teenage boys, and now it made this arrogant bully pause. I seized the moment.

"It's time for you to leave, Mr. Richards. If you have anything further you'd like to discuss about the tennis team or any other subject, I'd suggest you make an appointment with Mr. Gonzales, our principal, who will be happy to address your concerns."

For a moment none of us moved. In the silence a clock somewhere in the room ticked out the seconds. Mr. Richards hesitated another instant, then erupted with a bellow, kicking a desk out of his path. It toppled over with a crash. I jumped but held my ground.

Glaring at me, he halted inches from my face, at the last instant deciding not to strike me. He tried to stare me down. I stared back, partly in defiance, mostly just frozen with shock. Either way, it finally worked. He backed down.

"I'll do that. This isn't the end of this conversation," he said to Fred. "You fucking bitch," he added to me as he stomped by.

"Mr. Richards," I said, my voice quiet.

He half turned.

"Don't come back. If I see you in this hall again, I'll call the police first and ask questions later."

He didn't bother to reply. Cautiously, I followed him out the door, watching to make sure he actually went down the steps and out the double doors to the quadrangle. He did. I heard the crash the double doors made as he slammed through them, sending them banging in unison against their doorstops. He was halfway across the courtyard before the springs drew the doors shut again with a muffled clang. Silence returned to the hall. Not one teacher bothered to look out again, the cowards. I drew a deep, shaky breath, then returned to the classroom.

Fred had collapsed into the chair behind his desk, looking curiously shrunken and defeated. He stroked the smooth wood of his little desk clock with fingers that trembled as though with cold. The clock had been a parting gift from his coworkers when he'd left his original career to become a teacher some twenty years earlier. I wondered if he was feeling sorry he'd made the job switch. Noticing my glance, he set the clock back in its usual place on the corner of his desk, then let his hands drop into his lap.

"You know, I thought he was going to hit me," he said in a wondering tone.

I pulled up a chair and sank into it, taking the clock into my own hands, admiring it. It was a pretty little thing made of polished mahogany, about the size of my two fists held together, standing upright like a miniature grandfather clock. Along the bottom was a small drawer complete with lock and tiny key, and on the back an engraved plaque.

Now that the argument was over, I could feel a reaction of my own setting in. My fingers trembled enough that I decided to put the clock down.

"So what did he want anyway?" I asked.

Fred answered slowly, as though puzzled. "I'm not even sure. Something about wanting his boy, Eric, to be team captain. Which is ridiculous because I don't have anything to do with that. The kids vote for team captain. I don't think Eric even signed up to be in the running."

"What does the team captain do?" I asked.

I didn't care, but I didn't want to leave him just yet. I didn't like the gray hue of his face or the way he slumped in his chair—it made me wonder about the condition of his heart for the first time. For years he had been the head of our team of history teachers, a vibrant, passionate man, completely dedicated to his students and to the school. He and I argued occasionally over things like lesson plans, but I usually deferred to him in the end. I liked to tell him it was because I figured he'd been an eyewitness to most of the things we taught. But until now, I'd never thought of him as being old.

He didn't answer for a long moment. Then finally he looked up as though confused. "I'm sorry. What did you ask?"

I repeated the question.

"Ah, that. It's nothing much. The captain is responsible for little things like maintaining the calling chain and acting as my assistant for the away games. It's mostly just an indication of the other players' respect. I suppose it might look good on a résumé," he added as an afterthought.

I frowned. "Then I don't see what he wanted. If he tries to bully you again, Fred, you need to call someone. Preferably the police."

"Oh, I don't think that will be necessary," he said, not quite meeting my eyes. "A one-time occurrence, tempers getting a bit out of hand. Nothing to worry about."

"Nothing to worry about? Fred, that guy was two seconds from hauling off and hitting you. What exactly is going on?"

"Nothing. No, it's nothing." He rose abruptly, glancing one last time around his classroom, taking in the rows of desks, the whiteboards, the newly hung maps and posters on the walls. Everything appeared neat, clean, and ready for the first day of class tomorrow. Even the air held the scent of lemon polish and new books, the smell of a new school year, sweet with promise. "I'm going home. Nothing left to do that can't be done tomorrow."

Always a gentleman, he held the door open for me, leaving me no choice but to precede him into the hall. He pulled the door shut behind us, locking it and then nervously scanning the hall, then the stairwell.

"Fred—" I started, but he cut me off.

"I'll see you tomorrow, Jocelyn." He walked to the stairs, then turned. "Thank you for . . . well, just thank you." Then he hurried away, pattering lightly down the stairs. Maybe he wasn't getting old after all.

I watched him go, feeling dissatisfied.

There should be a special place in purgatory for whoever had designed James Bonham High School. In the main academic building, the upper-floor corridors were lined with painted metal railings and provided a perfect view of the floor below, which in a high school was just an open invitation to spit. The architecture reminds first-time visitors of something they can't quite place—I was there a whole year before I figured it out, and then only did because I'd just seen *The Shawshank Redemption*. Contracts to build schools go to the lowest bidder, and in this case the winning bidder's most recent project had been the state correctional facility. And it showed in every loving detail, from the concrete floors to the cinder-block walls to the unheated and un–air-conditioned hallways. You could practically hear the clang of the bars and the shouts of the guards.

I suppose to the casual visitor, it might not seem so bad. The campus was spacious, liberally sprinkled with trees and consisting of four main buildings that enclosed a central concrete courtyard. Closer observation revealed that these main buildings were surrounded by what we less than fondly referred to as portables, which were basically double-wide mobile homes, each stripped of appliances and other niceties and divided in half to make two uncomfortable classrooms, poorly heated in the winter, poorly air-conditioned in the summer. Of course, this wasn't much worse than in the permanent structures. Only the administrative building had central air-conditioning. The rest had individual heating and cooling units in the classrooms only, leaving the hallways to the mercy of the Texas weather. In fall and spring, the heat was stifling. In winter, the cold and damp turned fingers blue and cheeks red.

Now, I fought back the feeling of vertigo that I get from heights and leaned over the rail for a moment to watch Fred's little white head disappear through the same doors that Mr. Richards had barged through just minutes ago. I was just straightening when a number of strangers walked in, led by the principal, Larry Gonzales. I leaned out again with interest.

Larry was doing his Lord of the Manor walk, which meant these were visitors of particular importance. All the teachers could tell the exact status of a visitor by Larry's walk, and my friend Laura and I had set up a rating system. The all-purpose Brush-off was used for students and teachers alike—long quick steps, eyes focused on a sheaf of papers or a cell phone, a pretense of deafness. The Brush-off got him through the halls with minimal interruption and maximum efficiency.

The PTA or "Tight-ass" walk was for parents—short quick steps, arms stiff against his sides, stern gaze focused on a vague point on the horizon. This walk conveyed a sense of mission and importance, although the shortness of the steps allowed a determined parent to keep up without breaking into a trot. The Concerned Administrator was reserved for groups of parents or teachers with actual grievances who needed to be "handled" to avoid unpleasantness, which meant anything from bitter letters to the editor to full-blown lawsuits. It was hardly a walk at all and involved slow, measured steps, a lot of head nodding, and the occasional sensitive touch on the shoulder or forearm, which let you know what a great and concerned guy Larry was. And finally, there was the Lord of the Manor—head thrown back, arms gesturing expansively, voice booming—the walk Larry reserved for visitors who needed to be impressed, which meant visitors who could do something for Larry.

I wondered who they were and what Larry wanted from them. Unlike the usual Lord of the Manor candidates, these three weren't terribly impressive at first glance. A skinny blond guy with a ponytail was holding some sort of electronic device at arm's length and swinging it this way and that. He walked beside an earnest-looking young woman with serious black-framed glasses that she apparently did not need because she kept pushing them down to the tip of her nose and looking over the top of the frame. And finally, a slightly older man in jeans trailed behind about ten paces, making notes on a legal pad. As they moved directly beneath me, I could hear the woman saying, "Yes, this will be absolutely perfect. Just fantastic."

Then they turned a corner, and I decided to go back to my room instead of following them, feeling sure I'd hear about it sometime soon. Anything that rated a Lord of the Manor walk was bound to make its presence known and probably bite the rest of us in the ass.

I picked up the chair, which I'd knocked over when I raced out, and returned to the poster I'd been hanging. I'd saved this one until last, putting it in the corner where it could be seen by all my students. It was a picture of lemmings jumping off a cliff with the words, "Those who cannot remember the past are condemned to repeat it."

Stepping off the chair, I looked around with satisfaction, feeling my room looked almost as nice as Fred's. Of course, mine didn't smell of lemon polish because it would never have occurred to me to dust with more than a damp paper towel, but still everything looked pretty good. Tomorrow was the first day of the new school year, August 24. A little later this year than in past years, but still the height of summer. Long days, cloudless skies, sizzling heat. There wasn't a kid on the planet who wouldn't have rather been at the pool, but at least I was ready for them.

I returned to my desk and started looking over the lists of student names again. This year, my day was made up of four history classes, two French classes, one planning period, and one lunch period. Which meant I had about 180 students. Going through the lists in advance made it easier remembering who was who when I finally met them all. I prided myself on my ability to know every kid's name by the end of the first week. I was just going through the list a second time when the door to my classroom opened, and my best friend Kyla Shore walked in.

Although most people assume we are sisters, Kyla and I are first cousins. Our fathers are identical twins and we look enough alike to be twins ourselves. Maybe not identical twins, but we'd been mistaken for each other before, a fact that drove Kyla absolutely crazy. She would never admit there was anything more than a remote family resemblance. For my part I would have been happy if we looked even more alike, or rather if I looked more like her. Because, although I wouldn't break mirrors, Kyla was drop-dead gorgeous—the kind of beauty that made men stop in the middle of the street to pick their jaws up off the ground. She was no fool either, and was fully aware of the effect she had on men. In fact, she shamelessly used it to her full advantage, telling me once that she hadn't bought a drink for herself in five years. It might have made her obnoxious, but she was also completely charming. And to be fair, it didn't seem to mean much to her other than as an entertaining diversion. She'd graduated with honors in computer programming and now worked as a lead developer for a software company, raking in money and bonuses.

Today she looked glum. And beautiful, of course. And stylish and elegant. August in Austin, Texas, meant the temperature outside was at least ninety-five degrees. It meant that touching a steering wheel could leave grill marks on your palms.

It meant that the thirty seconds it took to dash from an air-conditioned building to an air-conditioned car could leave your shirt clinging to your back like a professional wrestler's. However, in her white and yellow sundress, Kyla looked as cool and together as an ice sculpture. Even her dark hair curled and bounced around her shoulders with a life of its own. My own hair was pulled back in a limp ponytail, and I looked sourly down at my denim capris and oversized T-shirt. We could have been the Before and After shots in a makeover commercial.

Now, she dropped her purse on my desk with a thud and flopped dramatically into a chair with a groan.

"That doesn't look like good news," I said. "How did it go?"

Kyla had recently had a little trouble with the law.

"Pretty good. I guess. I got community service," she added with a frown.

I whooped. "Hey, that's great! You couldn't have hoped for much better than that."

She looked at me sourly. "The best thing would have been for them to give me a fucking medal for protecting myself and the public in general."

"Well, yeah. But you pulled a concealed weapon on Sixth Street. They couldn't exactly let that go," I pointed out.

A look of outrage lit her sapphire eyes. "I don't see why not. Was I supposed to just let those assholes carjack me? I don't think so."

"No, of course not."

"If it wasn't for me, those little bastards would still be out there, taking someone else's car, maybe hurting someone." Her finger jabbed the air at every word.

Now she was glaring at me like it was my fault.

I held up my hands. "You know I'm one hundred percent on your side. It's just that carrying a gun down in that area is illegal. They had to do something. Think about it—community service is really just a slap on the wrist. It's a good thing."

"I don't see what the good is of having a concealed-carry license if you can't carry around bars. That's exactly where you need to have a gun," she grumbled.

"Yeah, maybe everyone should just walk around with holsters and six shooters on their hips."

I was being sarcastic, but she considered it. "Not a bad idea. An armed society is a polite society."

"Robert Heinlein," I responded, impressed she knew the quote.

She rolled her eyes. "Whatever. Anyway, you'll never guess what I have to do."

From her tone, it was pretty nasty. "Pick up trash on the highway? Clean urinals at the bus station?"

"Worse. I have to teach a six-week seminar about girls in technology. You know, encourage high school girls to go into the sciences."

I stared at her blankly. "You get arrested for carrying a concealed weapon, and the punishment is teaching children?"

My whole life, my whole career, reduced down to a community-service penalty.

Kyla was oblivious. "Yeah, does that suck or what? But here's the good part. I got them to let me do it here."

I choked a little. "Here?"

"Yup. Twice a week for six weeks. And you have to help me. I don't know what to say to the little monsters."

Which probably meant that she expected me to do it for her. I threw up my hands. "I have a full schedule. You know, my own classes."

"Yeah, yeah. It'll be right after school, so your classes won't interfere. We can go get dinner and drinks after," she said by way of bribery. "It'll be fun."

I sighed. "I'll help with the first one, but then you're on your own."

She decided not to argue, but I could see she was already thinking of ways she could get me to do the whole thing. She's devious that way.

The afternoon sun threw golden rectangles of light across the desks and floor, lighting up tiny motes that twinkled in the glow like fireflies. Outside, I could hear the roar of a mower accompanied by a dull thumping of rap music from the groundskeeper's radio. I consoled myself with the thought that the owner could look forward to an adulthood of early deafness and pounding headaches.

"So how's Alan doing?" Kyla asked, changing the subject. Conversations with her often bounced around with very little in the way of segues.

I winced a little as though at a sore tooth, then shrugged. "Okay, I suppose."

She looked at me. "That doesn't sound good."

Alan was my . . . well, boyfriend, I guess. I felt a little old to have a boyfriend, but there didn't seem to be a better term in the English language. What do you call someone whom you've been dating for a few months, but who lives in a different city and who never seems to be around?

I'd met him when Kyla and I had taken a tour of Egypt, a tour that had gone disastrously wrong and ended up with both Alan and me almost getting killed. That kind of experience usually draws people together, I suppose, but I had to admit I wasn't completely happy with the way things were going right now. For one thing, Alan had not yet moved to Austin, although he kept saying he was going to as soon as he could make the arrangements to move his travel company from Dallas. For another thing, because he was the owner of WorldPal Tours, he seemed to be on the road a lot. He was extraordinarily attractive, which made up for a lot, but on the other hand, I was still spending most of my evenings alone, with only a glass of wine and my fat elderly poodle for company.

I finally admitted, "I haven't seen him in three weeks, but we're going to Port Aransas for Labor Day."

"That sounds fun," she said with patently fake enthusiasm. "Wait, no it doesn't. Why Port A? You can do that any time. Why doesn't he take you somewhere awesome? He owns a tour company, for God's sakes. You guys could go anywhere in the world."

I gestured to the empty desks around us. "Not in three days. I have a job, remember? Besides, I want to pay my own way. I can afford Port Aransas."

"Pay your own way?" she said with outrage. "Why? Is he

that cheap? He sure isn't racking up any boyfriend points, is he?" She looked thoughtful, as though struck by a sudden idea. "Are you going to kick him to the curb?"

"What, are you waiting to snap him up?" The question wasn't quite as far-fetched as it sounded. She'd had her eye on him when we'd been in Egypt, although admittedly since I'd been dating him, she'd been strictly hands off.

Now she snorted. "Ew. I don't need your sloppy seconds, thanks very much. Especially not some cheap bastard. But there's this new guy in my office who's sort of cute, and I could introduce you. You might like him."

"Alan's not a cheap bastard, and no, I'm not kicking him to the curb," I said. But even I could hear the uncertainty in my voice.

Kyla ignored this. "It wouldn't hurt you to meet this guy. Just for drinks or something. It's not like you and Alan are exclusive."

I frowned. Of course we were exclusive . . . weren't we? Thinking about it, I supposed we'd never formally talked about it. No promises on either side, that sort of thing. Part of it was the distance. When you only got to see each other a weekend or two each month, things tended to move pretty slowly. It seemed like we spent half our time each visit getting reacquainted. Not that the reacquainting wasn't a lot of fun, but I was getting tired of the dry spells in between.

"No, I don't think so. Alan and I are doing okay. At least," I added, "I want to give us a chance to do okay."

She shrugged. "Think about it. Sherman's a nice guy. And smart. And funny."

"His name is Sherman?"

"He can't help that. Besides, he's a hottie. Or he would be if he had someone to tell him how to dress."

"Why don't you want him?" I asked suspiciously.

"I thought about it," she admitted. "But I have to work with him. It would be awkward, especially since I'd have to make him buy a new wardrobe and change his name. You know I could never go out with a guy named Sherman."

I decided to leave it at that. We spent the next hour going over what she could say in her first class. I made her take notes and reminded her that she'd have to do it on her own, but we both knew I'd be doing most of the real work. By the time we left, I'd already forgotten about Larry and his VIP guests. And about Coach Fred.

Austin is the best city in the world, I thought for about the millionth time as I drove home. On this August afternoon, the sun was gliding slowly down to meet the blue tops of the hills to the west and throwing a brassy golden light over the dusty live oaks and cedars that filled every undeveloped bit of land. Heat pulled color and shape into the air above the road, and made it shimmer and undulate like miniature underwater reefs. With the air conditioner blasting icy air in my face and my radio playing Brad Paisley's "Mud on the Tires," I didn't care. Like most Texans, I'd take a miserably hot July and August over a miserably icy January and February any day.

I'd been born in Texas, although I hadn't grown up there. Until his retirement, my father had been in the diplomatic corps, and my two brothers and I had spent much of our childhood in France, Italy, and Spain. Moreover, my mother was French, and as a result I was fluent in French and Italian, and had a fairly decent grasp of Spanish. We'd returned to Austin at the beginning of my high school years, and I'd been able to go to school with Kyla, which had been a bit of a mixed blessing. On the one hand, she'd resented me for looking so much like her and had stolen my very first boyfriend for no other reason than to prove she could. On the other hand, we'd somehow managed to become best friends anyway. We'd roomed together at the University of Texas, and even after we'd graduated and gone into separate careers, we still spent most of our spare time together.

The phone was ringing as I walked through the door, and my fat little poodle was barking and spinning in circles. A present from my parents for my sixteenth birthday, Belle was a small blob of black curls who weighed about ten pounds soaking wet and who had apparently been purchased without the optional brain pack. Knowing that no command of mine would stop the yapping, I grabbed the phone on my way to the back door and ushered her to the back door, where she galloped across the dry grass, intent on patrolling the perimeter, making the yard safe from squirrels. One of the evil ones liked to sit on the fence and chitter at her, a pastime that never got old for either of them.

"Hello?"

"Hi. I was just about to hang up." The deep voice was that of Alan Stratton. I loved that voice.

I smiled. "Just got back from school. How was your day?"

Actually, I could just as easily have asked, "How was your week?" He didn't call as often as I would like, but I didn't want to be one of those clingy women. I glanced through the door to my bedroom where my suitcase lay on the floor, already half-packed for our trip to the coast.

"Better, now that I'm talking to you," he said gallantly, "but not good overall. Vittoria has broken a leg, and she was supposed to start the "Tastes of Italy" tour on Saturday. She'll be out of commission for at least six weeks, and I have no backup. It means I'll have to go to Rome myself."

"That's terrible," I said, trying to feel sympathetic for someone forced to go to Italy. Then I did a mental double take. "Wait, you mean *this* Saturday?" The Saturday that he and I were supposed to go to Port Aransas for a beach weekend? I held my breath.

"I'm afraid so. I'm really sorry." His voice was sincere and full of regret, but it didn't help much.

I thought about banging my head against the wall. "Me, too. I suppose you couldn't postpone the tour?"

"No, all my clients have booked their tickets, either through WorldPal or on their own. Nonrefundable, nonchangeable. I suppose you couldn't get away and come with me?" he asked. "I could really use someone who could speak Italian. All expenses paid, salary thrown in," he added persuasively.

So tempting, but so impossible. It would mean not only losing my job but never working in Austin as a teacher again. And I liked my job. Bitter disappointment made me speechless.

He must have thought I was considering it because he

added, "You know, you could work for me permanently. It would be so great to have you based here in Dallas."

"You know I can't. I have a job. With a contract. I can't just give two weeks' notice and scamper off, even if I wanted to. And anyway, I thought you were in the process of moving down here," I reminded him.

Silence on his end. My stomach sank to my toes, bounced up against my esophagus, and then settled down to a wicked churn somewhere in the middle.

"Yes, I am. But it isn't as easy as I originally thought," he said at last. "I've been looking into it, don't get me wrong. But it might be easier if you could come up here."

Yeah, easier for him. "We've had this conversation before," I said finally. "Maybe we need to spend some more time together before either of us uproots our lives."

"No, don't say that. I don't mean it that way," he protested. "Damn, it's impossible talking on the phone. Look, I'll come down there the minute I'm back from Rome. We can figure out what we're going to do then, all right?"

I agreed, and we left it like that, neither of us happy. Funny how you can hear the death rattle of a relationship so clearly when you know what to listen for. I'd clung to the corpse of my first marriage for months after I'd heard that sound, and I wasn't going to go through that again. Like seeing the future in a crystal ball, I knew he would come visit, we'd talk, he'd get angry, I'd cry, and then it would be over. No harm, no foul. At least I wouldn't be stuck in a strange city when it happened, with no friends and no job. Much better this way, really.

I went to the back door to let Belle back inside and got a beer from the fridge. Passing the suitcase filled with brightly colored shirts, beach towels, and a swimsuit, I gave it a kick and then burst into tears.

Chapter 2

DEATH AND DIVAS

The next morning, the first day of the new school year, I drove into the parking lot at seven o'clock, a full hour and a half before classes started. I liked getting to school at that time. I liked having my pick of the best parking spaces in the teachers' lot, which were those under a couple of massive live oaks. Trust me, shade in August is worth any amount of bird droppings. I also liked the relatively quiet time before most of the kids and teachers arrived. I always stopped in at the front office to chat with Maria Santos, who besides being my friend was also Larry's secretary and knew more about what was happening at the school than he did. Then I would wander down the foreign-language hall and check in with Laura Esperanza, my friend and fellow early bird who could usually be counted on for some good gossip. And then I would head to my classroom, where I would spend the remaining time grading papers or helping kids with their homework. Not that I'd be doing that on the first day, but I was looking forward to catching up with my friends.

I knew something was wrong the minute my tires rolled with a crunch onto the pitted asphalt of the parking lot. A small group of kids milled around the tennis shed, a half-size portable building that stood beside the tennis courts and was used for storing tennis equipment and as a makeshift office. At this time of day, I might expect to see one or two kids dropping off their racquets, which were too big to fit into the school lockers. Five kids huddled in a tight circle meant trouble, especially since one of the girls appeared to be sobbing. When they saw my car, two of them ran straight at me, waving their arms. I stood on the brakes, making my little Civic skid to a stop. Heart pounding, I opened the door.

"What the hell are you doing? I could have hit you!"

They ignored this.

"Ms. Shore, come quick!" said the dark-haired boy, a kid named Dillon Andrews whom I'd had last year for American history.

The taller boy, skinny and blond, added, "It's Coach."

Fear is more contagious than any virus. It took maybe five seconds to cover the distance from my car to the open door of the shed, but in that tiny space of time, a nameless dread made my mouth go dry and filled my stomach with lead. I didn't know what to expect, but I knew it would be bad.

It was. And it wasn't. Other than a spilled bucket of tennis balls, the shed was almost preternaturally neat. Metal shelves lined the walls, loaded with neat stacks of towels, cans of tennis balls, and cases of bottled water and sports drinks. A handmade wooden stand held half a dozen battered tennis racquets, and an old desk stood in one corner, clean except for a small brass lamp and an empty in-box made of black plastic. I took two steps inside, far enough to see around the sets of shelves, and stopped. The only thing out of place, really, were the tennis balls and Fred.

He lay on his back on the floor, and even from that distance I could see that he was dead. I rushed forward anyway, my feet kicking against tennis balls with every step, and knelt by his side. Poor old Fred. He lay on his back, legs twisted a little to one side, arms thrown wide. I thought about feeling for a pulse, but a single touch on his wrist told me he was already cold. And stiff. I wiped my fingers on my skirt, not so much to remove the contact but to feel something warm.

I sat back on my heels, taking in the scene. Fred's eyes stared blindly at the ceiling, already covered by a strange milky cast. On his chin, right beside the left corner of his mouth, a dark bruise and a small dried cut marred the marble pallor of his skin. Near his hand lay an overturned white plastic tennis ball bucket, the kind he bought on sale at Walmart for ten bucks each, always out of his own pocket. I don't know why that was the thought that finally made my eyes fill with tears, but I had to blink hard as I rose.

I turned back to the kids who were standing in the doorway like young deer, ready to flee. "Have you called 911?" I asked.

Apparently not. Five phones materialized like a Vegas show trick. I held up a hand. "Just one of you." I singled out the kid I knew. "Dillon, you call. You," I pointed to the girl who wasn't actively sobbing, "what's your name?"

"Brittany. Brittany Smith." Her voice was tight and squeaky, struggling not to cry. I liked her for it.

"Okay. Brittany. Do you drive?"

She looked puzzled, but gave a nod.

I said, "Here are my keys. Go park my car in the teachers' lot, then come back. We need to make room for the ambulance."

She hurried away. I stepped outside, closing the door behind me, then turned to a tall blond boy, who was now standing just a little apart from the others.

"What's your name?" I asked him.

He looked at me blankly for a moment, as though he couldn't quite remember, then said, "Eric, ma'am. Eric Richards."

Ma'am. Wow. New kid for sure. He had to be a freshman. Then the last name registered. Was this the son of that arrogant bully from yesterday? I looked at him more closely, but couldn't see any resemblance in face or build. This kid had the long, loose limbs common among so many of the best tennis players, but he was stick thin and had none of the bulk and sheer bullying presence of his father.

"Eric, do you know where the office is?"

"Yes, ma'am."

"Okay, good. You run there and find either Mr. Gonzales or Mrs. Santos and very quietly tell them what happened. Then come back, would you?"

He was gone like a shot, golden hair bright in the morning sun, long legs flying. When I'd said run, I hadn't meant it literally, but it wouldn't do the kid any harm. Dillon was off the phone now, and all of them were staring at me for further instructions. The only problem was that I didn't know what to do, other than to wait for the ambulance.

"Which one of you found him?" I asked, more for something to say than because I thought it mattered.

The crying girl raised her hand like limp bird, then let it flutter back to her side, bursting into fresh sobs.

"I know you, don't I? Aren't you Melody Mills's sister?"

She nodded through the tears. "McKenzie," she whispered.

Snot was collecting in a little pool around her nose and her face was mottled and red. She looked just about as bad as it was possible for a teenage girl to look, but the fact that the boy beside her still hadn't removed his arm from her shoulders told me that this girl was probably exceptionally pretty under normal circumstances.

"I had Melody last year for World History," I went on while she gulped and sniffed.

She seemed to be calming down a little. Brittany returned with my car keys and my purse, thoughtful girl, and I thanked her and pulled out a little pack of tissues and handed them to McKenzie. She pulled out two and buried her face in them. I gave her a moment, then laid a hand on her shoulder.

"McKenzie, when you went in the shed, did you move anything?" I asked her. I don't know why I asked. Mostly just to get her to talk rather than cry.

She looked scared. "I . . ."

I hastened to reassured her. "It's not a big deal. I just wondered if the tennis balls were already spilled or maybe if you dropped them. Wouldn't blame you if you had," I added quickly. "I would have dropped anything I'd been carrying if I'd walked in there unprepared."

But she was shaking her head. "No, those were already there. I almost stepped on one when I went in to leave my racquet. I was just picking them up when I saw him."

I nodded. Fred must have kicked the bucket when he fell, I thought, then wished I hadn't. God, the brain came up with horrible things under stress.

I thought about the way he'd fallen and wondered if he'd had a heart attack. Despite the white hair, and despite my teasing words to him, he really wasn't that old. Maybe sixty, give or take a year or two either way. And in pretty good shape, except for the smoking, of course. Still, heart attacks could hit you at any age, and he definitely hadn't looked good yesterday after the encounter with Mr. Richards.

"I picked up the racquet stand," Brittany was saying.

"What?"

"The racquet stand. It was knocked over. The racquets were on the ground."

That was a little odd. The racquets weren't anywhere near where Fred had fallen. In fact, they were on the opposite side of the bookshelves that had initially screened his body. And not at all in a direct line from the door, so it wasn't as though he would have bumped into them by accident. Of course, maybe he'd been standing beside them and then had started feeling faint. Maybe he'd been trying to get to his desk to sit down or possibly call for help. I looked at the wires stretching to the tennis shed. There was electricity, but was there a phone line? And wouldn't he just have used his cell phone? I hated the thought of him dying all alone like that, unable to summon help.

In the distance a police siren began to wail, faint at first, then louder. A couple of minutes later, a black and white Crown Victoria rolled up, blue and red lights flashing, followed closely by a yellow and blue EMS truck. The medics pulled a medical case from the back, then hastened after the police officer into the shed, only to emerge a moment later shaking their heads. They spoke briefly together, then said something to the police officer and began repacking their equipment. Nothing could have said more clearly that Fred was beyond their help. The police officer joined the kids and me just as Larry Gonzales sailed in, head up, the light of battle in his eye. Behind him, long-legged Eric was trotting to keep up. A variation of the Brush-off walk, I thought critically, guessing that Larry probably hadn't moved this quickly since the chem lab exploded three years ago.

Larry spoke to the police officer first, interrupting him as he was asking us his first question. The officer politely and firmly refused to allow Larry to go anywhere near the shed. Thwarted, Larry turned on me.

"You should have called me right away," he said under his breath, as though the kids and policeman standing three feet away couldn't hear him.

"I sent Eric," I pointed out.

Larry gave the officer and kids a brittle smile over my shoulder and pulled me a few paces away. I could smell his cologne, a strong musky scent, probably marketed as being manly.

"You should have called me before you called the police," he said. His eyes were darting back and forth like Ping-Pong balls at the state finals.

"I don't have your number on speed dial, Larry. And it seemed a little more important to call for help first." I didn't see any point in mentioning that Fred had been way beyond needing help.

"Ah, yes." He cleared his throat, then raised his voice slightly. "Well, certainly these children don't need to be standing around here. I suggest you accompany them to the office, Ms. Shore, and see about calling their parents."

I can't think of anything that he could have said that would have made those kids want to stay around more. You'd think a high school principal would know better than to refer to the students as children. Kids yes, children no. They began to protest, but luckily for them, the policeman had other ideas.

"These folks are witnesses, sir. I'm going to need some information from all of them."

He asked our names first, which we provided one after another. After ascertaining who had been the first inside, he was just beginning to go over the details with McKenzie, who, I'm sorry to say, looked like she was beginning to enjoy the attention, when another car drove up.

The man who stepped out was dressed in neat khaki pants and a pressed shirt. Dark hair, dark sunglasses, a ruddy tan that spoke of some serious time in the sun. He wasn't old enough to be a dad arriving for a kid, and although he could have been an older brother or an uncle, I somehow didn't think so. He had an indefinable air of authority. Larry followed my gaze and then hurried forward to intercept.

"You can't park there," he said, waving his hands.

The man gave him a cool gaze and produced a badge from his pocket. It silenced Larry far more effectively than anything else could have. He consulted briefly with the officer, then approached me.

"Detective Gallagher, ma'am," he said, flashing his badge again.

I didn't even glance at it. He'd removed his sunglasses, revealing blue eyes under thick black lashes and brows, the same color as the hair that fell across his wide, high forehead. His long jaw was clean-shaven, though it showed the faintest trace of a blue shadow. Despite the Irish name, his voice was pure west Texas.

He paused as though waiting for something, but I just stared at him like an idiot. He blinked, then went on. "You were the one who found the body?"

"No, that was McKenzie," I said, gesturing to the girl, who obediently moved to my side.

He gave her a single glance, scrawling something in a small notebook. "But you went into the shed?" he asked me.

"Yes."

"And your name?"

"Jocelyn Shore. I'm a teacher here," I added.

"Okay, very good. Look, if you could stay for a few minutes, I think we can let everyone else get in out of the heat."

He glanced at the first officer, who took the hint and began herding the kids and Larry toward the school, Larry protesting the whole way. Another officer arrived and began diverting traffic away from the tennis shed. By now the school buses were beginning to arrive, interspersed by a stream of cars rolling into the school driveway. Lots of parents drove their kids to school on their way to work, but never more than on the first day of the school year. Parents of freshmen could be counted on to drop their kids off with quivering farewells and sometimes a photograph or two. When they drove away, their eyes were too full of tears to notice their embarrassed offspring scurrying away with eyes averted, hoping none of their friends had seen the display.

Now the stream of cars was moving more slowly than ever as their occupants craned to see what was going on. Some actually parked, and a crowd of kids and parents were gathering on the sidewalk in the front of the school, staring our way. Larry broke away from the police officer and went to deal with them, probably thinking that this at least was something he could control. He began waving his arms and shooing the gawkers away like a farmer protecting new seeds from a flock of crows. And like any self-respecting crows, they drew back while the arms were flapping, and then crept forward the instant they stopped.

The air was already beginning to heat up, not yet unpleasantly hot but warm and dry. A little breeze stirred across the sere yellow grass that covered the field and the drainage ditch that ran along the back of the tennis courts. I looked at the sagging, frayed nets on the nearest three courts and again felt a tightness in my throat. Poor Fred. He'd spent much of the last year campaigning for new nets. He'd never get them now. My eyes pricked, and I blinked hard, trying to force the tears back where they belonged. A single drop escaped anyway, and I hurriedly wiped it away.

To my surprise Detective Gallagher touched my arm briefly. "You all right, ma'am? Would you like to sit down?"

I would like to sit down, I thought, but there wasn't anywhere to sit. And what was with the "ma'am" stuff? He was surely older than I was, even if only by a couple of years, and coming from him it made me feel as though I was one step away from support hose and puffy blue hair.

"I'm fine," I said more sharply than I intended.

He ignored this and led me to his car. Opening the passenger door, he gestured for me to sit. "Here you go. If you don't mind waiting, I'll be back in a second," he said.

I did mind, and I didn't want to wait. But I wasn't sure what else I did want to do. Should I go into my classroom? Should I go help with the tennis kids, maybe call their parents? Should I pace up and down and howl at the unfairness of it all? The last one seemed the most appealing, but I didn't think it would do my self-image any good. Plus this bossy detective seemed to assume that I would be cooperative, and I figured I probably ought to be. So I sat.

Detective Gallagher returned to the shed, said something to the officer standing guard at the door, and slipped inside. As more people gathered by the school, another police car arrived, and the second officer began directing traffic. At least I wasn't sitting in the marked car, which would have convinced everyone that I was under arrest. Feeling impatient, I glanced at my watch and then back toward the shed wondering when Detective Gallagher was going to return.

"What's going on?" asked a voice behind me.

I jumped. Turning, I saw a face peering in the open driver's side window, the face of Roland Wilding, the assistant drama coach. I suppressed a groan.

Roland was the acknowledged school heartthrob, the focus of schoolgirl crushes, the apple of the senior drama coach's eye. He was almost ridiculously good-looking, and he had something that I could only call presence. When he walked into a room, or, I should say, when he made his entrance into a room, every eye turned his way. The fact that half those eyes turned away again to avoid dry heaves somehow didn't seem to register.

"What are the police doing here? Are you in some kind of trouble?" he asked, his eyes sparkling with amusement at the thought.

Much as I tried, I couldn't think of a reason not to tell him. After all, it was hardly something that could remain a secret.

"Coach Fred is dead," I said, then winced at the unintended rhyme.

He gave a low whistle, then walked around the car so he could lean against the back door beside me. "What happened?"

I shrugged, willing him to go away. He chose not to notice.

"Who found him? You?"

"No, one of the kids was dropping off her racquet. What difference does it make?"

"None. I was just curious. Must have upset the poor kid," he added as an afterthought, probably because he thought he should, not because he really cared. "Heart attack?"

"How would I know?" I said.

At that moment Detective Gallagher returned. He looked Roland Wilding up and down, then glanced at me. I'm not sure what he saw in my face, but his lips twitched.

"Can I help you, sir?" he asked. His tone was dismissive, but I could have told him that subtlety wouldn't work on Roland.

"I was just trying to find out what was happening, officer," said Roland. "Such a tragedy. How did he die?"

"We haven't been able to determine that yet, sir. Did you know the deceased?"

"Well, of course. I know everyone around here. I'm a teacher. Although I know I don't look the part," he added with a self-deprecating laugh and ran a hand through his already artfully tousled hair.

I closed my eyes so he wouldn't see me roll them.

"And your name, sir?"

"Ah, I am Roland Wilding." He gave a ridiculous little flourish with one hand. "I'm the drama teacher here."

"Assistant drama teacher," I corrected.

"Well, yes. Assistant drama teacher," he admitted, throwing me a cool look. "Only my second year, have to work my way up the ladder, you know, while I'm building my reputation as a screenwriter," he added with a flash of white teeth.

"Hmm. And when did you last see Mr. Argus?"

I liked that Detective Gallagher knew Coach Fred's name without having to consult his notes.

"Yesterday," said Roland brightly. "He was here on the courts, and I was just over there with the drama club. We were cleaning the stage area, painting props, that sort of thing. Preparing for the new season. The play we have planned is going to be something extraordinary. I've written the adaptation myself." He drew breath, apparently to expound on the glories of the Bonham theater season and his own scriptwriting skills.

Detective Gallagher headed him off just in time. "And did you notice anything unusual? Did he appear to feel well?"

Roland shrugged. This was far less interesting than the theater. "As far as I could tell. He was working with the kids. Seemed fine."

"Other than the tennis players, did you see anyone else in the area?"

"Not exactly, but people were coming and going all day yesterday. Most of the clubs had practices or work days. Why are you asking? Is something wrong?"

Other than a dead teacher? I stared at him with distaste, but Detective Gallagher took it in stride.

"Not at all. It's just policy to try to find out who might have seen him last."

"We were here until about ten o'clock last night, but I left through the front door." He gestured. "I didn't notice anything over on this side of the building, but then it was dark and I wasn't looking. Want me to ask Nancy if she saw anything?" He glanced toward the school where a small crowd had gathered.

Nancy Wales, the head drama teacher, was instantly recognizable. For one thing she was a huge woman, well over six feet tall, and built like a linebacker. Then, too, she favored bright colors and loose-fitting clothing, which would have made her stand out even if she'd been petite. Today, she wore a turquoise and cobalt silk caftan that billowed gently in a breeze of her own making. Her blue-black hair was thick and long, and today she had it swept up into a twist and fastened with a claw clip, which made her seem even taller. When she was in a good mood, she glided through the halls like a barracuda, silent and watchful. In a bad mood, which was her default, she was more like a shark preparing for a really good feeding frenzy, sniffing for the first sign of blood in the water. Freshmen scattered like minnows when they saw her coming. Now, though, she looked concerned, even a little frightened. Was it possible that she actually felt something because of Fred's death? Or was she—and this I considered to be much more likely—worried that the police had discovered that she was actually an escaped convict who'd had an only partially successful sex change and had arrived to haul her back to prison?

Roland began waving to her without waiting for Detective Gallagher to respond. She looked aghast, skittered a little like a nervous horse on the verge of bolting, and then reluctantly approached.

"Hey, Nancy!" Roland called, his actor's voice easily carrying over the sound of traffic. "Did you see Fred here last night when we were leaving? This officer is trying to find out who spoke to him last."

She reached us, shaking her head with certainty even

before he'd finished speaking. "I park out front. I never come over this way."

Detective Gallagher asked for their names and made notes in a small notebook. "All right. Well, thank you both." He handed them each a card. "If you think of something that might be relevant, you can contact me at those numbers."

Nancy took her dismissal with obvious relief and pattered back toward the school a good deal faster than she had arrived. Roland accompanied her with less alacrity, the top of his golden head scarcely reaching her cheekbone. Detective Gallagher glanced down at me, then walked around the car and slid into the driver's seat.

"Coach Argus was a good friend of yours?" he asked.

At his kind tone, my eyes again filled with unexpected tears, and I closed them tightly to hold back a flood. "He was a really good guy," I said finally, my throat tight and dry.

"He have any trouble with anyone around here?"

I sniffed, wishing I had a tissue, but I'd given mine to McKenzie. Detective Gallagher reached across me to open the glove compartment, and I caught a faint scent of soap rising from his body. He pulled out a box of tissues and handed it to me. Gratefully, I took two and began wiping my eyes, hoping my mascara wasn't turning me into a raccoon. It was bad enough knowing my eyes and nose were probably as red as a baboon's hiney and twice as attractive.

"He didn't have real trouble —everybody liked him, and he was a great teacher. He had the usual fusses we all have."

"What's a usual fuss?" he asked, eyes crinkling a little with amusement.

"Oh, you know," I said, and then realized he probably didn't. "Disagreements with other teachers over the teaching plan, requests for funds for the tennis team that were always turned down. It used to make him so mad." I smiled a little through my tears, then thought of something else. "Just yesterday he had a parent in his classroom yelling at him about the tennis team. I guess that probably shook him up, but I never thought it was enough to . . . well, to give him a heart attack."

"What parent? Do you know what happened? Was it something serious?"

"I was there," I said. At his inquiring look, I described the argument briefly, and then asked, "Why does it matter?"

"It probably doesn't. Almost certainly doesn't. We have to be thorough when there's an unexpected death, that's all," he said with a shrug, making a few more notes on his notepad. "Do you know this parent's name?"

"Mr. Richards. I don't know his first name."

"And the other teachers? The ones he had disagreements with?"

I didn't know whether to laugh or sob. "Me. I was the worst. He and I used to go round and round over things that don't seem very important right now. He always won," I added, remembering. And Fred had enjoyed our discussions, enjoyed showing me why his way was best, enjoyed sharing his long years of experience. He couldn't stop teaching, even when his student was another teacher.

"Anyone else?"

"Not really. Well, he had an ongoing battle with Nancy

Wales. But that wasn't about lesson plans. He thought she worked the drama kids too hard."

Detective Gallagher made a few more notes, then glanced out the window. A white Chevy minivan with flashing red lights and the words "Travis County Medical Examiner" in red was just pulling into the school driveway.

"All right, ma'am. And how can I contact you if I have more questions?"

I gave him my cell phone number, then asked, "What kind of questions?"

He smiled. It transformed his face, making him look younger and far more human and making my breath catch in my throat.

"Won't know until I think of them. You have someone who can give you a ride home? You shouldn't drive when you're upset."

Of course I didn't have anyone to drive me home. For one thing, I wasn't going home. It was the first day of school, and I had a classroom that would be filling with thirty confused freshmen by now, and I didn't even have their names memorized yet. However, it would have taken too much effort to explain all that, so I just nodded and got out of the car. He hurried across the parking lot without looking back, intent on speaking with the medical examiner, and I made my way into the school, taking the shortcut through Building A.

As I crossed the open courtyard on my way to class, Larry Gonzales sprang out of the administrative building like a sweaty jack-in-the-box. He was now wearing his suit jacket, which he normally kept hanging on a hook in his office, probably so that he'd look good for the news reporters who were sure to show up any minute. I tried pretending I hadn't seen him and kept walking.

"Jocelyn!" he called, and I had no choice but to stop and let him catch up.

Around us, dozens of students, happily oblivious to the death in their midst, were talking and laughing, calling greetings to friends whom they hadn't seen for weeks, comparing class schedules and lunch periods. First-day excitement, new clothes, new supplies, new backpacks. The whole year starting fresh with limitless possibilities. This should have been a very good day, I thought sadly.

Larry hurried to my side, still moving at unwonted speed, things on his mind and loose ends to tie up. He drew close enough to speak in low, private tones, and I noticed his comb-over was lower than ever this year and gleamed with a fresh application of gel.

"Jocelyn, I want to apologize to you for suggesting that you should have called me sooner. The children on the tennis team let me know how efficient you really were. All of us here appreciate that very much."

"Thank you," I said, looking at him with some alarm. What did he want? Larry seldom gave out compliments, and never without an ulterior motive.

"Obviously, we're all upset by the tragedy of Coach Fred's death," he went on. "He was a fine man, and will be sorely missed. Of course, at this point in the day, we can hardly cancel school."

"No," I agreed. Besides the fact that 2,200 kids were

already pouring onto the campus, the school's government funding depended on attendance, and Larry wouldn't have canceled a day of classes unless two or more buildings were on fire, and even then he would have tried to get a roll call first.

"We will be arranging for a substitute teacher for Mr. Argus's history classes." He paused, as though waiting for me to say something.

"I'll be glad to go over the lesson plan with whomever you get," I offered.

"Ah, yes. Good. Thank you." He paused again, waiting for me to continue, but I had no idea what else he could want. We stared at each other for an awkward moment.

He cleared his throat. "The tennis team seemed to think quite highly of you."

"That's nice of them." I wondered where he got that idea.

"Yes, well." He floundered for a moment, then finally bit the bullet. "I would like you to take over as the tennis coach."

Tennis coach? I almost laughed out loud, but suddenly realized he was serious. Was he out of his mind? I wasn't a coach.

He must have read my thoughts in my face because he quickly continued, "And you know the game. You were outstanding in the faculty tournament last year. You played in college, didn't you? And it would be temporary, of course. Just until we can find a suitable replacement."

"Why not just cancel practice for a few days?" I asked.

"Tennis is run as an eighth-period class as well as an extracurricular activity. At least half the team is taking it for credit, with the other half then joining them directly after school.

I looked at your schedule. Eighth period is your planning period."

Yes, it was. Something I'd pulled strings to achieve. Like most teachers, I put in far more than a forty hours week, arriving early, staying late, working into the night grading papers. But there was nothing better than leaving school at three thirty on a Friday afternoon, and I'd planned my schedule around that one goal. I definitely did not want to give that up to teach tennis. Still, Larry was in a bind, and I probably was his best candidate. And at least he had the tact to ask rather than order me to do it, which he probably could have done.

With reluctance, and feeling I would surely regret it, I said, "Okay. Sure, yes, I can do that for a few days. But seriously, you need to find someone else. I don't know enough about coaching to be a good choice long term."

He looked relieved. "Of course," he said, and hurried away before I could change my mind.

At twelve thirty, my AP World History class filed out noisily, leaving me feeling very pleased. I could tell already it was going to be a good class, full of bright kids with good attitudes. I'd already spotted the two I'd have to keep my eye on and the three quiet ones who would never volunteer an answer, but who would always know them. The best part was that the group dynamic had felt right, and I could tell we were going to have a good time of it.

I was just pulling my lunch out of my desk drawer when Laura Esperanza poked her head in the door.

"*O-la, señorita,*" she called. "*Quieres almorzar?*"

Did I want to have lunch? I burst out laughing and waved her in. Laura was born in Midland, Texas and, despite her last name, was no more Spanish than I was. Not only did she have what was possibly the worst Spanish accent in the history of Spanish accents, she also had a hard time understanding spoken Spanish. Which was a little ironic considering she was one of two Spanish teachers at Bonham High. However, she was completely fluent when it came to the written word, and her students consistently aced their standardized tests.

"*Con mucho gusto. Adelante,*" I responded.

She paused. "What? I mean, *qué?*"

"Come on in," I repeated in English, setting my sack lunch on the desktop.

"You're never going to believe this," she said without preamble.

"Try me."

"That bitch Nancy Wales is at it already."

I started laughing. Laura never referred to Nancy as anything other than "that bitch Nancy Wales," at least not in private. It sounded especially funny coming from someone who barely topped five feet and weighed about as much as my poodle.

We pulled a couple of desks to the side of the classroom where we couldn't be seen through the window in the door and popped the tops on the two cans of Dr Pepper she'd brought. Laura proceeded to unload her lunch sack, pulling out a huge roast beef sandwich, a pack of Fritos, a banana, a pudding cup, and three cookies wrapped in plastic. As usual, I could only wonder where someone so tiny put it all. Hardly larger than your average twelve-year-old, Laura's head barely reached my chin, and her arms and legs looked like knobby twigs. Maybe she needed it to grow all that hair, I thought, admiring the long brown tresses that flowed straight and shiny from the crown of her head to her waist. I wondered how on earth she washed it and how she managed to go to the bathroom without dunking it in the toilet.

"What has she done this time?" I asked.

"Tried to block the FLS cultural recital. She thinks she owns that theater, the stupid whore."

The Foreign Language Studies cultural recital was Laura's special project and dear to her heart. Each year, she cajoled, pleaded, and threatened the other language teachers into rounding up various groups of kids who were more or less willing to go onstage and do something, anything relating to a foreign country. The tango club was always the headliner, and the German club could be counted on to find a couple of boys willing to put on lederhosen and clop around with eight to ten girls. Very occasionally, a kid with real talent would pop up. One year, a skinny boy with a battered twelve-string guitar had perched on a rickety stool and played "Malagueña" so well that he got a standing ovation from the audience, who had been almost comatose by that point in the proceedings.

"What do you mean, block it? She can't stop us from having a recital."

"No, but she wants us to use the cafeteria. Or the gym. Anywhere but her precious theater. She says the set of the musical will be too big to be moved this year, the stupid *vaca*." Laura's face was getting red as she spoke.

"That's ridiculous. She can't commandeer the theater for

the entire semester. Lots of groups use it." I thought for a moment. "And don't you mean *vaca?*"

"Cow. I mean cow. She's a stupid cow."

"True," I agreed soothingly.

"Anyway, that's what she's trying to do. I've already set up an appointment with Larry for this afternoon. And if he doesn't have the balls to stand up to her, I'll get the parents' groups involved," she added grimly, taking a savage bite of her sandwich. "I'd like to see her take on Candy Wells."

Candy Wells, the president of the PTA, ate teachers for breakfast.

"It would be like *Alien vs. Predator,*" I said with awe.

She paused to process this, and then burst out laughing.

A knock sounded on the door, and we turned to see Ed Jones, the ninth-grade algebra teacher. I hadn't seen him all summer, and he'd obviously been busy with his personal grooming regimen. This fall, he was sporting a snappy mustache-goatee combo in a lemon-cream-pie color at least two shades lighter than his hair. He looked a little like Colonel Sanders, but with less animal magnetism. Definitely the kind of guy who took the sting out of being single.

He bustled in, ignoring Laura. "So I heard you're going to be the tennis coach," he said pointedly.

Laura gave me a surprised glance. "Really? That's great."

Ed snorted. "No, it's not great. She doesn't know anything about tennis. Or coaching."

This was more or less true, at least about the coaching, but Ed didn't know that, and I resented the assumption. "What do you want, Ed?" I asked.

"I should be tennis coach," he said. "I've had my application in for two years."

We stared at him. His thin knit shirt revealed all too clearly a meager expanse of chest set off by a pair of small yet perky man-boobs. He also had a flesh-colored nicotine patch peeking from under one sleeve.

I said, "I always thought of you as an athlete, Ed."

Surprised and pleased, he preened a little, diverted for a moment from his righteous indignation.

Laura wasn't distracted quite as easily. "Why weren't you helping Fred, then?" she asked. "He was doing everything all by himself. I'm sure he could have used the help."

Ed looked annoyed. "I tried," he admitted sullenly. "He said he didn't need an assistant."

This only meant he hadn't wanted Ed. Hardly surprising, since Ed managed to combine petulant officiousness with rampant ineffectuality in one scrawny package. Laura gave a discreet snort, and he glared at her.

I thought briefly about Ed as tennis coach and didn't like the thought. Whether or not he knew anything about the sport, he was not a good teacher. He had a hard time maintaining discipline in his classes, and an even harder time teaching any but the brightest kids. I knew he consistently got complaints from both kids and parents each year because he whined about it fairly frequently. If Ed took over the tennis team, I suspected most of the players would quit and the school wouldn't be able to continue sponsoring it. Tennis was the only sport at Bonham that accepted any kid, regardless of experience. Competition and winning had been almost a side issue as far as Fred was concerned. Sportsmanship, leadership, and fun had been higher on his list. The tennis team was a place where students could belong to an athletic group without having to devote their lives to it, something I supported completely. Which didn't mean I wanted to be the coach, but definitely did mean I didn't want Ed taking over. Besides, the temptation to mess with him was irresistible.

"I'm pretty excited to be coach," I said. "I have tons of new ideas. I figure with a little work, we'll be heading to State."

A blatant lie. The Bonham Breakpoints were consistently in the lower third of the Austin high school league, and they'd be lucky to be that high with me in charge.

Ed almost ground his teeth. "You've never wanted that job," he accused.

"It was always Fred's," I pointed out. Which wasn't a denial.

He stood there, trying to think of something cutting to say. "I'm going to talk to Larry about this," he said finally.

I nodded. "Good idea."

He looked at me helplessly for a moment, then stormed out.

Laura turned to me. "I didn't know you wanted to be tennis coach."

I grinned. "I don't. But I couldn't give that little weasel the satisfaction. This way he'll sweat about it. Besides, I think we owe it to women everywhere to prevent that man from appearing anywhere in tennis shorts."

"True," she said with a little shudder. She paused, then added, "I'm really sorry about Fred. I know he was your friend."

"Thank you. Yeah, it was a shock this morning. You don't think about someone you know dying like that." I said. "It feels very weird to be going on with the day, but I don't know what else to do."

Laura shrugged. "There's nothing else you can do."

Except maybe protect Fred's team, I thought, but I didn't say it out loud.

Chapter 3

COACHING AND COERCION

I was exhausted by the time three thirty rolled around. It was always like that during the first few days of school. For me, the long summer break was not exactly a break. I filled my time by taking continuing education courses at Austin Community College, by reading, and by working on my teaching plans for each of the classes that I'd be teaching during the next year. Still, there was no doubt that my schedule was much more relaxed during the summer months, and getting back into the pace and demands of teaching could be a shock to the system. And here it was, eighth period, and by all rights, I should be gathering my purse and heading for the door. As it was, I made my way down the stairs and through the throngs of kids clattering through the un–air-conditioned halls. The smell and humidity were identical to that found inside a teenage boy's sneaker, and the din was incredible. Lockers slamming, boys shouting good-natured insults at each other in a continual stream of obscenities that would have made June Cleaver go into convulsions, but meant no more to these kids than "gosh darn it" had meant to Barney Fife.

I hurried straight across the open courtyard where the heat reflecting up off the concrete turned my face red in seconds, crossed through Building A, which housed the gym, theater, and cafeteria, and then across the parking lot to the tennis courts. It probably wasn't a good thing that I felt winded already, and practice hadn't even started.

A group of kids clustered in front of the tennis shed. The door was shut, a strip of yellow tape and a sticker over the lock the only sign it had contained a dead man just a few hours earlier. The kids themselves were dressed in their tennis clothes, but they did not look ready to play.

I introduced myself and scanned their faces, recognizing McKenzie Mills, Eric Richards, and Brittany Smith from this morning. I did a quick roll call, checking off names.

"Where's Dillon?" I asked.

Most of them looked around uncertainly, then Brittany answered, "He comes after eighth period. He's not in the class, just on the team."

"Ah. Okay, then."

"Ms. Shore, our tennis rackets are in there," said Brittany, pointing with one finger to the shed. "We didn't know if we should go in."

I didn't know if they should go in either, but I was glad the tape had stopped them. I had no idea what state the little room was in after the police had finished their investigations, and I didn't want the kids to be the ones to find out. I would go in later and take care of things.

"That's okay," I said. "In light of everything that's happened, I wasn't planning to have a real practice anyway. Come on, let's go find some shade."

I led the way to the sidewalk beside the building where the temperature was a good ten degrees cooler, although still by no means cool. While it might have been even more pleasant under the live oaks by the parking lot, we'd almost certainly have had to contend with fire ants, and I wasn't in the mood. The kids flopped on the ground like wilted lettuce, only less ambitious, and stared at their own hands or feet glumly.

"There's no way I can replace Coach Fred. No one could. We're all going to miss him so much. I don't know how many of you know this, but I teach history here, and Coach Fred was the lead teacher for my department. I worked with him very closely, and he was my friend."

My voice cracked a little as I said this, and I struggled to push back tears. A few eyes turned toward me, and I could tell they were all listening. I went on.

"If tennis was just a team and not a regular class, I'd cancel practice for a week and let us all grieve for Fred in the way he deserved, but that's just not an option. And maybe it's not even something he would want. Of all the work he did at the school, he was the most proud of his tennis team. Of you. He thought the world of you. He talked about you all the time, of the progress you've made over the past couple of years, of the fun you have together, and the fun he had being your coach."

By this time the boys were staring grimly at their shoes and the girls were all perilously close to tears, but these things had to be said. I looked away to give us all a little time. Overhead in the cloudless blue sky, a lone turkey vulture spiraled lazily on an updraft, wings motionless, outstretched feathers quivering. The steady thrum of traffic competed with the lazy summer sound of cicadas in the trees. I drew a deep breath of the sweltering air and felt a trickle of sweat run down my back.

"So, for today, any of you that have your own cars can go ahead and leave. Anyone who needs to wait for the bus or for a ride can either go to the library or you can come to my classroom and get a head start on filling out the bajillion first-day forms that I know you have. Then tomorrow, one way or another, we'll have regular practice."

This seemed to meet with general approval. A handful of the twenty took off, and the rest, mostly freshmen and sophomores, followed me up to my room, a subtle vote of confidence, which I appreciated. On the way, McKenzie Mills caught up with me.

"Ms. Shore," she said hesitantly. "I . . . um, I have a problem, and Coach Fred was going to help me, but I don't know if he had a chance before he . . . before he . . . ," she trailed off, not knowing how to say "before he died."

"What's up?" I asked.

"Well, it's stupid, but . . ." Again, she had trouble finishing her sentence.

"Hang on. Let me open my room, and then we'll talk." We had arrived at the classroom, and I unlocked the door to let everyone else in, and then closed the door so McKenzie and I could talk in the hall. The blast of cold air from the room made the hall seem doubly stuffy, but it was a whole lot better than outside. Across the way, Coach Fred's room was already dark and locked.

I turned to McKenzie, who was wearing a pink and white tennis outfit, her blond hair pulled into a ponytail. I'd been right. Without the reddened eyes of this morning, she was very pretty. And right now either worried or embarrassed.

"Coach Fred was going to take care of something for you?" I prompted.

She nodded. "Uh-huh. See, I auditioned and got a part in the musical." She looked at me with pleading eyes, as though this was a problem I could solve.

"That's wonderful. Congratulations."

Not what she wanted to hear.

"Thanks, but see, Ms. Wales said I'd have to drop tennis, and I don't want to. Rehearsal is right after school, but only until the performance in September."

I thought about this. "I don't see why you'd have to drop tennis. Just come to eighth period like a normal class, which is what it is, and then go on from there to rehearsal. You'll miss the extra tennis practice and maybe a few tournaments, but that's no big deal. Didn't Coach Fred tell you that?"

"Yeah, he did. It's Ms. Wales. She doesn't want me showing up ten minutes late because I've taken a shower, but she also doesn't want me coming on time but being sweaty. She says I'll have to be putting on costumes."

"But tennis is a class. You can't just drop it."

"I told her that, but she said I could take it in the spring or next year to get the gym credit. Or even better take something that practiced earlier." McKenzie looked miserable.

I could feel my own temperature rising, and it had nothing to do with the heat in the hallways. That bitch, Nancy Wales. I could almost hear Laura's voice in my head. Couldn't wait to tell Laura this one.

Out loud, I said, "So what did Coach Fred tell you?"

"He said he'd talk to Ms. Wales and work it out. But now . . ." She trailed off.

The anxieties of a high school freshman. So intense, so painful, and in this case, so entirely justified. Nancy Wales was the worst teacher in the school, not because she didn't know her subject but because she was a bully. Kids who had talent got parts, yes, but only if they were part of Nancy's inner circle. And she only liked the kids she could control. Stand up to her or question her in any way, and you were out. Every year parents lined up outside Larry Gonzales office to complain, and every year he did absolutely nothing about it. From his point of view, the drama department was a well-oiled machine, consistently winning awards at the district competitions. And unlike other departments, they never had any infighting among the teachers, mostly because it was just Nancy and her toady Roland Wilding, who was a world-class ass-kisser.

I took another look at McKenzie. She must have an amazing voice to have been chosen for a role as a freshman. Even more unusual, she must also have her head on straight if she wanted to stay on the tennis team instead of just caving to Nancy's ridiculous pressure. My respect for the girl rose a notch.

"I'll go and talk with her," I said. "She can't expect you to give up tennis, especially since you won't have to come to the after-school practices while you are rehearsing. I'll work it out with her."

She looked both relieved and anxious, and I could tell she didn't entirely believe I could make good on that promise. Which was reasonable, because I didn't entirely believe it myself. I'd never yet had a battle with Nancy, but I'd heard the war stories from the other teachers. Especially Laura, who butted heads with her every year over the use of the stage.

When the final bell rang, I returned to the tennis courts to meet the rest of the team and gave them a shortened version of the same speech, telling them that practice would begin for real the next day. They scattered like cockroaches, a few running to catch the buses, the rest rushing toward the student parking lot. I watched them go, wondering what I was getting myself into. If things had gone according to plan, I would already be home, stretched out on the couch in the air-conditioning, maybe going over the next day's lesson plan, maybe just reading a good book. The tennis shed, with its closed door, was a grim reminder that I should be counting my blessings instead of my annoyances. I stared at it, wondering whom I should contact about the tape and seal. Detective Gallagher sprang to mind.

Like a salmon swimming up an exceptionally crowded stream, a big Crown Victoria inched its way up the school drive, braking every few seconds to avoid kids heedlessly streaming across its path. At last it turned into the side parking lot and rolled to a stop beside me. Detective Gallagher got out, reflective sunglasses hiding his eyes completely. The crisp pressed shirt of this morning had wilted only slightly, but he had loosened the tie around his neck in acknowledgement of the heat.

"I was just about to call you," I said as he approached. "Is it okay to open up the tennis shed yet? The team is going to start practice again tomorrow and all the equipment is in there."

He glanced over, mirrored lenses reflecting the yellow tape, before returning to reflect me. It was disconcerting to see a double image of myself, and I had to suppress an urge to adjust my hair.

"Yeah, we're finished in there. I left the tape on so I could be here when you went in. I wanted to ask you a few questions."

"About what?"

"This and that," he answered evasively, and I gave him a sharp look.

I lifted a hand to the door, then hesitated at the tape, but he reached around me and tore it down, then peeled the sticker off the doorjamb without ceremony.

"We would have left someone to guard the door if we hadn't been finished in here," he explained, stepping aside to let me open the lock. He watched as I punched in the code.

"That's the first question," he went on. "How many people know the combination to this door?"

"I don't know. Not exactly, anyway. Probably a lot of people know it. Every kid on the tennis team for sure, and it hasn't been changed in at least a couple of years." Actually, it hadn't been changed since it had been installed, but he didn't need to know that.

"You know it," he pointed out. "And you said you weren't

involved with the team this morning." His voice was light, as though he was just making an observation, but I could feel his eyes watching me.

"Well, yeah. A lot has changed since this morning. Then, I wasn't involved. Now I'm the new coach," I said. "But I already knew the combination, because a couple of years ago, Fred was away at a tournament and called to ask if I'd go into the shed and get him a phone number from the roster."

"You remember a combination you'd heard only once two years ago? Pretty impressive."

I didn't care for his tone, which was a combination of fake respect and complete disbelief. I kept my own voice level.

Pointing to the giant electric Bonham High School sign at the foot of the driveway, I said, "What do you see?"

"Bonham Students are Winners?" he said, reading the scrolling message of the day.

"Below that. Look at the address. 7203 Live Oak. That's the combination. 7-2-0-3."

He looked from me to the sign, then back again. "You've got to be kidding. Why didn't he just leave the door wide open?"

"He said the lock was there to stop temptation, not theft," I said with a shrug, remembering. "He had a boundless faith in the goodness of people, especially kids."

Detective Gallagher snorted a little and shook his head.

I glared at him. "He was a good guy, and he wasn't stupid. He knew people, but he was an optimist. And the shed was never burgled."

"He was damn lucky, and you know it. I bet you told him to change the combination."

I'd not only told him to change it at least every two weeks but to install a secondary keyed lock so that he could control when other people could open the shed. However, I wasn't going to give Detective Gallagher the satisfaction.

He went on. "So basically, anyone could have known or guessed the combination."

"Basically," I agreed.

I pushed the door open, and we looked in. Most surfaces now had a fine dusting of black powder on them.

"You dusted for fingerprints?" I asked. "What's going on?"

"It's standard procedure for unexpected deaths," he said. "In fact, we go to every death that occurs outside a hospital."

"We?"

"Homicide," he answered.

"You're a homicide detective?" I had missed that part somehow.

He nodded but added reassuringly, "Don't read anything into it. We go to every unattended death. Murders, of course, but also suicides, heart attacks, accidents, whatever."

"And all this?" I asked, gesturing to the powder.

"Again, we have to treat every unattended death as a possible crime scene. We take photographs. We collect evidence. Most of the time, it's not needed, but we only get one shot at the scene, so we have to be cautious."

"But now you're back," I said, puzzled. "You've had all day to examine the shed, but you're back. Is that standard, too?"

"I just wanted to clear up a few final details. It's nothing to be concerned about."

I did not believe him. "How did Fred die?" I asked suddenly.

"Was it a heart attack? Or a stroke?" I racked my brain. What else caused people to drop dead without warning?

"We don't have the results of the autopsy yet," he answered evasively.

Which was not an answer at all. Now that we were inside, he had removed his reflective glasses, but it made no difference. I could read nothing at all in his eyes.

He moved forward, past the rows of tennis racquets, around the metal shelves. "This filing cabinet was locked, but we found the key in his desk. Do you know what he kept in it?"

Was this a test? "Well, no. I assume forms and maybe papers about tournaments or the team lineup. Why, what's in there?"

He pulled the top drawer open so that I could see a collection of files, each labeled in Fred's meticulous, tiny handwriting. He closed it and pulled out the bottom drawer, which was filled with a couple of cartons of Marlboros.

"Did you know he was a smoker?"

I almost laughed. "Everyone who came within ten paces of him knew he was a smoker. The reek from his shirt could make your eyes water. So what? What difference does it make?"

He didn't answer. Watching me, he pulled out the two cartons and laid them on the desk. Then he opened the bottom one. Tucked in between two packs was a slim, poorly rolled joint.

"That's not Fred's," I said automatically. "He would never smoke marijuana."

In response, Detective Gallagher opened one of the cigarette packs. It was full of the same slim little joints, lined up inside the package just like miniature cigarettes. I stared.

"Fred must have confiscated those from one of the players."

"You think so? Are you sure?"

"Of course. What else could it be?"

He simply shrugged. I looked at him, appalled. "No way. You can't possibly think these were Fred's. He was a straight arrow. He . . ." I started to try to explain, then stopped abruptly. I'd finally caught an expression in Detective Gallagher's blue eyes.

He pulled a plastic evidence bag from the top drawer of the desk where it had been stored, and put the packs inside. It was already labeled and ready to go.

I asked, "So, you left this here for me? Why?"

"I wanted to know if you knew about Mr. Argus's drug habit. You say you didn't." His voice was carefully expressionless. It was anyone's guess whether he believed me or not.

"Fred did not have a drug habit." I enunciated each word with as much force as I could, trying to control my temper. "If this is important, then you need to look elsewhere. Hell, even if it's not important, you need to look elsewhere. Fred would never, ever be involved with drugs in any way whatsoever."

"The tox screen might tell a different story."

I glared at him in frustration. Then another thought occurred to me. "Wait, what is this really about?" I said slowly. "You aren't going to pursue drug charges against a dead man."

For a moment I didn't think he was going to answer, then

he said, "We've noticed a few anomalies about this death. It's probably nothing, but we have to look into it."

"Anomalies? What does that mean? Are you saying you don't think Fred's death was natural?"

"I'm not saying that. I'm just saying it is my job to thoroughly investigate the scene of a death. That's all I'm doing." He started inching toward the door.

I followed him. It was all I could do not to grab his arm and shake him. Or kick him in the pants. "You cannot possibly think that Fred Argus smoked marijuana."

"I didn't say he smoked it. But he might have been dealing."

This was even worse. "Never!" I all but shouted. "Never, never, never. You don't understand."

A cheerful voice from the door interrupted. "Here you are! I was looking for you everywhere."

We both turned, a little startled. My cousin Kyla was standing in the door frame. For an instant, the golden August sunlight streamed over her dark curling hair and slim figure, lighting her up like a statue of a Greek goddess. I could almost hear Detective Gallagher's jaw hitting the floor.

I didn't know whether I was glad to see her or not. I absolutely could not let Detective Gallagher go on thinking that Fred had been a drug dealer, but on the other hand I didn't know how I was going to be able to convince him otherwise.

I swallowed hard and made the introductions. "Kyla, this is Detective Gallagher. He's here about Coach Fred. Detective, this is my cousin, Kyla Shore."

She advanced, holding out her hand. Like me, she's tall,

but like me, she had to look up to meet his eyes. She gave him a slow, warm smile. "It's nice to meet you, Detective. I hope I'm not interrupting. It sounded like you were in the middle of an argument."

"Not at all, ma'am," he said, looking from Kyla to me and back again. "Cousins. I can certainly see the resemblance."

Kyla frowned at him. "The light in here isn't very good," she said shortly. "Anyway, what's going on?"

"Do you work here at the school?" he asked her.

She snorted. "Not likely. I just stopped by to talk to Jocelyn." She directed a glance at me. "Your cell phone is off by the way."

I brushed this aside. "Coach Fred . . ." I started again, but Kyla interrupted.

"Who's Coach Fred? And what are the police doing here?" The first question was thrown at me, but the second was very clearly directed to the detective, and the tone suggested it was a welcome and happy surprise. The look she gave him would not have won any awards in a subtlety contest.

"Our tennis coach died today," I said. "Or last night. We found him today," I added, suddenly feeling unsure of anything.

Kyla blinked and glanced around, taking in the black powder on the desk and shelves. "In here?" she squeaked.

At Detective Gallagher's brief nod, she retreated to the door and stepped outside with quick light steps. We followed her. A hundred yards away, the football team was running drills, the boys bulked to twice their normal width by the padding in the black and gold uniforms. The flow of cars leaving the school had thinned to a trickle. I sneezed unexpectedly.

"Bless you," they said in unison.

"Look, you just can't think Coach Fred would have anything to do with that." I pointed to the baggie he carried.

"Of course. I'm aware there might be some other explanation, and I assure you that we'll look into every possibility."

I ground my teeth in frustration. "You have to understand who Coach Fred was. I don't care if you found him carrying a garbage bag full of marijuana and wearing weed pants, there would still be an explanation other than smoking or selling."

As an answer, the detective handed us each a card. "You can reach me at those numbers," he said, and he left without even a goodbye.

Kyla and I watched him go, I with frustration, she with appreciation. Then she turned to me. "Weed pants?"

"That complete ass is saying he found marijuana in Fred's desk."

"Hmm. Well, I'm sorry to hear about your friend. Not sorry to have seen that though," she tipped her chin after the detective's car. "That's one fine-looking man."

I looked at her in exasperation.

"What?" she asked. "He is nice-looking. Why shouldn't I say it?"

"What do you want?" I asked her, too disturbed to go into a conversation about the physical appearance of a homicide detective who thought my dead friend was a drug dealer.

She took the hint. "I've been trying to get hold of you for hours. A bunch of us are going out tonight. We're meeting over at the Dog and Duck for some beers. Sherman will be there," she added.

I must have looked at her blankly, because she went on. "You remember. The cute guy I was telling you about. Look, I can tell this hasn't been a good day, but honestly, you don't want to go home by yourself right now, do you?"

I didn't. But I also wasn't interested in meeting some new guy. For one thing, regardless of her opinion, I had not broken up with Alan. I tried to ignore the aggravating little voice that added . . . yet.

It was as though she could read my mind, because she said in a gentler tone, "Come on. Just come down there for one beer. It would do you good. You won't even have to talk to Sherman if you don't want to. Just get away from all this."

I finally agreed, mostly because she was right. I didn't want to go home alone just now. Then I remembered McKenzie Mills's little problem. "Shoot, I need to take care of something first."

She pulled out her iPhone and glanced at the time. "Well, hurry it up. We're meeting at six. You need any help?"

I shook my head.

"I'll save you a seat, then."

I watched her go, a slim, elegant figure who somehow always knew when I needed a lift, even when we hadn't talked. I couldn't remember the last time she had shown up when she couldn't reach me on the phone, but here she was. I pulled my five-year-old flip phone from my pocket and unmuted the ringer, then squared my shoulders and headed for the theater.

Inside Building A the cheerleaders were practicing in the long, wide hall that separated the gymnasium and cafeteria on one side from the theater, orchestra, and choir rooms on the other. Someone had propped open the door to the gym to let some of the air conditioning stream out into the hall. The squeak of tennis shoes on lacquered wood and the shouts of the volleyball team told of a practice going on inside. I dodged around a line of jumping girls and pulled open the doors of the theater.

Inside, all was cool, dark, and quiet after the bright activity of the hallway, and my eyes were slow to adjust to the dim light. Gradually, I began to see what looked exactly like an old-time movie theater, complete with numbered maroon plush seats, red-carpeted aisles, and faded velvet curtains pulled back to reveal a partially completed set. At center stage, a group of girls gathered around Roland Wilding, whose tousled hair gleamed like a blurred halo under the spotlights. Next to them a group of boys was arranging an odd collection of chairs and boxes. The sound of a handsaw competed with an electric drill from somewhere offstage.

I scanned the area for Nancy and had almost decided that she must be in her office when I spotted her sitting in the third row, off to the right. Beside her sat Pat Carver, the school accountant, a tall woman in her midforties, built like a fireplug, her pinched face made memorable by unusually pale eyes magnified behind thick glasses. Pat was in charge of all booster club funds, which meant that no club in the school could spend a nickel without Pat's approval. In theory, she kept the constantly changing stream of parent volunteers from breaking any of the district rules, but in practice she used her position to curry favor and retaliate against those who offended her. She and Nancy had their heads together, whispering in the dim light, and seemed oblivious to everything around them.

I waited at the back, glancing at my watch. I didn't want to talk with Nancy in Pat's presence, but at that moment, Pat rose and stretched, putting hands to lower back and arching like a cat. A very large, goggle-eyed cat. I started down the aisle, thinking they were done, but Pat bent suddenly, leaning close to Nancy's head, and I heard the words, "You better take care of it fast. That much money is going to be noticed."

She sidled out of the row, then stalked past me up the aisle, giving me a sharp glance from her silvery blue eyes. Nancy sat very still for a long moment, then began shuffling through a sheaf of papers, pulling her reading glasses from her head where they'd been perched like a headband. I wondered how she could see anything at all in the dim light.

I slipped into the seat beside her.

"Hi, Nancy," I said.

She must have seen me, but she gave a theatrical little jump anyway and said, "Ah. Jocelyn." She glanced from me, up to the stage, and back down to her papers as though trying to decide where to focus her attention. Somehow, I didn't think I was her first choice.

I decided to get right to the point. "I need to talk to you about McKenzie Mills."

Nancy gave me the unblinking stare of a python confronted by a medium-sized monkey and wondering if it could be consumed.

"McKenzie Mills," I repeated. "She's in your musical, but

she's also on the tennis team. Did Coach Fred have a chance to talk to you about her?"

Her eyes slid away from me again. I waited. I passed the time by wondering why she insisted on dyeing her hair black. It could not have looked more unnatural if she had chosen bright blue. And the way the short wisps stuck out on the top reminded me more than a little of Ursula the Sea Witch. Come to think of it, the puffy bosom and flowing caftan also added to the impression.

Eventually, she said, "Coach Fred? No, I haven't spoken with him at all this year. What's this about?"

"McKenzie Mills," I said for the third time, starting to feel frustrated. "She's in your play," I reminded her. At that moment McKenzie crossed the stage to join the other girls around Roland, her blond hair almost as bright as his under the lights. "Look. Right up there. In the pink shirt."

The basilisk stare flicked that way. "Oh. Yes, of course. What about her?"

"She's on the tennis team. She said that you told her she had to quit the team if she wanted to be in the musical."

Nancy's attention finally focused. She sat up a little straighter and the bulldog expression returned to her eyes and jaw. "Yes, that's right. I can't have my actors running late and being distracted by other obligations."

"I'm coach of the tennis team now. I'm here to work out a compromise so that McKenzie doesn't have to give up her eighth-period class to be able to participate in the drama club. I've already told her that she can skip the additional after-school practice and the tournaments for the duration of the play. There shouldn't be any reason that she can't continue with both." I smiled as pleasantly as I could, bracing for the push-back.

"The girl has a very large part. She's one of the Sateens." Nancy said it as though it would mean something to me. My expression must have convinced her otherwise, because she went on. "She's playing Sateen in two of the performances. The lead role."

I still had no idea what she was talking about, but it didn't matter. "Yes. Well, that's terrific. That's still no reason she has to give up tennis. She will be at rehearsal, ready to go at 4:40, just like everyone else."

"Drama kids are required to be present in the theater room at four thirty," she snapped.

I had her on this. "Official time for after-school practice is four forty. That gives the students time to put their books away or to shower after phys ed."

"Which is why McKenzie can't be in tennis. She has to be in the theater room at four thirty."

I drew a slow breath, willing myself not to reach out and strangle this woman. "Nancy, I'm here to ask you to make an exception for my player." She opened her mouth to refuse, but I held up a hand. "I think this is in everyone's best interest. Of course, we can pursue it with Larry if you prefer."

She thought about this. I could almost see the way her mind was working, wondering just how far I was willing to go, considering whether she could bully me into backing down, weighing whether she could win. I gave her credit. She read me correctly.

"I suppose I'd be willing to let McKenzie come in a few minutes late," she said at last.

I was impressed that she could get out that many words without unclenching her teeth.

"You mean, not as early as the others," I corrected, to make sure we were clear. "She won't be late."

"Yes." She bit off the word.

I rose, giving her a tight-lipped smile. "Excellent. Perhaps you can let McKenzie know so she isn't worried. Oh, and Nancy," I paused to give my words weight. "I'll be checking with McKenzie to make sure that tennis isn't interfering with drama."

She shot me a cold look but didn't answer. I left, feeling uneasy.

I'd heard rumors. Heard about kids driven out of the drama department when they fell out of favor, about kids losing parts even after they'd made it in auditions. It was such a subjective area: the teacher claiming the kid wasn't practicing hard enough, the kid claiming bias and retribution. All but impossible to tell from outside who was in the right. In disputes between teachers and students or teachers and parents, I usually found myself on the side of the teacher, but in this case, our two-minute conversation had been enough to make me afraid for McKenzie's continuing theater aspirations. I doubted whether the girl would ever get another part, and there was absolutely nothing I could do about that. The only thing I could do was make sure she didn't lose the one she had.

I returned to my locked classroom to pick up my purse. Hesitating a moment, I considered my options, then made a decision. Kyla would not be happy, but I simply could not face a loud, happy group of strangers. Not tonight. I pulled out my cell phone to tell her I wasn't going to be coming. Maybe I'd never intended to go. The only thing I wanted now was a Sonic cheeseburger, cheese tots, and limeade. Beer would have been better, but I needed to learn the official rules of high school tennis and maybe something about form and strategy. It was the last and only thing I could do for Coach Fred.

Chapter 4

EPITAPHS AND EPISTLES

Coach Fred's funeral took place three days later. Bowing to public pressure, our fearless principal dismissed school for the afternoon, which admittedly was more complicated than it sounded because he had to put classes on a shortened schedule and arrange for the school buses to arrive three hours early. However, to hear Larry moan about it, you'd think he was orchestrating an international peace convention single-handedly, instead of simply telling Maria, his secretary, to make the arrangements. Which was basically all he had to do.

I arrived early at the tiny church and chose a seat at the rear. It was an old building, simple and elegant. The pews were long wooden benches with very upright backs, recalling a simpler, slower time when women came to church wearing flowered dresses and tiny hats, plump legs squeezed tight under the shimmering grip of support hose. Despite the abundance of flower arrangements, the air smelled mostly of old wood and furniture polish. The worn carpet was a mint green color, which I supposed was supposed to be restful, and the only adornment on the walls was a large mahogany cross hanging on the wall behind the altar. In front of the altar, a wooden casket rested solidly on trestles covered with golden cloth; it was flanked by two candelabras, tiny flames shivering as though cold from the air-conditioning. I looked down at my hands.

Other people began arriving, and a couple of young men in suits escorted them singly or in pairs down the aisle. Some were members of the congregation or possibly distant relatives of Fred's. The rest were kids and teachers from Bonham High, wearing dark clothing, some with reddened eyes and noses. Many I knew, many more I didn't. One girl sobbed as she was escorted to her seat. Her suffering was all too theatrical and exacerbated by the bevy of friends who reached out to touch her shoulder or squeeze her hand. Dramatic by nature, teenagers are all too easily caught up by the form and ceremony of death and grieving. Their feelings are passionately intense and sincerely felt, at least in the moment. I figured there was at least a seventy percent chance the girl had actually known Fred.

A sound from the doorway made me turn my head in time to see Roland Wilding and Nancy Wales making their entrance. Something in their thespian blood must make them incapable of slipping quietly into a room. Even here, at a funeral, their gestures were large, their voices just slightly too loud, their postures a little too erect. "Look at me, look at me," they seemed to be saying. Or "slap my face, slap my face," which was the effect it had on me. However, upon closer observation, I realized that Nancy was, if not subdued, at least quieter than usual, and that it was Roland who was doing most of the grandstanding. He made a big point of asking the usher where he should sit and requesting that the boy take them closer to the altar. Nancy actually had the unexpected decency to resist, but he urged her forward. I looked away in disgust.

The low tones of recorded organ music began streaming softly through the speakers mounted in the corners of the chapel. The church was packed, every seat taken, a line of mourners standing along the walls in the back and flowing out into the foyer. A small group wearing black—two women, a man, and two small children—were escorted to the pew in the front. Fred's widow and children, no doubt, and the grandchildren of whom he'd been so proud.

The service was brief, although not brief enough. The minister said a few words. A young woman, probably a relative, stood in front of the altar with a boom box and microphone and sang "You Light Up My Life" with eyes closed, wobbling on the high notes. The phrase "funeral karaoke" sprang into my head and for a few minutes I had to struggle to suppress a wholly inappropriate urge to laugh. Fortunately, before she could start another song, Fred's son rose to deliver a surprisingly eloquent and moving eulogy, which had everyone in the congregation reaching for tissues. The minister said a few more words that no one heard, and then it was over.

Because I'd sat at the back, I was one of the first out the door after the grieving family, and I took my place in line to walk by and press their hands and express my condolences.

The heat of the afternoon hit me in the face like a blast furnace, the brilliant light blinding and welcome. After the dim, chill interior of the church, I'd almost expected the day to be dark and drizzly, the earth weeping along with the rest of us. Instead, the brilliant blue sky overhead, the August heat, and the happy raucous cries of the grackles fussing with each other in the grass all welcomed us back into the world of the living. Impossible not to draw a deep breath and thank God that we were still alive.

The line of mourners moved fairly quickly. When I reached Fred's widow, I murmured my generic, "I'm so sorry for your loss," and attempted to move on.

Unexpectedly, she gripped my hand. "Aren't you Jocelyn Shore?" she asked.

Surprised, I admitted I was. Of course, I had met her on one or two occasions over the years, but I hardly expected her to remember me. Her name was Edith, which I remembered only because it had been printed in the funeral announcement.

"Here, wait just a second."

She fumbled in her little black purse, a pretty thing, almost certainly bought for a special occasion—an anniversary or birthday celebration in a fancy restaurant—and not for her husband's funeral. I don't know why, but the sight of that purse made my eyes fill with tears again, and I tried to blink them away before anyone could see. The line of mourners behind me was backing up, and I could feel people craning to see what was going on.

Edith pulled an envelope from her purse, folded and somewhat crumpled. "Here, this was in Fred's jacket pocket," she said, her voice tight and breaking a little. "It was addressed to you."

I took it automatically, then stared at it, not sure what to do. She had to be curious, a last communication from her dead husband and it was addressed to another woman. On the other hand, I could feel the mounting pressure of the mourners behind me.

"Thank you," I said, and moved away.

I walked to the side of the building, where I could stand in the shade, and considered what to do with the envelope. I could see the widow staring after me, and I knew that whatever the envelope contained I would have to go back and share it with her. I tried to give her a reassuring expression. Farther back in line, I saw Roland, Nancy, Larry Gonzales, and Pat Carver, the accountant, followed by a stream of high school students. It seemed as though they were all staring at me as well. I moved farther away.

A figure approached from my left and stood beside me. I glanced up from the envelope. It was Detective Gallagher. He wore a pressed maroon shirt, tie, and black slacks, but not his badge. Giving me a quick smile that did not quite reach his eyes, he scanned the line of mourners intently then turned his attention to the envelope in my hand.

"What are you doing here?" I asked, not caring if it sounded rude. Somehow, it did not seem right that this man, this arrogant ass who thought that Fred was a dope dealer, should be allowed to attend his funeral.

He didn't appear to notice my tone. "I wanted to see who was attending the service."

"Why?" I asked. "What do you care? Just a fan of attending funerals for people you don't know *at all,* or are you maybe looking for addicts?"

He spared me a brief glance. "It bothers you, my thinking that Fred might have been involved in drugs?"

"What do you think? Yes! You're an idiot if you think that was possible." I glared at him.

His lack of reaction was annoying and made me think he was probably accustomed to being called an idiot.

"So, what's in the envelope?"

I thought about telling him it was none of his business, but decided that wasn't tactful. "I'm surprised you didn't open it yourself when you went through his belongings," I said instead, which was so much better.

"I would have, if it had been on him when we found him," he admitted. "He didn't have a jacket in the tennis shed."

He must have been listening like a dog waiting for the can opener if he'd overheard Edith telling me she'd found it in Fred's jacket pocket. "Fred always kept a jacket in his classroom. His room had an overactive air conditioner. If it was on at all, it was set to arctic."

I was oddly reluctant to open the envelope in front of him, but I didn't see any way out of it. Besides, I could feel Edith's eyes continually straying to me in between passing mourners, and one way or another I was going to have to show her the contents. I pulled up the flap.

Inside was a small key and a sheet torn from a yellow legal pad. I palmed the key and unfolded the note.

Jocelyn,
Here's the key. As we discussed, it's just a precaution.
Nothing to worry about. And thanks.
Fred

I looked down at the key, turning it over in my fingers. It was silver and smaller than a house key, but it was unmarked and there was nothing otherwise remarkable about it. I could feel Detective Gallagher's eyes burning a hole in my skull and he shifted impatiently, obviously wanting to snatch the note from my hands. I took pity on him and handed him the sheet without a word.

His eyes flew over the lines. "Key to what?" he asked immediately. "What did you discuss?"

I was puzzled, too. "That's the weird thing. We didn't have a discussion, and I have no idea what he meant. He must have been intending to talk to me the day he died."

"Could I see the key?" he asked, holding out his hand as though he had a right.

I hesitated. This wasn't really any of his business, but on the other hand, maybe he would recognize what kind of key it was. I finally passed it to him with reluctance, feeling unsure whether he would give it back.

He examined it as I had, turning it over and looking for a clue to its purpose. "Maybe a key to a safe deposit box?" he said almost to himself.

"Or a cash box." I was trying to remember other things that used small keys.

"Did he have a cash box? Maybe at school?"

"Not that I know of."

"We'll ask his wife," said Detective Gallagher.

"Can I have my key back? And my note?" I held out my hand. Damn, the man was nosy.

He frowned. "I'm sorry, no. I need them as evidence. Could you give me the envelope as well?"

"What? Why? Evidence for what?"

Drawing a breath, he raised his eyes heavenward as if looking for inspiration from above, and finally let his breath out slowly. "There were no fingerprints on the cigarette packs," he said at last, as though coming to a decision.

"So? What does that mean?"

"It means someone either wiped them down very carefully, or else handled them with gloves. Packs like that are a perfect surface for fingerprints. It raises a few questions. If Coach Argus confiscated the packs from a student, both his prints and the student's prints should have turned up. Likewise, if he was hiding the packs there so that he could distribute them—and I'm not saying he was," here he held up a hand to stop my instinctive protest, "his fingerprints should still be there. He would have no reason to wipe them off."

Roland and Nancy moved forward in the line, followed closely by Larry Gonzales. As they reached Edith, Roland expressed his condolences in a broken voice that I could hear from where I stood and pressed Edith's hands as though he were her long-lost grandson. Edith discreetly tried to pull away. He was acting the part of the heartbroken friend, and not particularly well. People were starting to stare. Even Nancy, who normally watched him like a doting tycoon watches his twenty-year-old trophy wife, looked as though she'd like to be anywhere else. Larry, for once taking charge, poked a finger into Roland's back and said something that made him move along.

Detective Gallagher watched them also. Turning back to me, he must have seen something in my expression, because one dark eyebrow lifted. "Were they friends of Mr. Argus?" he asked.

"They aren't friends of anybody," I said shortly. "But no, they never had anything to do with Fred one way or another. As far as I know," I added, thinking of McKenzie Mills.

"As far as you know?"

I shrugged. "Coach Fred was supposed to intervene on behalf of a student who committed the ultimate sin of wanting to play a part in their musical and still stay on the tennis team."

"And did he?"

"I don't think so. I had to take care of it." I didn't give a rat's ass about Roland or Nancy, and turned the conversation back to the interesting part. "So, what does it mean about the fingerprints?"

"I don't know yet." He was silent for a moment, then added, "I do know that Coach Fred did not die in the tennis shed."

I wasn't sure I heard him right. "What do you mean? That's ridiculous. He was absolutely dead when I found him."

"Mmm, yeah, but he'd been moved."

I felt my heart thud in my chest.

"Moved. What do you mean?" I whispered.

He shrugged.

"Are you saying . . ." I stopped, unable to utter the words. It seemed too ridiculous.

He gave me a quick, grim look. "It will be on the news tomorrow. But yeah, Coach Argus was murdered."

Chapter 5

PARENTS AND PESTS

Almost a week had passed, and tennis practice was going well even if not much else was. After the funeral Detective Gallagher and I had waited and shown the note and key to Edith, but she had no more idea than I what it was for or what Fred had meant by the phrase "just a precaution." Detective Gallagher had kept both, which irked me. I might not know what either was for, but they were mine and I wanted the key in case I ever found something that needed unlocking. So far, I hadn't, but that was beside the point.

I walked up and down the narrow aisles that ran between the tennis courts, observing the action and dodging the occasional ball. Bonham High had six courts, and I'd placed an upperclassman in charge of each. The older kids had stepped up, organizing their squads, suggesting exercises, coming up with techniques and drills all on their own. And even my half-trained eye could already see the improvement among my players. Eric Richards, somewhat to my surprise, was almost as good as his father claimed. His long limbs gave him a terrific reach, and he coupled that with impressive bursts of speed. But, to my relief, he was no prima donna, and in fact was showing signs of being a real leader, despite his short time with the team. He'd been the one to suggest working on a different drill on every court, each run by the team member who was strongest in that skill. Currently, he was providing instruction on the backhand stroke on Court 6 and I watched him demonstrate a sweeping move for a short freshman, then stand back to watch. On Court 3 a sudden shout made me turn in time to see the players pelting Dillon Andrews with tennis balls. He was laughing and covering his head with his arms. I decided to pretend not to notice.

I walked toward the tennis shed, thinking it was time for yet another cup of ice water from the giant orange cooler, when a black SUV pulled up directly in front of the shed door in a no-parking area. The driver emerged, a bull of a man, wearing a gray business suit and dark glasses. Except for the fine cut and quality of the cloth, he might have been an FBI agent. As it was, I smelled lawyer. He stood, legs spread, fists on hips, staring at the players with a grim expression, and then removed his glasses. With a jolt of recognition, I realized that Mr. Richards had returned. I approached with trepidation.

"Hello," I said. "Can I help you?"

"Gary Richards. I'm here about my son." He gave me a long stare, and then frowned in sudden recognition. "You. It's you."

That kind of statement is very hard to refute. "Why, yes it is."

An expression of outrage flickered across his massive face and the fleshy cheeks flushed. "*You* are Coach Shore? Eric told me a new coach had replaced that doddering old fool, but I had no idea . . ." Here he stopped as though words failed him.

I thought about taking him up on the doddering old fool comment, but decided it wasn't worth it. No point in poking the bear. Besides, having him off guard was an advantage I didn't want to lose.

"What can I do for you, Mr. Richards?"

He drew himself up and leaned forward slightly. Intimidation tactics and not very subtle ones at that, I thought with a certain amount of amusement.

"I am here to discuss Eric's future with the team."

"Of course," I answered promptly. "Would you like to step into the shed?"

He followed me for a pace or two, then balked like a startled mule. "No. That's the shed where . . ."

I turned, surprised. "Where what?"

"Where the old geezer died."

I thought about Detective Gallagher's theories on that subject, but I wasn't going to discuss those details with Mr. Richards.

"Yes, Coach Fred was found in the shed, but . . ." Even as I said it, I winced at the unintentional rhyme.

He cut me off. "We can talk out here."

I gave him a sharp glance. Not wanting to enter a room in which a death occurred didn't necessarily indicate anything more than a certain level of squeamishness or possibly superstition. Big men could be as susceptible to that as anyone else. On the other hand, it could indicate a guilty conscience, but, if so, was it because he'd been rude and threatening to the dead man, or was it something worse?

With a mental shrug, I led the way to a weathered wooden bench, which rested in a narrow strip of sere grass running along the courts and occupied a small but welcome pool of shade cast by the wall of the shed. A couple of feet away, a mound of crumbled earth marked the home of a colony of fire ants, the bane of outdoor life in Texas. From this distance and in this heat, the mound seemed quiet, but without a doubt thousands of the evil little insects were just poised and ready to swarm out and cover a hapless victim with burning, itching blisters. I made a mental note to complain to Larry about them again.

Feeling a trickle of sweat slide down my back, I courteously took the side of the bench nearest the ants, leaving the other available for Gary Richards. A mistake, because instead of sitting, Mr. Richards stepped directly in front of me, using his height and bulk to loom like a buzzard over a juicy piece of roadkill. I leaned against the wall of the shed, extending my legs and crossing one ankle over the other so I at least looked like I was relaxed, and was pleased to see an expression of annoyance creep into his eyes. Across the courts Eric stopped his instruction and looked our way, tension creeping across his shoulders like an icy hand.

"Eric's doing very well on the team," I said. "He's showing real leadership skills in addition to his performance on the court, which I'm sure you know is outstanding."

The bull snorted. "I don't give a flying fuck about his leadership skills. He's not here to lead, especially not this pack of beginners and incompetents." He gestured with his head toward my team. "He's here to advance his own game, to get a scholarship, and to play for his college. Maybe go pro."

I considered this while repositioning my outstretched legs slightly so that Mr. Richards either had to step back and ease up on the intimidation over me or else shift to the left, closer to the anthill. He chose to shift left.

"If that is Eric's goal," I placed emphasis on Eric's name, "then he would be better off with daily private instruction and belonging to the National Junior Tennis League."

"So you admit that your program is inadequate." His glare was vaguely triumphant, as if he had scored off me. I wondered again what his profession was. He had lawyer written all over him, and I should know, having been married to one of them for a brief, albeit painful, time, but it was possible that he specialized in something a little more cutthroat. Hostile takeovers maybe.

I leaned left as though trying to see around him, and he immediately moved to block my view.

Ignoring this, I said, "Not at all. This program is one of the best in the state. It's designed to provide an opportunity to learn and improve at a sport that will be a source of lifelong fun and physical activity. It's also designed to teach teamwork and leadership skills. It is not, however, a training camp for future professionals."

"Big words from someone who doesn't know what the hell she's doing."

I shifted again. And again he moved to the left rather than back away and give me some space. A swift downward glance showed a single enterprising fire ant starting to scale the polished wall of his shoe. I quickly raised my eyes.

"On what do you base that statement, Mr. Richards?" I asked in a pleasant tone, as though I really wanted to know.

He did not seem to know how to answer. I suspected he was used to making inflammatory statements to goad his opponent into a shouting match, as he'd done with Coach Fred that day in the school. Behind him, all the kids had now stopped their practice and were looking my way anxiously. They might not be able to hear our conversation, but even at that distance, the menace in Mr. Richards's shoulders and posture was obvious. I did not want them coming over.

I straightened my back, leaning to look around him one last time, thinking surely this time he would back off rather than move to block me. Then I could stand and speak with him on more equal footing.

He didn't. His right foot brushed the ant mound bringing down a miniature avalanche of dirt and white pupae. A flood of tiny but enraged brown bodies swarmed over his shoe and up his sock. In an instant he was hopping up and down like a madman, shrieking and swearing. I leaped to my feet and jumped out of his way. The kids raced over, then stopped abruptly when they realized what was happening. Half of them collapsed in laughter on the court. Eric hurried forward and began trying to brush the biting little creatures from his father's leg. Mostly to save Eric's hands, I grabbed up the big orange water cooler and removed the white top, tossing it to the ground.

"Stand back!" I shouted to Eric, and when he threw himself backward, I emptied the icy contents over Mr. Richards's leg.

To say he was less than grateful was an understatement. By this time he had pulled off shoe and sock and was busy rolling up his trouser leg, frantically brushing the clinging little insects away. I could see the ant bites welling up on his hairy calf, already red and angry. By nightfall, they would be tiny blisters. The cursing was perhaps a bit uncalled for, but I'd heard worse even if not at quite such an impressive volume. His primary goal seemed to be that of informing me and the world in general that I was a bitch, and I figured everyone pretty much knew that already.

The kids' response surprised me though. The two largest boys, Dillon Andrews and Travis Longman, positioned themselves between me and Mr. Richards, while Brittany Smith and McKenzie Mills came and stood beside me. I was more touched than I could say. For a moment Eric sat frozen in the dirt where he'd landed, horrified at his father's stream of profanity and rage, but then he scrambled to his feet and grabbed his father's arm. For a terrifying instant, I thought Mr. Richards would strike the boy.

"Get in the car, Eric!" he ordered. "We're going."

Eric took a single step backward. "No. I'm . . . I'm not . . . practice isn't over yet." He threw me a desperate glance.

"It is for you. And get your racquet. You won't be back."

Gently tugging away from McKenzie's death grip on my arm, I stepped forward. "I'm afraid that's not possible. Eric can't leave now. He is enrolled in the tennis class, and he's required to come every day. Besides, there's no way I can release him without a signed note from the front office. You'll have to go there and fill out a form first."

The second part was a lie. School had ended for the day, and the kids could come or go as they pleased, but it sounded official. Mr. Richards face turned a richer shade of purple. I waited for either an explosion or an aneurysm, but he whipped around and stalked away, kicking the orange cooler viciously on his path back to the black SUV.

In silence we watched him drive away, tires squealing on the asphalt as he turned and accelerated far too quickly out of the parking lot.

When he was definitely gone, I turned to my team, noting the shaken expressions with some concern.

"You all . . ." I stopped, not sure how to express my feelings. I finally settled for "Thank you."

They looked pleased. I glanced at my watch. The whole incident from start to finish had taken less than ten minutes, and it was hard to believe we still had another hour of practice left. I wanted nothing more than to go somewhere cool and gulp down a very large beer, but responsibility called.

"Okay, time for the games. Brittany, can you get the roster off my desk and tell everyone which court they're on today? And Eric, will you help me refill the cooler?"

Brittany ran inside to get the roster from my desk, and Eric, still very white, picked up the orange cooler where it lay on its side. The hard orange plastic was a little dusty, but showed no other sign that it had been kicked like a soccer ball. I scooped up the white lid, and we walked slowly toward the cafeteria.

"Coach, I'm . . . I'm really sorry," he said in an undertone, not meeting my eyes.

"Not your fault."

"I'll drop the class," he offered miserably. "I can get my PE credit some other way."

I glanced over at the hunched shoulders, the downcast eyes under the bright flaxen hair. He looked like a puppy who'd been slapped over the nose with a rolled up newspaper, and I didn't like it.

"I don't want you to drop the class. You are part of our team." I stressed the "our" ever so slightly.

"My dad . . ." he started.

"Yeah, your dad." I could not allow myself to say what I really thought, not to this unhappy boy. "He really does seem to want the best for you," I said.

He raised his eyes, a quick flash of bright blue, then lowered them again. "He does. He's always wanted the best for me . . . and for me to be the best. The thing is, sometimes we don't exactly agree on what that is."

I nodded. "You're not alone in that. Lots of gifted kids run into that problem with their parents."

This struck a nerve. "I'm not gifted!" his voice rose, then he looked ashamed. In a softer tone he added, "I'm not gifted."

"It's not an insult, kid," I said with a smile. "And I didn't mean it in the institutionalized, tested, and stamped sort of way. I just meant that you are smart, funny, and athletic."

"Oh," he said, relaxing a little, then turning red as he took in my words.

We had reached the cafeteria kitchen, and I pulled open

the giant ice maker. Eric set the cooler on the floor and began scooping ice into it.

I went on. "I've seen you on the courts. You're great with the other kids. They're learning a lot. They like and respect you."

"Not after today," he said, his voice flat. "They won't want to talk with me. They'll blame me for my dad."

"You're wrong there. I suppose that things might be awkward for a day or so with one or two of them, but most of them are already one hundred percent on your side. They want you to stay on the team, and they don't want to see your dad force you off. And you have to remember that there's not one person alive whose parents haven't embarrassed them in front of their friends."

He managed a small smile at that. "Not usually so loudly."

"Maybe not," I admitted, "but that's just a matter of degree."

He finished scooping ice and closed the door of the ice maker. He was a little taller than I was but his skinny shoulders, though promising future development, were still those of a boy. I doubted he would ever reach his father's massive girth and strength. It struck me how young and vulnerable he was.

I felt a flash of fear on his behalf. "Eric, how much trouble are you going to be in when you get home tonight?"

He looked honestly surprised. "None. He'll have calmed down by then. He gets pretty mad, but it doesn't last." He thought for a moment, then added, "He'll probably try to talk me off the team, though."

He put the lid on the cooler and lifted it with a grunt.

"Let me help you with that," I offered.

"Nah, I've got it."

We started back to the courts. "There's one more thing I have to ask you, and I don't want you to take it the wrong way. I also want you to tell me the truth. Does he ever hit you?"

Again, the flash of wide blue eyes, surprised but not evasive or alarmed as far as I could tell. "No, ma'am. He never has. He shouts a lot, and he kicked the door off a cabinet once. But he's never hurt any of us."

I supposed I would have to be content with this, although I hated the thought of the boy going home to face that man.

"Okay, then. You know if you are ever worried about that or anything else, you can always tell me. There are lots of things we at the school can do to help families."

This was a bald-faced lie. There was jack shit we could do, other than call Child Protective Services. On the other hand, I could always get Kyla to go over to his house with her little Glock and put the fear of God into the bullying bastard.

Eric shook his head. "Really, he's not like that. It's okay."

When we got back, I sent him out to join his friends on the courts. Catching sight of Eric, Dillon shouted for him to hurry up because he, Dillon, was getting his ass kicked. I had to grin. I wandered around the courts, offering occasional advice or rulings, but my mind wasn't on coaching.

Regardless of Eric's opinion, Gary Richards seemed to be always riding pretty high on the rage wagon. What if he'd returned to the school on the night of Coach Fred's death? What if he'd restarted the same fight, maybe threatened the old man, and finally lost his temper and taken a swing at him? A hard blow from a big man like Gary Richards might have been enough to kill Fred, especially if he'd struck his head on something. Like the desk in the shed. Or wait, Detective Gallagher had said that he didn't think Fred had died in the shed. I looked around. If Mr. Richards had accosted him in the parking lot, maybe his head had struck the asphalt, or something like a car bumper. There had been a moment back by the anthill when I thought he was going to hit me, and he'd been close to striking his own son. He wouldn't have meant to kill. Just lost his temper and then panicked. It wouldn't have been hard for him to pick up Fred and carry him into the shed. I didn't see how he would have known the combination to the shed door, although it was possible Eric had mentioned that it was the school's street address. But it was also possible that Fred had the door open because he was doing something inside.

I thought about Eric and didn't want the killer to be his father, but there was no getting past the thought that he was definitely a possibility. I was going to have to talk with Detective Gallagher.

Chapter 6

DIRECTORS AND DETECTIVES

Practice over, I returned to my classroom to pick up my purse and the stack of papers I still needed to grade. How had Fred done it all? I felt as limp and worn out as a napkin at a barbecue, and all I wanted was a cool shower and an evening on the couch. Which I wasn't going to get. I'd arranged to meet Kyla at Artz Rib House for dinner and drinks. Glancing at my watch, I thought if I hurried and if traffic wasn't too bad, there was time for a quick dash home to shower and change clothes. And maybe the routine would get easier if it ever cooled down. I walked back into the blast furnace that we in Texas liked to think of as a balmy August evening and stopped dead.

In my brief absence, a giant unmarked cargo trailer like those pulled by semis had appeared as though by magic, and now squatted solidly behind my car, a set of wooden steps leading up to the double doors on the back end. I couldn't have been out of sight for more than ten minutes. Hurrying over, I crossed behind it to examine my car, which was now trapped between the trailer and the trunk of a very large and very solid live oak. With less than three feet of brittle dry grass between my bumper and the shiny silver side of the trailer, my car wasn't going anywhere.

I went looking for the driver.

Fortunately, the sound of voices led me around to the back of the school, where a group of ten or twelve strangers was scurrying like especially industrious ants, setting up large lights on silver stands and dragging industrial electric cords through the dust. Several burly men in jeans had already discarded their shirts, revealing sweaty tattooed arms and backs. They squatted in the dirt, thin streams of smoke rising from the cigarettes dangling from their lips, busy laying rails that looked for all the world like miniature railroad tracks. A couple of others wrestled with microphones and a massive camera with a lens the size of my head. A film crew.

I caught sight of a skinny blond guy with a ponytail and recognized him as one of the trio who had been with Larry right before school had started. Sure enough, not far away was the woman with the glasses. So this was the reason behind Larry's Lord of the Manor walk—he'd been making arrangements for a movie crew to do some filming on campus. I wondered if they were making a commercial.

I stood for a moment trying to figure out who was in charge, when a voice at my shoulder said, "This area is off-limits. You can't be here."

I turned. Another ponytail was approaching fast. It belonged to a man somewhat older than the rest of them, maybe in his midthirties, who was bearing down on me with a hostile expression. He wore purposely distressed jeans, a shirt buttoned one button too low, and a two-day growth of stubble which I suspected he went to some effort to keep like that full time.

The unfriendly tone was annoying, but I just said, "I don't want to be here. Your trailer is blocking my car."

He gave me a disbelieving glance, then turned to look. Judging the distance between tree and bumper, then bumper and trailer, he pursed his lips and said, "You have plenty of room to back out. And you need to do it now. We're about to start filming. Go on now, or I'll call security."

Security? He was going to call security on me? That son of a . . . It was too much. With a flick of my wrist, I tossed my keys toward his chest with some force. Reflex kicked in, and he caught them at the last second with a startled look.

I said, "You back it out. And if you so much as scratch my car, you can deal with my insurance company . . . and my attorney. Oh, and what's your name so I'll know where to send the claim?" I pulled a small notebook and pencil from my purse and stood waiting.

After a long pause, he said, "Michael Dupre," and then looked at me expectantly.

I wrote it down and then stood back, waiting. We stared at each other in silence. I finally said, "Well? Are you moving my car or not? I'm in a hurry."

Without turning his head, he shouted, "Carl!"

A brown, sweating tattoo-covered roadie materialized beside him, cigarette dangling on his lower lip without visible means of support. His pants also had no visible means of support and hung dangerously low on his skinny hips.

"Carl, move this . . . woman's car for her, please," said Michael Dupre, handing him the keys.

The cigarette bobbed upward, tip glowing red on the inhale. "Be easier to move the trailer, boss," Carl answered, the words slipping out with the stream of smoke.

"Are you a professional driver or not? Move the goddamned car!"

Carl shot him a sidelong glance, then shrugged and started for my little blue Honda.

"Whoa," I said. "Plus shirt, minus cigarette." They both turned. "Hey, I don't want my seat soaked, and no one smokes in my car. You know, if you move the trailer, I could move my own car," I pointed out.

Carl shot a questioning glance at his boss, apparently saw the answer in his face, then stomped off to find a shirt.

Michael Dupre and I stood without speaking. Around us, the film crew continued setting up, calling to each other for power cords and the like. In the trees the cicadas buzzed their summer song happily and loudly. On the football field, coaches shouted at their players. But under the big live oak, all was silent, which tended to make a certain type of person very nervous. Michael Dupre was that type of person, because he started shifting from one foot to another. I could feel him staring at me, but I ignored him.

"I'm the director," he said at last. When I didn't respond, he added, "This is my movie."

He apparently wanted something, although I couldn't imagine what. "Ah," I said, nodding to show I could hear him.

He frowned at me. "You've heard all about it, I'm sure."

"Nope. Not a word."

His eyes widened in shock. "But . . . but we're shooting here. Right here. Here at your school," he stressed as though I didn't get it. "I assume you work here—I saw you on the tennis courts."

"True," I agreed.

"And no one has told you we're making a movie?" He was incredulous.

"No," I said cheerfully, then relented a bit at his stricken expression. "They don't tell us much. I'm sure there'll be an announcement tomorrow. Or the day after."

He reached up and gripped his shiny ponytail with one hand as though he wanted to pull it out by the roots. "But this is a big deal. This is a real movie, you know. Not one of those low budget indies. The working title is *Teenage Fangst*. Universal Studios is backing us. ILM is doing our F/X. For God's sakes, I'm Michael Dupre!"

Carl returned wearing a puke green T-shirt with only about six holes and the slogan "No Fat Chicks" scrawled across the chest. He took one final enthusiastic drag on his cigarette, the tip flaring to bright orange, paper visibly shrinking. With a flourish in my direction, he tossed it to the dirt and ground it under one foot, then opened the door to my car.

I hadn't been a teacher for six years for nothing. "Exhale *before* you get in," I ordered.

He looked at me guiltily, like a kid caught with a can of

spray paint. Reluctantly he exhaled an impressively large cloud, then slid behind the wheel, muttering under his breath. He started the engine and rolled the car forward six inches. Then he cranked the wheel hard left and reversed about eight inches. Wheel yanked hard right, roll forward. Repeat.

I turned back to Michael Dupre. "So what's your movie about? Teen vampires?"

His jaws snapped together with an audible click, and a small muscle by his right eye gave a convulsive twitch. "You know, that's just the kind of reverse snobbishness I'd expect from one of you pseudointellectual, straitjacketed, backward, Texas cowboy fucks."

I lifted my eyebrows. "Whoa, that really stings. Most of us backward Texas cowboy fucks like to think we've advanced beyond pseudointellectualism and have entered the realm of pseudophilistinism."

In front of us Carl continued to inch my car forward and backward, the nose of the small Honda gradually turning to the right . . . or rightish. Beside me Michael Dupre, director, processed my words for a good sixty seconds, and then to my surprise, gave a startled whoop of laughter.

The Honda's brakes flashed red for an instant and from the set heads turned, all eyes on the boss. With a collective shrug, they all went back to work as Michael continued to laugh.

"You know," he said, wiping his eyes with the back of a hand, "you're all right. What's your name, anyway?"

"Jocelyn Shore."

"Tennis coach?"

"Temporary. Temporary tennis coach."

"Teacher?"

"Yup."

He grinned at me. "Well, Jocelyn Shore, teacher and temporary tennis coach, how would you and your team like to be extras? Paid, of course."

Now it was my turn to be surprised. I considered for a few seconds, then answered, "Tentatively, yes."

"Tentatively?" This seemed to amuse him still further.

"Well, we'd have to ask the kids. And you still haven't told me what your movie is about."

Carl had finally freed the Honda. He emerged, red-faced and pop-eyed from the strain, and tossed the keys with unnecessary force to Michael.

Michael caught them easily and dropped them into my hand.

"Werewolves," he said. "It's about werewolves. Vampires are completely passé."

And laughing, he strolled back to the set. As I got into my car, he turned and shouted, "See you tomorrow evening."

Marveling at the change, I drove away. On my way out I passed Roland Wilding, who threw me a startled glance as he hurried toward the movie set at a half trot. He must have just realized the film crew had arrived and was rushing to do what he did best, which was sucking up. I wondered what kind of a reception he would get.

I hurried home, showered, and then found the card Detective Gallagher had given me. I dialed the handwritten number on the back. While I waited for it to ring, I went into the kitchen and scooped food into a bowl while Belle spun in small circles and yapped. The minute the dish hit the floor, she rushed forward to push her nose deep into the food. Not to eat, of course. At least not right away. She liked to scoop the kibble out of the bowl onto the floor, then eat them one at a time from there. I sighed as she scattered the bits on the clean tile. "You're lucky you're cute," I told her.

The call went to voice mail. I hesitated, then said, "This is Jocelyn Shore. It's probably nothing, but I had a run-in with a parent today that I thought you should know about." I said, feeling a little foolish. "I'm going to dinner, now, but I'll try to reach you again tomorrow."

I hung up, feeling frustrated, and wishing I hadn't bothered. Now that I was away from the stress of my encounter with Eric's father, it seemed absurd to think that he could have killed Fred anyway. Completely ridiculous. Mostly. Probably. On the other hand, I could not shake the vision of the way he'd almost struck his own son, or about the way he had tried to intimidate me. To be honest, he'd done a pretty good job. I was proud of the way I'd handled myself, but there was no denying that I would not want to run into him if no one else was around. As much as it angered me to admit it, something about the man gave me the cold shivers.

I was only about ten minutes late getting to Artz Rib House, and to my surprise Kyla was already there, sitting at a large round table in a nook with another woman and three men. At the sight of the group, I halted. I'd thought I was having dinner with Kyla alone. Trying to decide whether I was really up for a party or whether I should just slip out while the slipping was good, I hesitated just an instant too long. Kyla saw me and waved. Too late to back out now. I pasted a smile on my face and stepped forward for introductions.

Artz is just one two-step above a dive, a tiny building with a rusting tin roof on South Lamar that has become a favorite haven of music lovers and rib lovers alike. Inside, the long narrow dining area looks like it has been transported to the future from 1950s small-town Texas—flimsy tables covered in red-checked oil cloth, lazily spinning ceiling fans, a chalkboard with the day's specials written in a barely legible scrawl. Almost every night of the week and all weekend long, a variety of musicians jammed at reasonable hours, beginning as early as seven o'clock during the week. Tonight was the Texas Old Time Fiddlers Jam, and in the back of the restaurant, a group of men and a couple of women were busily tuning a variety of fiddles, banjos, and basses. The rich odor of smoked brisket, sausage, and beer filled the air, making Artz a little slice of heaven. Or it would have been anyway if I'd been able to sit in peace in a dim corner with Kyla and tell her about Mr. Richards and the film crew. But there wasn't going to be a chance for any of that.

Kyla rattled off the names of her companions in one long stream. "Matt, Veronica, Jim, and Sherman." At this last name she gave me a rueful glance, and I wondered if she'd planned this dinner as a way to get me to meet Sherman from the beginning. A waitress appeared with a round of drinks for the table, and after she passed them out, I ordered a Shiner Bock and sat beside Kyla.

"I was telling everyone how great it is here, and they all

decided they had to see for themselves," she said, as though reading my mind. "Completely spontaneous."

She had been right about one thing, I thought. Sherman was extremely cute and probably was exactly the kind of guy I'd be eyeing if I wasn't still interested in Alan. Which I was, God help me. And it was a little too much that Kyla was already trying to set me up with someone else before Alan and I had called it quits. I hoped it wasn't going to be awkward and that she hadn't said anything to Sherman about me. However, closer inspection revealed that Veronica was practically sitting in Sherman's lap, and he must have dropped his keys down her cleavage because he didn't seem able to look anywhere else. I gave Kyla a smile and settled back in my chair, relaxed and ready to enjoy the music. She grinned back, relieved that I wasn't annoyed.

We'd just started eating and were listening to an enthusiastic rendition of "General Longstreet's Reel," when I realized the pair of dark pants at my elbow did not belong to the waitress. I glanced up to see Detective Gallagher watching me with a faint smile playing about his lips.

He pulled a chair from a neighboring table, inserted it backwards between Kyla and me, and straddled it, leaning his arms on the top rail. Even though he had loosened his tie and hidden his badge, he stood out in that sea of blue jeans and T-shirts.

"What are you doing here? How did you find me?" I asked, completely at a loss.

At the same time, Kyla leaned forward and said, "Good to see you! Detective Gallagher, right? Will you join us for dinner?"

"Colin," he answered. "And thanks. That would be great."

The waitress appeared with a menu and a set of flatware rolled in a napkin. He took the flatware, but waved away the menu. "Dos Equis Amber and the rib plate," he said.

"You got it," she nodded, not bothering to write it down.

"Seriously." I pulled at his sleeve. "How did you find me? Are you watching me?"

"Oooh, are you?" asked Kyla. "That's so cool. Is she a suspect?"

"That is not cool!" I glared at her across Colin's chest. A broad chest, I might add.

He held up his hands. "The answer is no to both. I'm not following you, and you're not a suspect . . . unless you know something I don't?" He added with a grin to Kyla.

She laughed.

"Still not amused here," I said.

"I am a detective, you know. I got your message. I knew you were going to dinner."

"I didn't tell you where. What, you've been checking every restaurant in the city?"

"I'm a detective," he repeated. "It's my job to find people. Anyway, what was it you wanted to tell me?"

I folded my arms across my chest and stared at him in stony silence.

Kyla said, "I know that look. You'll have to tell us how you found her if you want her to talk. Besides, I'm dying to know."

The waitress returned with his beer. He used it as an excuse not to answer, then took another look at me. He considered, then finally shrugged.

"It was a lucky guess based on my knowledge of the parties in question. You said you were going to dinner. I checked Facebook. Didn't find you, but I found your cousin. Her status said she was here."

Kyla looked pleased. "Wow, that thing actually works. And I tagged you, so he knew you were coming."

"Wait, what? You tagged me? What do you mean?"

She held up her iPhone. "Facebook Places." At my look of incomprehension, she continued, "Say you go somewhere, and you want your friends to know where you'll be. You check in to a location, and you can tag whoever is with you, so all your friends know what kind of party is going on. Pretty neat, huh?"

"Yeah, if you're a frickin' stalker. Why? Why would you do that?"

"It's fun."

"Well, don't. And don't include my name again. Ever."

She looked sulky. "You are so paranoid. Anyway, if you don't like it, you can block it. Although I don't know why you even bother to have a Facebook account if you're not going to use it."

Colin interrupted. "Anyway, back to the point. What did you want to tell me?"

I glanced around the table, but by this time the others had finished their meals and had pushed their chairs back so they could watch the musicians. Besides, what I had to say wasn't exactly a secret anyway. Kyla, of course, leaned closer to hear everything, her long hair almost brushing Colin's shoulder. He didn't seem to mind.

I recounted the confrontation with Mr. Richards, glossing over the bit about the anthill. I ended by saying, "It's probably not anything, and I'm overreacting. But he seemed very . . ." I groped for the word. ". . . menacing."

Colin pulled a slim notebook out of his pocket and scanned through a few pages. "Gary Richards. Yeah, I looked him up. He doesn't have any kind of a real record, other than a complaint by a neighbor."

"Complaint?"

"He said that Gary had threatened him."

"See? Violent."

"Threatening to hit someone and doing it are two different things, but I take your point."

I couldn't tell what he thought about Mr. Richards and wondered if I'd been foolish to make such a big deal of it.

Kyla spoke up. "This guy sounds like a first-class asshole, but I guess you can't arrest people for that. You really think he killed that guy, that tennis coach?"

They both looked at me, Colin with increased attention.

"I don't know," I said at last. "I don't have any reason to think that, except that he gave me a really bad feeling, and I know he'd been fighting with Fred. It crossed my mind that he could have hit Fred in a moment of anger. I'm not saying he would have wanted to kill him," I added hastily, "but he seems out of control. He might have done it almost by accident."

"I'll look into it," Colin said. He closed his notebook and

slipped it back into his pocket, then pushed back from the table. "I can get my food wrapped to go," he said.

"You're not leaving, are you?" asked Kyla. "Why don't you stay and finish your beer? You can't still be on duty."

I could see the way she was looking at him, and I couldn't blame her. He was a nice-looking guy.

"Yes, stay," I urged, pushing back myself. "You might as well eat here. I need to get home, though. Papers to grade," I added by way of explanation, hoping they wouldn't notice that I hadn't eaten yet either.

He looked from me to Kyla and back again, then settled into his chair. "I'll call you as soon as I learn anything," he said.

My telephone was ringing as I walked in the door, and my heart leaped. Maybe it was Alan, I thought dashing across the living room. I knew it couldn't be—it was the middle of the night in Italy—but nevertheless I yanked up the receiver without looking at the caller ID, eager not to miss the call.

"Jocelyn? Finally," said a voice on the other end. "I've been calling for hours."

Well, there was a voice once heard never forgotten. And just about the last person I expected to hear on the end of a phone line, now or ever. Not only was it not Alan, it was the absolute opposite of Alan. The anti-Alan. My ex-husband, Mike Karawski. The letdown was spectacular.

"*No hablo inglés,*" I said.

"Ha, ha. Nice try."

"What do you want, Mike?"

"Great, thanks for asking. And how have you been?"

Typical Mike. Funny, yes, but always with a sting.

"I'm sorry, where are my manners? So lovely to hear from you. How are you? And how is your lovely wife? What's her name again? Bubbles?"

"Tiffany," he answered shortly.

"Tiffany. That's right. Silly me." I kicked off my shoes, and then opened the back door to let Belle outside. She waddled out sleepily.

"Heard you had a murder at your school."

"Oh, are we done with the chitchat? Yes, we had a murder."

"What do you know about it?"

"Why are you asking?" I countered.

"I'm interested."

"Yeah, but why?"

"There's a murder at a school in my town, and I can't be interested?"

"Not without an ulterior motive."

He was silent for a minute, which surprised me. Normally, he had his lies planned out in advance. "I've joined the district attorney's office."

"You're a prosecutor now?" I asked. Another surprise. The last I'd heard he was becoming something of a star as a defense attorney.

"That's right."

"What the hell? There's no money in that, Mike."

"I'd had enough of private practice. I wanted to serve the community."

I laughed out loud. "Uh-huh. I forgot what a humanitarian you are."

I could almost hear him grinding his teeth. "Regardless, I'd like to know about this murder."

"Why? Besides, there's nothing to know. They haven't found who did it yet. Nothing there for a lawyer to do."

"The public needs to be protected. Murders in our schools. It's outrageous. I need to be current on incoming cases."

"Oooh . . . I get it. The public needs protection. Your protection. You're thinking about running for office, aren't you?"

"That is certainly something I'm considering," he answered stiffly. "I believe the citizens of Travis County could use a judge who . . ."

"Wow, a judge?" I interrupted. "Shooting pretty high, there, Mike."

". . . who isn't afraid to take a strong stand against crime."

"Impressive. Were you shaking a cop's hand while you said that on your infomercial? And I've always wanted to know—do you use real cops or do you hire actors for shit like that?"

"Look, can you cut the crap for just once? I need to know a few things before I make a statement. Now, there are rumors going around that the dead guy was selling crack out of some kind of tool shed on school property . . ."

I hung up.

This was bad. I paced around my tiny living room, ignoring the stack of papers that was calling my name. Mike was an idiot, but a connected idiot, and his facts were wrong, but not wrong enough. This meant that the cops were still pursuing the drug angle, looking for ways that Fred had brought about his own destruction. It meant that instead of focusing on the murder, they were focusing on finding out about Fred's possible illegal activities, which was bad enough. But if Mike was planning a political campaign around fighting corruption in public places, maybe in our schools, it meant that Fred's reputation was going to be skewered, and he would be remembered forever as the teacher who was murdered while selling drugs to children.

I could not let that happen.

A scratching at the door reminded me that Belle was still outside, and I opened the door to let her in. She waddled to the couch and bounced beside it a few times before finally getting enough momentum to jump onto the cushions. Curling into a small ball, she settled down to watch me with beady, watery eyes.

I sat beside her, running a hand over her curly head and thought back almost seven years ago to my first day of student teaching. I'd been so nervous that day, wanting to do well but afraid I would have a hard time reaching the kids. After all, I wasn't that much older than the students. My hands had been like ice when I reported to the office, but Fred Argus was already there, waiting for me with a cup of terrible coffee from the teachers' lounge. He told me to watch what he did that day, especially during third period, which was his trouble class. He was a master at maintaining order. At the beginning of each period, he stood at the doorway, saying good-bye to exiting students, usually with some funny word or silly warning to behave. Then, as the next class arrived, he greeted each student by name, telling one kid to remove his hat because "gentlemen do not wear hats inside a building," then telling another that she had impressed him with her last paper. Talking in his class was forbidden, participating in class was mandatory. His students were relaxed and engaged. He had a gift for recognizing each kid as an individual, for making the lessons interesting and relevant. I learned more in those few months with him than I had done in all my years of education classes. Not only about how to be a good teacher but about how to be a good human being. I know that when I applied for a position at Bonham, Fred had been the main reason I was hired over all the other applicants. I owed him more than I could say.

And now, I could not let his name and reputation be ruined by rumor when he was not able to defend himself. Not after all he'd done for me. I rose and began to pace, wanting to stomp out my frustration on the wood floor. Belle raised her head briefly, then turned her back to me before going back to sleep. What could I do? How could I stop a rumor mill once it started grinding?

Maybe, just maybe someone had seen something. I thought back to the day we'd found Fred. Roland and Nancy had been at the school late the evening before. Maybe I could start with them, try to find out if they'd noticed a strange car in the parking lot—maybe something like Richards's black SUV. Or possibly they had seen Fred speaking with someone and just hadn't thought anything about it. Also, I could talk with the tennis kids about the shed, about Fred's cigarettes, and about anyone who might smoke marijuana. I had a pretty good relationship now with several of the kids. They might be able to tell me where the joints originated, especially if I was able to convince them that I didn't care whose they were, as long as we could prove they weren't Fred's. And then I would talk to anyone else I could think of. Something that Detective Colin Gallagher ought to be doing, I thought bitterly, but apparently wasn't since he seemed to be too busy spreading rumors to wannabe judges about Fred instead of working. I wished he were here so I could kick his shins.

I flopped down beside Belle and stared at the stack of papers unenthusiastically. It was already almost ten o'clock, and I was tired, but putting it off would just make the next day's stack that much higher. I pulled a sheet from the top, and started reading.

Chapter 7

DRAMA AND DEFENSE

In the morning, careful to park at a safe distance from the film crew, I went looking for the drama practice room, sometimes known in the teachers' lounge as Nancy's Lair. Despite cutting through Building A every day on my way to class, I hadn't been down there in several years, not in fact since my first days at the school when I'd been given the grand tour, and I had only a vague idea of where it was. Around me the school was starting to wake up. In the wide hall that ran between the theater and orchestra rooms, the flag team was gathering for practice, two boys using their flags to reenact the light saber battle from *Star Wars* while the girls took turns calling words of encouragement or derision, depending on their preferences. In a corner, a couple of moms were opening the Tiger's Den, a miniature storefront at which the PTA sold school supplies and spirit items like Bonham bumper stickers. I'd guess they sold roughly thirty-five cents worth of stuff each morning, making it totally worth their time.

Passing the doors to the theater, I turned left along a narrow corridor that ran from the main hallway toward the front of the building and ended with doors that opened to the outside. These doors were supposed to be locked at all times, although most days someone propped them ajar with a brick. Peeking through the first window, I saw the risers used by the choir. The second window was dark and appeared to be a storage closet. But yellow light streamed through the window of the third, and I pushed it open. I'd found the Lair.

The large room was divided into different zones. Nearest to the entrance was a walled-off office with a door and two desks, each piled high with papers, and one holding a single ancient computer. There was no sign of Nancy or Roland. I stepped farther in, easing the door shut behind me so it wouldn't slam. To my left, a large wooden platform about fifteen feet by twenty took up much of the floor. A practice stage, I thought. Directly across from the stage, a blank whiteboard hung on the wall above a circle of chairs. And at the back of the room, a partition concealed another area. Hearing voices, I went in that direction.

Nancy Wales was standing with her hands on hips, speaking in low cutting tones to a girl who looked like she was about to cry. Nancy was dressed in a black pants suit with a brightly colored silk shawl draped around her shoulders, a dramatic outfit that accentuated her height and bulk. She towered over the girl.

The girl saw me, and her eyes widened, but Nancy didn't notice.

She was saying, "It's your choice. Either come to practice or leave the production."

"But Ms. Wales, I do come to practice. I've been to every practice. But my mother wants me home before ten . . ."

"Your mother is not in theater. You are. All actors must stay for the entire rehearsal, no exceptions."

Ten o'clock at night? Was this a joke?

"Good morning, Nancy," I said, and was pleased to see her give a start.

She turned and gave me a sharp look. Probably wondering how much I'd heard. "That's all, Megan. You can go."

"But . . ." Megan started.

"Now," said Nancy.

The girl slid past us, head bowed, shoulders hunched, trying not to sob aloud. I watched her go, then turned back to Nancy.

"Trouble?"

"It's always something with these kids," she said evasively. "Lazy and unmotivated. Back in my day, we couldn't get enough rehearsal. But never mind that. What can I do for you?"

I decided to get what I came for first. "Last Monday night, the evening Fred was killed, you were having practice up here until fairly late, right?"

She stiffened visibly, then made a great show of thinking about it. "Hmmm, last Monday. Last Monday. Why, yes, we did have practice that night. Why?"

"I'm not sure the police are making much progress. I was thinking if we all pooled our information, we might come up with something that could help them."

She gave me the same look she would give a dead rat. "I hardly think so. I've already told the police everything I know.

And so has Roland. I didn't see the poor man at all that night. In fact, I don't recall seeing him at all this year."

"He was holding tennis practice every day for the previous two weeks," I pointed out.

She waved a hand. "I'm sure he was, but you can hardly think I pay any attention to sports. I believe the football teams were out there too, and you could hardly walk ten paces without tripping over someone carrying a tuba, but I simply do not have time to notice every person on campus. We are in the middle of rehearsals for the most important production we've ever had here at Bonham. My time is best spent here."

"Still, Roland said you were here until dark. There couldn't have been too many people about at that time. Maybe you saw someone when you were walking to the parking lot?"

Her eyes flashed with annoyance, carefully suppressed. "No, no one at all. I simply went to my car and drove home. I wasn't even parked on the tennis side of the building."

"But maybe there were a few other cars still in the parking lot?"

"I saw no one. I don't know how to be more plain on that point. I already told the police as much, and I don't really want to go over it again with you. Now, I have work to do," she said pointedly.

I decided I wasn't going to get anything else out of her. I'd have to make sure to tackle Roland later when she wasn't around, or she'd stop him from speaking to me. Especially after what I was about to say.

"So, Nancy, I couldn't help overhearing part of your conversation with your student. Practice until ten o'clock? Really?"

Her face hardened, jaw jutting like a bulldog's, only a good deal less friendly. "You must have misunderstood, Miss Shore." She stressed the "Miss" part, I guess to make sure I knew we were no longer best friends forever. Heartbreaking of course, but I would have to live with that.

"No, I heard her quite clearly. In fact, it sounded like her mother was pretty unhappy about it. Can't say I blame her. I mean, when are the kids supposed to do their homework? Or eat?"

Her face reddened and a muscle worked in her jaw. "I don't think you need to be concerned about it," she said. "You can be sure I take care of my students. There're always one or two who are whiners, that's all."

"I'm sure you do. I was just mentioning it because I would hate to see your department get into trouble with the University Interscholastic League. They have pretty strict rules about after-school practice. I know, because I've had to be careful with the tennis team."

This was nothing more than the truth. The UIL had disqualified teams before, sometimes on the very eve of a contest or match. Which didn't always prevent ruthless coaches from overworking their kids, but it did at least slow them down.

She eyed me narrowly, trying to decide if I was threatening her or just trying to be helpful. I kept my face pleasantly concerned, or at least I tried. I admit, I've been advised by friends not to play poker. Apparently, this was one of those times.

Nancy decided to go the intimidation route, and I was reminded sharply of Mr. Richards. What was it with these large angry people? She took a step toward me to make the most of her height and bulk.

"I appreciate your advice, but this isn't any of your business."

"I have to disagree. Teachers are responsible for the wellbeing of students."

"I run this department, and I decide what the practice schedule is. This show is special, the most ambitious we've ever done, and it requires 110% effort from everyone involved. I will not tolerate anything less, not from the kids, not from myself." Little flecks of spit sprayed out, narrowly missing me.

"You can stay up here 24/7 as far as I'm concerned. The kids can't." I glared at her. "And you know they can't, Nancy. Why are you doing this?" I turned my back on her and returned to the corkboard beside the door where the rehearsal schedule was posted. I yanked it off its thumbtack and read it aloud.

"Monday, four thirty to ten thirty. Tuesday, four thirty to ten thirty. Wednesday, Thursday, the same. Ooh, and look, on Friday, it's four thirty to eleven thirty and then all day both Saturday and Sunday." I flapped it at her. "Are you kidding me?"

She tried to snatch it from me, but I put it behind my back and, short of tackling me, she couldn't reach it.

I said, "You're not going to need this again. I want to see a new schedule up there. No more than eight hours of practice Monday through Thursday. Total. You know the UIL rules."

She looked horror-struck. "You can't do that! You have absolutely no authority over me or this department. I run this theater. It's mine." Her own words seemed to enrage her. "Mine.

I decide the productions, I decide the casting, I decide the rehearsal schedule. End of story. Now get out!" Her voice rose to a shout.

"Yell all you want. You'll change the schedule to comply with the guidelines or I will report the violation. And even if Larry doesn't do anything about it"—which was a likely scenario—"the UIL will. You'll be barred from competing at Regionals."

She drew back in shock. "You can't be serious."

"Of course I'm serious. Look," I pointed to my head, "it's my serious face."

She decided on a new tack. "It's just for the next couple of weeks. We have to get this play in shape by the tenth." Her voice was almost pleading.

"The tenth? Since when do you put on a play in early September?"

"It's a special case, it's . . ." she struggled to find an explanation.

"Hey, what's going on?" a deeper voice broke in, and we both turned. Roland Wilding had made his entrance, but neither of us had noticed.

He looked from Nancy to me and back again, handsome face inquiring, golden hair gleaming in the fluorescent light. He was so ridiculously good-looking that his expressions always looked somewhat fake. Even the way he stood, hip cocked, one thumb casually hooked in a belt loop, reminded me of a male underwear model.

Nancy sputtered for a few seconds, trying to find the words. Annoyed, I realized I had just blown my chance to ask Roland about Coach Fred. I was now public enemy number one, or soon would be.

I flapped the practice schedule in the air. "Change it, Nancy. I'll be checking with the kids to make sure you do." And I left.

I was ashamed to find my hands were trembling. I hated confrontations, and I was more upset than I would have wanted Nancy to guess, both about having to be a hard-ass and about the way Nancy and Roland were given license to make kids miserable. Why should I have to keep an eye on them? Where was Larry, our fearless principal? This was his job. I considered whether I should take the matter up with him anyway, but I doubted whether he would do anything about it. No, somehow this had become my problem and the only thing I was sure about was that, like the monster in a slasher flick, it would rise from the dead and return to bite me in the ass.

Chapter 8

GLOCKS AND GRIEVANCES

The talk with Nancy made me later than usual getting to my room, and four of my tennis kids were already waiting in the hall. Students who arrived at school early had few places where they could go to finish homework or simply wait for the day to begin, and they often went to their first period classroom if the teacher arrived early enough. Lately the tennis team, even those who did not take a class with me, had taken to meeting in my room, a subtle vote of confidence that I recognized and appreciated. They'd started calling me Coach J, too, which cracked me up. Within the next ten minutes, a good portion of the team arrived, some working on assignments I was sure they should have finished the night before, others sitting together in the back, talking quietly. Right in the center of the group, as always, sat Dillon Andrews, friendly, smart, and popular. The perfect kid. Well, for my purposes anyway.

"Mr. Andrews," I said. "Could you come with me, please?"

He looked up, startled. One of the best things about

being a teacher is the power to give orders without explanation. I could see him wondering what he had done, thinking back over all the pranks—and I was sure there were several—for which he might be called to account. He assumed an angelic expression of innocence, which immediately made me suspicious that he actually did have something to feel guilty about.

We stepped into the hall, and I closed the door behind us. There were several ways I could play this, but I decided on the most direct approach possible. After all, these kids had liked Coach Fred.

"Dillon, you know everyone on the team, right?"

"Well . . . yeah, I do," he admitted cautiously.

"Pretty good kids, right?"

"Yeah," he nodded, more confident at this.

"I have a question for you that might be hard to answer. Actually, it's hard to ask, so let me start by giving you the background. In confidence. Do you know what that means?"

"Um, yeah, I'm not three. You don't want me to tell anyone else."

"Except your parents. You can always tell your parents anything."

He blinked with surprise. "What?"

"I'm serious. Nothing happens in this school that you shouldn't be able to tell your parents. Anyway, where was I?" I'd lost the thread. "Oh yeah. Look, Dillon, you know the kids on the team pretty well, right?"

He nodded again.

"The police found some items"—that sounded vague

enough—"that I think Coach Fred must have confiscated from some kids, but which the police think might be his."

"What kind of items?" he asked, eyes brightening with curiosity.

"Just . . . items." This was harder than I thought, especially with him looking at me like a squirrel spotting an acorn. "Okay, fine. Joints."

He gave a shout of laughter, loud enough to make me jump. "Coach Fred? You've got to be kidding." He looked in my face and realized I wasn't, adding firmly, "No way, no how. The police must be ar-tards."

I grinned at him. "Yeah, well, they aren't stupid, but they didn't know Coach Fred like we did. Anyway, what I'm asking you is, do you think they belonged to someone on the team?"

He stopped laughing and assumed a thoughtful expression. A group of girls came up the steps, long tan legs bare under very short skirts, ankles wobbling on platform shoes. Dillon's expression became decidedly less focused.

I snapped my fingers near his head to regain his attention. "I don't care about the joints. I'm not looking to get anyone into trouble. But if we could show that they weren't Fred's . . ."

"Yeah, I get you. But the thing is, I don't think they belong to anyone on the team either. I'm not saying it's not possible, but as far as I know we're all clean. And believe me, if Coach Fred had found a joint on someone, he would have kicked that someone off the team. He told us that on the first day of practice. Every year. Repeated it about once a week. He hated drugs."

"I know he hated drugs. But if it really came down to it,

would he really have kicked one of you off the team? Or would he have tried to work with that person?"

Dillon shrugged. "I'm pretty sure he would have kicked us off. He sounded serious."

"Okay, so where did the joints come from?" I asked, more to myself than to Dillon.

He gave me a jaded look. "He probably took them from some kid in a bathroom. All he'd have to do was hide in a stall for about three minutes to overhear a deal going down."

I made a mental note to go into the kids' bathrooms more often, something I usually avoided because they were disgusting. For some reason, the floors were always wet and at least one toilet in every one of them was more or less permanently stopped up. And I didn't even want to think what the boys' bathrooms must be like.

"Great," I said. "Well, if you think of something that might help, let me know. And Dillon, don't tell the other kids about the joints. I don't want anyone thinking of Fred that way."

He shook his head. "I could get on the PA and announce it to the entire school, and no one who had ever met Coach Fred would believe it for even one minute. But don't worry, I won't tell."

After wolfing down a turkey sandwich I'd brought from home, I spent the remainder of my lunch period asking questions, starting with Stan the Parking Nazi. Stan's official title was school monitor, which gave him the dignity and authority of a roaming mall guard. Among his many mostly self-imposed duties was the chore of verifying that kids who left the campus for lunch were actually seniors, which was a school policy. I found him on a grass island near the front entrance, stopping each car as it went out to demand to see IDs. Red-haired, with freckles on top of his freckles and a pear-shaped body that had never seen the inside of a gym, Stan was an impressive specimen of manhood. He had the raw intelligence of a piece of broccoli, but he was cheerful, and he loved his job. The kids called him the Parking Nazi more on principle than out of animosity, and it was a favorite campus pastime to slip one over on him.

I waited as he finished with one carload of giggling senior girls. "Stan, you got a minute? I need to ask you about that day Fred was killed."

He glanced up at me, face breaking into a grimace. A trickle of sweat rolled down his cheek, and he lifted the collar of his official James Bonham High School polo shirt to wipe it off. I caught a glimpse of a white undershirt and a sprinkling of red chest hair in the gap before I could avert my eyes.

"That was awful. Poor Coach. He was a real gentleman." Stan waved the next car by, obviously recognizing the driver, then held up a hand to stop a red Mustang. The driver rolled his eyes, but obediently slowed to a halt.

"Yeah, he was," I agreed. "Anyway, I want to know if you noticed anyone around that day who didn't belong. Maybe a car that was in the lot late that night?"

Stan snapped his fingers to demand ID from the kid driving the car. I glanced in the back window and saw a blue blanket spilling off the seat and over a large kid-sized lump on the floor. The lump quivered a little as though suppressing snorts of laughter.

"Don't really remember anything. Nothing that stands out." He waved the car on without noticing anything untoward and turned his attention to the next.

Across the parking lot, a group of boys headed toward a big Chevy Impala. A few of them clustered casually around the trunk, which opened and then quickly closed behind them. The number of boys remaining to climb into the car had been reduced by at least two. I glanced over at Stan to see if he'd noticed. He hadn't.

"What about visitors? There was at least one parent who came to the school because he was mad at Fred. Did you see him or anyone else like that?"

Stan tilted his head and looked up as though there might be an answer in the cloudless blue sky. I could feel the sun soaking into the concrete at my feet, feel the warmth settling into my hair and skin. The air carried the summer scent of warm grass and earth, overlaid by waves of exhaust and melting asphalt. Two cars slipped by without stopping while he pondered.

"There were lots of visitors. Kids, parents, teachers, workmen. I think that film crew was stomping around that day, measuring stuff around the back of the school. I wish I'd seen something!" he added, voice suddenly intense. "I wish I'd been there that night with Fred!"

The last statement was so heartfelt that I reached out and patted his shoulder, something I instantly regretted. It was like touching a sweat sock.

"Thanks anyway, Stan." I said, then decided that kindness in Fred's memory deserved to be rewarded. "Hey, just a suggestion—check the trunk of that Impala."

He looked surprised, then his eyes narrowed, predator instinct kicking in. He shot me a look of gratitude and triumph, and I left with a wave.

I stopped in at the administration office, welcoming the blast of icy air that spilled over me as I opened the door. This was the only building on campus that was properly air-conditioned. Or improperly, depending on your point of view. The two women working behind the large front counter were both wearing sweaters, and I could hear the hum of a space heater behind one of the eight desks that filled the large open area.

Maria Santos, secretary to Principal Larry Gonzales, looked up as I walked in and waved me over eagerly.

"Look!" she said, holding up both hands. "Blue. The tips of my fingers are actually blue. I beg Larry to turn up the temperature, but he tells me that women are always cold. Yeah, I tell him. When it's forty below zero, we are always cold. He just laughed."

I laughed, too. I couldn't help it, she looked so indignant. She glared at me for a moment, then relaxed into a giggle, her dark eyes crinkling with amusement. She spoke English perfectly, but with a rich Hispanic accent that lent her words an exotic flavor.

I sat down on the orange plastic chair beside her desk, looking around with some interest. I didn't often come back here, and the view was somewhat different. For one thing, there was a large portrait of Larry, looking very dignified and grim, hanging on the wall to the right.

Maria followed my eyes. "Lovely, right? He had it in his office for a long time until Coach Fred asked him if he had pictures of himself in his wallet, too. After that, he moved it out here." She smiled at the memory. "Poor Coach Fred."

"I bet he does have pictures of himself in his wallet," I said.

She nodded agreement, then shot a glance at the only other person in the room. The school accountant, Pat Carver, glared at us with her odd silvery eyes, narrowed and malevolent. She reminded me of a very large toad, wide stocky body perched atop long skinny legs. Even her face looked like a toad's, wide mouth, rubbery lips, and moist pale eyes behind thick glasses. Pat was in charge of auditing the fundraising efforts of the myriad student organizations and clubs and somehow had a lot of control over what could be collected and distributed. I thought about upcoming tennis events and gave her a big smile. She met my eyes with the warmth and humor of a python gazing at a mouse, then looked away.

"I did want to talk with you about Coach Fred," I said, lowering my voice so Pat couldn't hear. "Did he ever come in here to report anyone in his classes or on the tennis team for taking drugs?"

She looked thoughtful. "I don't know about drugs, but I think there was something going on. He came in two or three times during the week before school started—closed-door sessions with Larry."

I raised my eyebrows. Coach Fred hadn't liked Larry much,

often expressing the opinion that Larry was a worthless paper pusher who couldn't make a real decision to save his life. And that was what he said within Larry's hearing. He was even less flattering in private. He certainly hadn't been dropping in to shoot the breeze.

"And you don't have any idea what they talked about?" I asked.

An acid voice from across the room said, "That is none of your business, Ms. Shore. And I'm sure Ms. Santos understands that she can't reveal confidential information." Pat Carver glared at us both with her unblinking eyes.

My God, the woman had the hearing of a bat, I thought. She must have been straining with every fiber of her being to listen to our low conversation.

Maria was more direct. "Blow it out your ass, Pat."

Pat shot her the finger, then turned back to her computer.

At my slack-jawed expression, Maria explained, "Relations have deteriorated between Pat and me over the last few weeks."

"Really? You both hide it well."

Switching to Spanish, she said, "I'll tell you about that bitch sometime. You won't believe it." Then in English, she said loudly for Pat's benefit, "Confidential or not, I don't know what Fred wanted. You might want to talk with Larry."

I shuddered at the thought, but asked "Is he in?"

She laughed cynically. "Of course not. He can sense when someone might want to talk with him. He left a half hour ago."

• • •

Kyla was waiting at the door when my seventh-period class ended, a frantic look in her eye. She pushed through the exiting stream of students and hurried to my side. Several of the kids did a double take, looking from her to me and then back again. I wondered if real twins had it so bad. I saw a couple of them grab friends by the arms and wondered if they thought that keeping their fingers close to their chests while pointing made it either polite or subtle.

Fortunately, for once Kyla was oblivious. And panicked. "My class is today," she wailed. "You have to help me."

"It will be fine," I soothed, starting to gather up my things. "They aren't monsters. Just remember what I told you—they can sense fear. And don't get your fingers too close to their mouths."

Then I laughed my best evil genius laugh. How I wished I could be a fly on the wall when she walked into a room full of cynical teens and tried to talk to them about careers in science, but go with her I would not. For one thing, I was due on the tennis courts, and for another she'd somehow arrange things so I would be doing her job.

"Oh, my God. I'm dead." Kyla sank into my chair and swung her purse onto my desk, where it landed with a loud thunk.

"What do you have in there? Bricks?" I asked.

She shrugged, her eyes sliding evasively to the side. "You know, the usual. Phone, camera, wallet."

I wouldn't have thought much about it if she hadn't looked

so guilty. After all, my own purse weighed as much as a well-fed toddler. So why was she . . .

"You do not have your gun in that purse," I said, realization dawning.

"Of course not!" she denied, snatching it back and hugging it to her chest.

"Because carrying a gun on school property is a felony. And you've already been arrested once for carrying illegally."

"I know. I'm not stupid."

"Then tell me you don't have a gun."

"I don't have a gun," she said, blue eyes wide and ingenuous.

I didn't believe her. She was packing her 9mm Glock 19 in that bag. At my school. I considered. Short of wrestling with her for possession, there wasn't much I could do about it. And at least I now had plausible deniability, something that was critical in any dealings involving Kyla. I comforted myself with the thought that at least she knew how to handle it and she wasn't a crazed loner.

"I've got to go," I said. "Tennis practice."

"Are you kidding me? You can't go to tennis. You have to come and help me. You said you would."

"That was before I became the tennis coach, and besides, I did help you. We came up with a lesson plan, remember? And you're a big girl. You can do this."

She snorted twin puffs of air through her nose, but, for reasons known only to herself, didn't argue with me.

I locked my desk. "Come on, let's go."

She rose, then glanced at me slyly. "So what's up with you and Detective Gallagher?"

"Maybe I should be asking you that. What did he have to say after I left?"

"Not too much. He asked how often you have trouble with parents."

"What did you tell him?" I asked, curious.

She said, "I said I didn't think you had much trouble, because you would've bitched about it if you had. We didn't talk very long. Another group started playing, so we pushed back and listened. It was nice. Anyway, why did you scamper off like that?"

I didn't answer for a moment, not exactly sure myself. I finally shrugged. "He irritated me, finding us like that. And I really did have work to do." Both reasons were true, but even I knew they were just excuses.

"Uh-huh. I thought so." Her expression was both smug and condescending.

Annoyed, I said, "What do you mean?"

"You know the sparks were flying between the two of you."

I had been moving toward the door. Now I stopped. "What the hell are you talking about? The only sparks were from me being pissed off at the two of you for being stalker and accomplice. Seriously, Kyla—I can't believe you routinely post your location for anyone to see."

"I changed the setting so only friends can see now. Of course, Colin is now a friend, but that's beside the point. And don't try to change the subject. You have to admit he's one fine-looking man."

Well, yes he was, but I wasn't going to give her the satisfaction. "He thinks one of my good friends was a drug dealer.

He's an idiot. And a blabbermouth," I added, thinking of my conversation with my ex.

"An idiot with a heart of gold? Or at least a bod of gold? Besides, he didn't strike me as being stupid. At all. And he couldn't keep his eyes off you."

This was somewhat more interesting, but she didn't need to know that. "Now who's being stupid? He's the cop in charge of a murder investigation. I'm a . . ." What was I? A witness? A suspect? "I'm an involved party," I said with dignity. "If he looked at me, it was only to pry information from me."

"You're oblivious. Why don't you look around once in a while?"

"If you think he's so hot, why don't you give him a call? Or tweet him or whatever it is you do."

She changed the subject. "So how about Sherman?"

I laughed. "You mean Sher-monica? He couldn't keep his eyes off those shirt bunnies."

"A temporary infatuation," she said, a little frown creasing her perfect brows. "Veronica doesn't have the brains to keep him interested very long."

"I think his interest lies somewhere south of that. Besides, I keep telling you, I'm dating Alan." I started edging for the door.

"So you say. Odd how he's never around though. Sherman has a lot of good qualities." She paused, thinking. "What the hell were his parents thinking? Do you think he'd be willing to change his name?"

"Um . . . no. Look, we've both got to go. We'll be late."

"I just can't do this," she whined.

"Yes, you can. Go on. Just start by introducing yourself and then make each of the kids introduce themselves and say why they are interested in technology. That will kill half the time right there. And look, if it'll make you feel better, I'll get the tennis team started and come check on you in about twenty minutes."

"Yes, that would make me feel better. And make it ten minutes."

She followed me out the door reluctantly, her normal jaunty step replaced by a dejected shuffle. I laughed all the way to the tennis courts. That is until I reached the shed and saw Roland Wilding waiting for me.

He leaned casually against the doorjamb, one hand again in a pocket, artfully tousled hair stirring in the light breeze. Something in the way he stood made me expect him to produce a bottle of men's cologne and start talking about how women just would not leave him alone. I glanced at the courts. While the boys had their minds on tennis, the girls kept stealing not so subtle glances his way. All except McKenzie, who very carefully kept her head turned any other direction.

"Hi, Roland," I said, wondering if he was here to talk about the drama practice schedule. I didn't know how deeply he was involved in making the decisions about the drama club, or whether Nancy ruled alone, but either way, I doubted I was on his best buddy list.

"Jocelyn," he said stiffly, not smiling.

I walked past him into the shed, and turned on the light on the desk, looking around for my clipboard with the day's practice plan. As bright as it was outside, the tennis shed was dim and stuffy, smelling of moldy plywood, new tennis balls, and feet. Nothing at all remained to remind anyone of Fred's death. I'd long since cleaned up the fingerprint dust, righted the tennis racquets, picked up the balls. The only thing that had changed since that day was the addition of a few cases of bottled water and sports drinks intended for our first match, courtesy of the tennis mothers. The calendar above the desk was still marked in his handwriting with the dates of our upcoming matches. The roster still hung beside the phone, his name and number listed prominently at the top. I suppose all the reminders should have upset me, but I found them oddly comforting.

Roland followed me inside and stood awkwardly beside my desk, looking around as though he'd never been in the place, which he probably hadn't.

"I need to talk to you," he started.

I cut him off. "Hang on, will you? I need to get the team going."

I hurried out to the court and called the team over, redistributing them on different courts and starting the drills. "Ten minutes, then we switch," I reminded them. "Brittany, will you let us know when time is up?"

I returned to Roland, who was now standing outside, and tried to decide whether I should move into the shade, which would be more comfortable, or instead stand with him in the sun, which might shorten this conversation. I chose the sun.

"What can I do for you?" I asked him, trying to sound helpful and pleasant rather than suspicious.

He flashed a brilliant smile, and ran a hand through his hair. "I wanted to talk to you about the acting arrangements."

He gestured in the direction of the giant silver truck at the back of the parking lot.

I followed his gaze. As far as I could tell, the film crew was taking a break. I saw a couple of roadies smoking under a tree, but everyone else had either left entirely or had escaped into one of the air conditioned trailers. These California types had no appreciation for our Texas summers.

His choice of topic was not at all what I expected. "You mean the movie they're filming?" I asked.

"Yes, exactly. The movie. *Teenage Fangst*. I spoke with Michael Dupre yesterday." I could hear a touch of wonder in his voice over the name. "Michael Dupre. He told me he already had all the actors he needed. That he'd made arrangements with you for the tennis team to be his extras."

I hadn't exactly forgotten, but I'd had other things on my mind. "Oh, yeah. Neat, huh? I think the kids are probably pretty excited."

"Probably?" He pressed his lips together like a cranky spinster taking a bite of a lemon.

"Definitely," I corrected. "They were definitely excited. I handed out the release forms yesterday. Guess I better see about collecting them and getting them over to the set." I made a little note on my clipboard.

"Do you even know who Michael Dupre is?" he asked.

I'd meant to look him up on the Internet, but I'd forgotten. "Of course," I bluffed. "He's a director, very up and coming."

"And a screenwriter. Name one picture he's made."

"Oh you know, that one with the actors. I can't remember the name."

One of the blue eyes twitched, and he rubbed his temple. "Maybe you've heard of *Midnight Moves?*"

Bluffing was becoming too much work. "Um, no."

"It won the Grand Jury Prize for Dramatic Film at the Sundance Film Festival," he said, trying to jog my memory.

"Impressive."

"It also won Best Screenplay at Cannes." His voice was almost pleading.

"Still not ringing any bells, Roland. I'm sure it was great."

"Michael Dupre is a genius, the most watched young director of this decade."

"Well, I'll be sure to check out his movie the next time I'm renting. Thanks for the tip. So, was that all you wanted?"

"No!" he almost shouted. Then, in a quieter tone, said, "No. I want to talk to you about the roles your kids have in the movie."

"What about them?"

"Don't you think it would be better to have drama students in those roles? You know, kids who are actually interested in acting?"

I considered this. In a way he had a point. Drama students would certainly have seemed a logical choice when casting extras, but on the other hand, extras by the very nature of their parts did not usually have to have any particular acting talent. And anyone would think it was fun to be in a movie.

"My kids are interested. They're really excited."

"I'm sure everyone would understand if you withdrew and let the drama department have those roles."

"Um, the only people who would 'understand' would be you, Roland. There's no way we're withdrawing. Why don't you talk with their casting people? They could probably use other extras."

"I did talk with them. They said their needs are met."

"Well, there you go. I'm sorry, but . . ."

"You don't even want to do this!" he burst out. His words were those of a petulant child. "You don't care."

He obviously did. His blue eyes glittered with suppressed rage, and he'd forgotten to hold his casual, underwear-model pose.

"I might not care all that much, but the kids do," I pointed out.

"You planned it! You waited around so you'd be the first one to see the crew arrive and then you swooped in to steal those parts from us. You did it out of spite, didn't you? You have some vendetta against the drama department. I heard what you said to Nancy, trying to keep us from practicing, trying to keep us from doing well. You'd love to see us fail, wouldn't you?"

He was so mad, he was spitting, and I took a step back to remove myself from the spray zone. It was too bad I'd had maintenance spread all that ant poison the day before. Where was a really good anthill when you needed one?

"Go away, Roland."

"You . . ."

"I mean it. Go away. I've got practice, you've got rehearsal. And this conversation is over."

I walked away without a backward glance, although turning my back on him me feel oddly uneasy, and not just because it was rude. I moved around the courts slowly, watching the kids, giving the occasional tip. I'd been viewing a lot of tennis training videos lately and was entering into that phase of having just enough knowledge to be a nuisance to anyone who really knew what they were doing. It made me feel like a pro. When at last I turned around, Roland was nowhere in sight. I permitted myself a sigh of relief.

Chapter 9

FILMING AND FEARS

Belatedly remembering my promise to Kyla, I told the kids I'd be right back and returned to the school to find the room she'd been assigned. Right now, between classes, the halls were deserted and the silence broken only by a low hum of muted voices coming from behind the closed classroom doors. I peered through the window in the door, and somewhat to my astonishment saw a group of girls shouting with laughter, focusing rapt attention on my cousin. She stood in the front of the room and was talking fast, making broad gestures with her hands. I watched for a moment, but I couldn't make out what she was saying. Somehow, I doubted it was a technology story. Kyla caught sight of me, and gave me a huge thumbs up. I grinned back at her, glad she needed no assistance.

The staccato tapping of heels made me look around to see Laura Esperanza stepping down the hall at her usual brisk pace. Today her long hair was braided into a glossy rope as thick as my arm, its beribboned end swinging level with her hips. The shoes she wore added a wobbly four inches to her height, which brought her head level with my chin and somehow made her look like a preteen playing dress up.

Catching sight of me, she called, "Hey, *queso pasa, mi amigo?*"

I laughed. "Cheese to you, too, man."

"What?"

"*Queso pasa*. That's good."

She looked puzzled, but then shook it off. "What's up?"

I spared a fleeting feeling of pity for her Spanish students.

I indicated the window just as another burst of laughter spilled from the room. "Oh, just checking on Kyla. Looks like she's doing great with her class. I'm not convinced she's staying on topic, but there you go. Hey, you'll never guess what happened with Nancy Wales."

Laura's eyes lit up. "You had a run-in with that bitch? I hate her. I hate the air she breathes. I hate the food she chews. What did she do now?"

I told her about the confrontation we'd had, and ended by saying, "My only regret is that I'm not going to be able to quiz Roland about Coach Fred. His panties are all in a twist about the tennis team getting roles as extras in that movie."

"He'll get over it. It wasn't like you planned it."

"No, but he thinks I did. What a twerp."

"If I have a chance, I'll ask him about Fred," she offered. "I have to go talk with one of them about getting the stage for the FLS again, and it might be easier to tackle him anyway. Assuming he's halfway human about it, what did you want to know?"

"Mostly if he'd noticed anyone else in the school who shouldn't have been there. Maybe a parent." I was thinking of Gary Richards. "Look, don't bother. I'm sure the police have already asked the same questions, and it's not like Roland ever looks much beyond the nearest mirror anyway."

She shrugged. "It won't hurt to ask. Hey, what's this I hear about Fred keeping pot in the tennis shed?"

I looked at her, appalled. "Where did you hear that?"

"I don't know. It's going around. Some of the teachers were talking about it in the lounge. I don't know where they got it. Is it true?"

I thought about pulling my hair and gnashing my teeth, but instead I asked, "Do you think it's true?"

She considered this. "I wouldn't have thought so," she said at last, "but then again, I didn't really know Fred. He always seemed like a good guy."

"He was a good guy. It's true the police found pot in his desk, but he must have confiscated it from some kid. I know it wasn't his. I just hate it that this is getting around. You'd think there'd be a law against spreading rumors or discussing crime scenes. That stupid cop." I thought about what I'd like to do to Detective Colin Gallagher if I ever saw him again.

Laura patted my arm. "Try not to worry about it. People who knew him won't believe it, and it will all be forgotten as soon as the next interesting bit of gossip pops up." Glancing at her watch, she added, "I better scoot back to class. The little monsters are probably destroying something."

I nodded, and she tapped off carefully, like a deer crossing a frozen lake. I could not imagine how she managed to stand on those things all day long.

When I returned to the courts, Carl from the movie set had arrived, cigarette on lip, tattoos gleaming through a sheen of sweat. He was wearing a rag that at some point had been a T-shirt before either he or a grizzly bear had ripped off the sleeves.

"Goddamn, it's hot here," he greeted me.

"It's warmish," I agreed.

Actually, it wasn't all that bad for early September. We'd already had the first cold front of fall, and the temperature was in the low nineties.

He looked at me sourly, but asked, "You got all the release forms? We want to get a shot in today."

"Yes, they're right here." I retrieved them from my desk in the shed, and handed them over.

He gave a grunt, which I assumed was meant as thanks. He was a charmer, that's for sure. On the other hand, he seemed to be Michael Dupre's right-hand man, which implied he was sharper than he seemed.

Thoughtfully, I asked, "Hey, Carl, when did you guys get here? I mean, what day?"

"Some of us been here about a week. Trailer and such came yesterday. Well, you know that," he added with a small grin.

"Were you here the Monday before last? August 23?"

"Maybe. Why do you want to know?" He looked at me suspiciously.

"If you were around Monday evening, I was wondering if you'd seen the old tennis coach. The guy who was here before me."

"You mean the dead guy?" He perked up with interest at that. "Yeah, I saw him. Old geezer wearing white shorts and a Gilligan cap."

"That's right," I agreed. I wondered how he would describe me and decided I didn't really want to know. But it confirmed my hunch that he was both alert and observant.

"What about him?"

"Did you happen to notice him talking to anyone in particular? Besides the kids, I mean?"

He took a pull on his cigarette, making the tip flare and the paper retreat toward his face. He held the smoke deep in his lungs for a long moment and then blew it out, courteously turning his head away from me. Not that it helped much. The breeze blew it directly into my face.

He noticed and coughed apologetically. "Sorry 'bout that. Yeah, old dude had some sort of argument with a guy. I could see his hands waving. Sorta funny, that's why I remember."

I could feel my mouth hanging open and made an effort to close it. "What did the other guy look like? Do you know who it was?"

He shrugged. "Nope. He was just a guy."

Grinding teeth, I said, "Do you remember anything about him? Was he tall? Short? Wearing a skirt? Anything?"

He grinned at me. "Wearing a skirt. That's good. Probably remember that. Nah, he was just regular. Big ass, though," he added as an afterthought. "For a dude."

"Big, but not fat? Wait! Did he have man-boobs? And look like a Chihuahua?"

He blinked. "Now that you mention it, he did have man-boobs. And the Chihuahua thing—yeah, you could say that. You know who it is?"

"I've got a good idea." I did indeed. Ed Jones, math teacher and wannabe tennis coach. I would have to have a talk with Mr. Jones.

Ever alert, the kids had stopped playing and were watching us eagerly. I beckoned to them and they galloped over, shoes slapping on the concrete.

Carl flicked through the forms. "Okay, good enough. Let's go."

He led the way toward a school bus, and I frowned. "Wait, where are we going?"

"We've got the cameras set up over in the park . . . um," he consulted his notes, ". . . Slaughter Creek Park."

"We're going to a park?" No one had told me that.

"Yeah, there's a terrific wooded path there, lots of trees, real isolated. Perfect for a foot chase."

I looked over at my kids, dressed in their tennis clothes, carrying racquets. "Um, I'm not objecting, but just out of curiosity, in what universe would a tennis team be running through the middle of an isolated park?"

He grinned. "Don't worry. By the time we get done with the edits, it'll look like the path is right beside the courts."

I shook my head, but retrieved my purse from the shed and locked the door. Despite what I'd said to Roland, I had to admit this was pretty exciting. I'd never been on a movie set before, and the kids were almost beside themselves, talking and laughing as we all piled on to the bus. As we rolled out of the parking lot, I spared a sympathetic thought for Roland and the drama club. No wonder he'd been green with envy.

Carl drove the short distance to the park without much regard for either the speed limit or the laws of physics. We were all gripping our seats with white knuckles to avoid being flung into the aisle when at last he pulled into a parking lot beside an enormous playground where a few moms sat in the shade, watching their preschool kids playing. They looked up curiously as we disembarked—I somewhat shakily and the kids with a great deal of laughter.

"This way," said Carl, and led the way along a path of crushed red gravel that ran beside the soccer fields and into the trees.

Just past the seventh tee of the disc golf course that ran beside the path, our way was blocked by a strip of yellow tape and guarded by a large young man with a clipboard and a wireless headset. He acknowledged Carl with a nod and opened the tape for us to pass, announcing us into the microphone as we went by. The path narrowed and wound through a thick grove of live oaks, elms, and cedars. Dense undergrowth filled the gaps between the trees and made any thought of leaving the path all but impossible. Dusty green and blue shadows spilled around the brush, growing long as the sun sank toward the western horizon. The crunch of tennis shoes on gravel drowned out the natural songs of cicadas and mockingbirds.

The young woman I'd seen on the first day hurried over,

long brown hair pulled back in a ponytail, thick black glasses perched on her head.

"Hi," she said in a bright voice. "I'm Amanda Finch, the casting director."

She looked us over, eyes bright and an inquisitive as a hamster's, then beamed at us. "Oh, yes. You're perfect. Come this way." She started off at a brisk pace.

We followed, looking around in wonder. The soccer fields and playground were less than two hundred yards away, but you would never know it. To all appearances, we had entered an isolated wilderness.

"I wasn't at all sure about it when Michael said he'd hired you," she said over her shoulder, "but I should have trusted him. He has a really good eye. Okay, let's have you stand just here. Might as well take advantage of the shade, right?"

She walked down the line of kids, looking at each one individually.

"You're just perfect," she said finally. "Very authentic. I have no changes whatsoever. Now, I don't know if anyone has told you yet, but you'll need to wear these exact clothes for every take. Exact. Right down to your underwear." She smiled, an unexpected dimple flashing like a star on her smooth cheek then vanishing as quickly as it came. "No, I'm just kidding about that. But everything that shows. Even your socks. Audiences are very sophisticated these days. They notice the minutiae. I'm going to take a picture of each one of you so that we can be sure everything is right if we need to film on another day. So, if you are wearing anything you don't want to be wearing, take it off now."

She began taking pictures of each kid, and I took the opportunity to walk forward just a bit farther. The path made another serpentine turn, and rounding the bend I came into an opening where the film crew was setting up. A small group of people was dancing attendance around a massive camera with a lens as big around as a tennis racquet. A few paces away, Michael Dupre consulted with the cameraman, pointing out something and shaking his head. Someone with a light meter was taking measurements and calling them out.

My phone rang in my purse. Instantly, every head on the set whipped around to glare at me. I felt like a gazelle accidentally stumbling into a pride of lions. Lions with serious anger management issues. Backing away, I dug in my purse and yanked the phone open without even looking to see who it was, then hurried away into the cover of trees as quickly as I could.

Raising the phone to my ear, I heard a voice on the other end saying "Hello?"

"Hello? Who is this?" I asked. The voice sounded vaguely familiar, but I couldn't quite place it.

The West Texas accent of the next few words identified him as much as what he said. "Colin Gallagher. Are y'all all right? You sound like you're running."

I gave a muted laugh. "One more ring and I would have been the victim of a lynch mob."

I kept walking to be sure I was out of hearing range of the crew. The path took a sharp turn to the left, then merged with a long low ramp of concrete serving as a bridge over the creek for which Slaughter Creek Park had been named. We'd had a particularly rainy summer, which meant that the water, though not flowing, still formed a puddle or two nestling in the rocky bed. The stones were mostly limestone, white and lumpy, ranging in size from softballs to M&M's. One or two trees leaning from the bank were gently turning from green to gold, and a breeze stirred like a whisper through a soft fall of brown leaves at their base. I stopped on the bridge, enchanted.

Colin sounded amused. "Lynch mob, huh? What, are you at a library?"

"Better than that. I'm on a movie set," I said and explained where I was. Halfway through, I stopped in midsentence, suddenly remembering that I was furious with him. "I'm sure you don't care about this. Why did you call?"

If he noticed the ice in my tone, he did not give any indication. "I wanted to ask you a few more questions. Would it be all right if I came by?"

More questions? Now what? "Now's not a very good time. I have to stay with the kids. Can you ask me quickly?"

"No, but it can wait. When will you be done there?"

"I don't know."

From a little way away, I could hear the sound of feet on the gravel path drawing closer. I wondered if someone from the film crew was coming to tell me to keep it down. I walked down the concrete embankment and into the dry streambed, thinking that I surely wouldn't bother anyone there.

He thought for moment, then said, "They'll have to be wrapping it up before it gets dark. Tell you what, why don't you give me a call when you're done, and I'll swing by?"

I hesitated, torn between curiosity and the desire for

petty vengeance. At last, I said, "Okay. But I can't promise when it will be."

"I'll be here," he said in a cheerful tone.

I hung up without saying good-bye. That will teach him, I thought, then almost laughed out loud. Detective or not, he was still a man. He probably hadn't even noticed.

I was just turning back toward the film crew, intending to rejoin my kids, when I heard a sound behind me. One stone clicked against another, very close. With a flash of fear, I jerked around, but not fast enough. I saw only a blur of movement, a raised arm against the blinding brilliance of the sun, then a blow to my temple.

I fell hard, stunned and helpless, my phone flying out of my hand and clattering against the stones some distance away. Blood streamed instantly and profusely into my eyes, blinding me. I tried to rise, or at least lift my head, but the world swayed back and forth, leaving me sick and dizzy. I clutched the rocks of the streambed, trying to figure out what had happened. A figure moved beside me, and out of blurred eyes I saw an arm holding a rock the size of a grapefruit raised above me. Instinctively throwing an arm over my head, I curled into a protective ball, which probably saved my life. The second blow, harder than the first, glanced off my upper arm and shoulder, an agonizing strike that drew a cry from my lips. A blow meant to kill. Scrubbing at the blood in my eyes, I tried to roll away, but my body didn't seem to want to obey my screaming mind. I managed to flop into a puddle, but I knew it wasn't far enough. A splash told me my attacker had leaped after me. I knew I was dead.

A scream and the sound of running feet from the direction of the movie set saved me. My attacker checked, aimed a last savage kick into my side, then turned and fled. I tried to see who it was, but could only make out a figure in blue. Sobbing and gasping, I lay still for what seemed a long time, head spinning, trying not to throw up. My arm and shoulder felt like they were on fire and my ribs ached, but the worst was my head, where there was more throbbing going on than in a romance novel.

Move, I told myself. Nothing happened. It felt like the horrible dream that comes halfway between wakefulness and sleep when your body is paralyzed. Move, I told myself again. And this time, slowly and reluctantly, my body obeyed. I couldn't stand, but I made it onto hands and knees and crawled out of the puddle and across stones to the concrete rise. I wasn't sure I could make it up the three-foot incline, but somehow my tennis shoes scrabbled against the rough surface and found purchase. I dragged myself to the top. Disoriented, I wasn't sure which way to go, but the sound of voices to my right pulled me in that direction.

The feel of crushed gravel cutting into my palms provided the incentive I needed to try to stand. I pushed myself up, the world dipping and whirling as I did so. Swaying, I made it to an upright position and staggered forward. Blood still poured freely down the side of my face, spilling onto my white shirt and dripping onto my legs and the ground, although at least now I could see out of one eye. A few more paces, and I made it around the bend in the path, reeling drunkenly into the clearing where the camera crew waited.

To my shock, I was met by a chorus of screams, and a

herd of panicked tennis kids sprinting toward me, looking over their shoulders as they ran as though being chased. Terrified they would run me over, I held up bloody hands to ward them off, and they balked and scattered like startled horses, parting and flowing around me. As they passed, I thought I saw huge gray shapes in hot pursuit, running beside a camera rolling like a freight train on silver rails. I caught one glimpse of Michael Dupre's astonished eyes, and then I collapsed.

Chapter 10

MUGGINGS AND MOTIVES

The next bit was pretty much a blur. I heard someone yell, "Cut!" and within seconds I was surrounded by a chorus of disembodied voices. I was vaguely aware of Brittany's face, then Dillon's, but I couldn't seem to focus on anyone in particular. In the background Michael Dupre was yelling at someone in a particularly penetrating voice.

"Was this your idea? No one fucks with my shots, do you hear me? Did you plan this? Did you actually think it would work?"

Wow, someone was in big trouble. I wondered who it was.

Then someone said, "I think she's really hurt."

"Is that real blood?"

"For God's sakes, someone call an ambulance."

Someone was hurt? Was it one of my kids? I tried to lift my head to find out, then realized they were probably talking about me. It didn't really feel so bad lying on my back like this.

I just wished everything would stop tilting and that other people would stop shouting. I wanted to tell them about the guy who'd hit me, to tell them to go after him, that he was dangerous and needed arresting, but I must have gone to sleep instead. I have a fuzzy memory of being lifted onto a stretcher, of riding in the back of a rocking ambulance, and of getting very sick over someone's very white shoes. Other than that, I have no idea where the next few hours went.

When I finally became myself again, I was lying in a hospital bed, and Kyla was sitting in the visitor chair reading a magazine. She looked pale and uncomfortable, shoulders loosely wrapped in a hospital blanket, hair slightly askew on one side as though she'd been asleep. I looked at her fondly, absurdly glad that I wasn't alone.

I stirred, trying to find my voice, but she was instantly alert and at my side.

"How are you feeling?" she asked, then went on without waiting for me to respond. "Everything is fine. You are doing great, nothing to worry about at all. You're in the hospital."

I opened my mouth again, and she continued, not giving me a chance to speak. "The tennis kids have gone home, I've taken care of Belle, the school knows what happened, and I decided not to call your mom and dad since you're going to be just fine."

I closed my mouth and looked at her, impressed. In two sentences she'd told me everything I really needed to know.

"Not bad," I croaked out, throat as dry as summer. "How long did you work on that?"

She looked taken aback for a second, then broke into a

wide grin. "Guess you're not brain damaged after all. Or at least not more than before."

I gingerly raised my right hand to my head. The left was hooked up to about a thousand tubes. Well, one tube, but it felt like more. I hated needles. My head seemed to be wrapped in bandages, and, despite whatever was dripping into my arm, it ached like a hillbilly's last tooth.

"So how bad is it?"

"Just a mild concussion. Not even a linear fracture, whatever that is, although they seemed to be worried about it for a while. No internal bleeding. All is well. Except, according to some kid named Dillon, you looked like 'Freddy Krueger's latest' when they brought you in. That's a quote, by the way. He was pretty hyped up."

"He's not still here?" I asked, alarmed.

"Not anymore. He and the rest of them insisted on coming with you to the hospital, and if you'll believe it, that film crew loaded them on the bus and brought them. Michael Dupre himself even stopped by," she added in an impressed tone.

"I . . . wait, you know who Michael Dupre is?"

"Well, duh. Everyone knows who Michael Dupre is. He's pretty hot, too," she added with a gleam in her eye. "Even in person. So many of those film types look tiny off screen, but he's all right."

"So glad you approve. What happened to the kids?"

She shrugged. "A nurse came in and had a cow when she saw them, so they left. I assume the film crew dropped them back at the school. Anyway, who cares about all that? What happened to you? No one can figure it out. One minute you were wandering off, talking on your cell phone, and the next thing anyone knew you were covered in blood. Did you fall?"

I stared at her, appalled. "Well, only after someone tried to kill me. Are you telling me no one is out looking for the guy?" I struggled to sit up.

"Hey, don't do that!" she protested, putting a hand on my shoulder. "You shouldn't be moving around yet."

"I have to call the police," I told her. "Someone tried to kill me."

For a moment I could see that she wasn't sure whether to believe me, but then her expression hardened. "Look, promise me you won't move, and I'll go and call Detective Gallagher. He's been by twice, asking after you. He wanted me to call him the minute you woke up anyway."

"He did?"

"Yup. So, let me go call."

"Call here."

She looked embarrassed. "They threatened to confiscate my cell phone if they caught me talking on it again. I'll be right back."

In my semidazed state, this seemed reasonable until the door closed behind her and I actually thought about it. Then I caught sight of the bedside phone and realized that she hadn't wanted me to hear whatever it was she was going to say. I wasn't sure what that meant. A number of unkind thoughts crossed my mind, ranging from thinking she needed privacy because she did not believe me and wanted to say I was raving or that she wanted to flirt with Colin. Either way, I decided I did not have enough energy to worry about it and found myself drifting into a light doze.

The next time I opened my eyes, Colin Gallagher was sitting in the chair by my bedside, thumbing through a magazine. Someone had turned off the glaring overhead lights, and the room was lit by the bluish fluorescent glow from the light strip above my bed. A curtain was drawn across the window to my left, but a slim gap revealed a night sky. Kyla was nowhere to be seen.

Colin looked up from his magazine and smiled. He was wearing a pale dress shirt, tie loosened and collar unbuttoned. The unnatural hospital lighting cast odd shadows, stripping the color from everything it touched, streaming over his high cheekbones and the planes of his face, turning his eyes into black pools under their dark brows. He looked tired.

He said, "Awake at last. How are you feeling?"

I struggled to sit up, feeling the sharp ache return to my head, but not as bad as before. Colin leaned forward and pushed a button, raising the head of my bed a few inches.

"Too early to tell. What time is it?"

He glanced at his watch. "About three o'clock. In the morning. I sent your sister home—she was beat."

"Cousin," I corrected automatically. But I was glad Kyla had gone home.

Colin rose and poured me a cup of water without being asked. I sipped gratefully, pretty sure some animal had crawled into my mouth and used it as a litter box while I slept. Lifting a cautious hand to my head, I explored the bandages stretching across my forehead and temple.

"It's not too bad," he said. "You have a pretty good shiner, but the swelling is already going down."

"A shiner? You mean a black eye? Me?" My voice squeaked in alarm. "Mirror. I need a mirror." I threw back the blankets, then realized I was still attached to tubes.

He put a hand on my shoulder and pushed me back in alarm. "Don't try to get up."

I frowned, then had another thought. "Purse. Where's my purse? I have a mirror in there."

A wardrobe was built into the wall on the far side of my bed. He hurriedly opened the door. "Nothing here."

"Someone stole my purse?" My voice rose to something uncomfortably close to a shriek.

He made placating gestures with his hands. "No, no. I doubt it. I'm sure your cousin took it for safekeeping. Now why don't you calm down? The black eye isn't going anywhere. You'll be able to see it in the morning. It'll probably be even more impressive then."

I glared at him. "If that's supposed to be comforting . . ."

"No, no. I just meant . . ." He stopped and took a breath and started over. "Just calm down and tell me what happened. Then, when we're done, I'll get a nurse in here, how about that?"

I didn't think much of it, but the need to report my attack slightly outweighed concerns about my appearance. Slightly. Besides, if it was three o'clock in the morning, he had to be exhausted.

I told him exactly what had happened in the creek bed, which didn't take long. He listened without comment, jotting down notes. When I had finished, he looked thoughtful.

"So you don't know which direction the guy came from?"

I tried to remember, but at last shook my head, then wished I hadn't. A stabbing pain behind my eyes told me not to do that again. "I was facing the creek, looking away from the path. I didn't realize he was there until the last second."

"And this was while you were talking to me?"

"Yes, we'd just finished when I heard him. No, wait." I tried to think back. "No, I'd heard someone a minute or two before then. I heard shoes crunching on the gravel. You know what I mean? But, I looked and didn't see anyone, so I turned away again."

"So it's possible he was waiting in the bushes for a few minutes. I'll go out there in the morning when it's light and see what I can see. It's unlikely I'll find anything, but we'd better make sure."

"Yeah," I said, sighing.

After all, other than a few drops of my own blood, what would there be to find? The rocks of the creek would not hold footprints. Footprints. Foot. The memory of that last nasty kick suddenly returned. "You know, whoever did this was really . . . mean."

"Mean? You think someone who brutally attacked you without warning, who struck you hard enough to give you a concussion, and who was apparently trying to kill you was . . . mean?" He mimicked my word choice and voice with some accuracy.

I wanted to be offended, but despite myself my lips twitched.

He saw it and went on. "Wow, I'd hate to have you on my

jury. I bet you think that Ted Bundy was quite unpleasant and Jack the Ripper! Well, Jack was just downright naughty."

His blue eyes crinkled as he grinned, the first real smile I'd seen from him. It changed him—the grim, tired cop transforming into a warm, attractive man. My eyes dropped briefly, taking in the long jaw, darkened slightly with a day's growth of stubble, then moving along the width of his shoulders. Catching myself, I quickly looked away.

"Stop!" I told him, mostly because holding in laughter hurt my head. "You know what I meant. Kicking me after I was down was . . ." I fumbled for what I was trying to say.

He sobered, realizing what I meant. "You mean it was personal. More than just a mugging?"

"It was so angry." Even now, I could still feel the rage and desperation that had poured from my attacker.

He thought about this, rising from his seat and pacing back and forth in the tiny space at the foot of my bed. I leaned my head back against the pillows and watched him, trying to keep my eyes from focusing on his butt. He had very longs legs and a flat stomach. Not even a hint of man-boobs.

He glanced at me. "What are you smiling at?"

"Nothing," I said. "Hey, did you interview Ed Jones? I found out he'd been talking to Fred out by the courts the day Fred died."

His eyes narrowed at the change of subject, but he let it go. "How did you find that out?"

"I hear things. Anyway, did you?"

"The name doesn't ring a bell, but I talked to a lot of people. Why?"

This question stumped me. After all, did I really think Ed Jones, he of the tight knit shirts and watery eyes, had anything to do Fred's death?

I didn't answer. Colin shot me a curious glance but returned to the subject of my attacker.

"You think someone targeted you specifically. You weren't just the first person on the path who looked alone and vulnerable?"

"I wasn't carrying my purse, because I'd left it on the bus. I was wearing shorts and a T-shirt, so it should have been pretty obvious that I wasn't carrying much. If the guy was a mugger, surely he would have at least been looking for wallet or keys. He didn't even bother to go through my pockets."

"Okay, then that brings up the standard cop question. Do you have any enemies?" He made it sound like a joke, but he also wanted an answer.

Yesterday, I would have laughed and said no. Today, in a hospital bed, IV dripping clear liquid into my veins, I had to pause and think. Did I have enemies? It seemed completely ridiculous. After all, I was cute and lovable. Then I thought about everyone I had annoyed in the past few days.

Gary Richards wasn't happy with me about the tennis team, but he couldn't know for sure that I'd maneuvered him into that anthill, and no one would harbor a grudge over something like that anyway. A strongly worded letter of complaint to the school board, maybe, but a sneak attack in a park? As for everyone else, Ed Jones desired the coaching position I had claimed, Nancy Wales was pissed off because I'd stopped her from running a theater sweatshop, and Roland Wilding was ticked because I'd stolen a chance for his club to be the extras in a movie, however inadvertently. But so what? Those were small things, the minor grievances of daily life in a school. Plus, did any of them really have the rage it would take to become physically violent? In fact, usually the only thing I associated with violence was drugs. Which did bring up the joints in Coach Fred's desk—the lumpy, poorly wrapped tubes of marijuana concealed in Marlboro packs. And even those hardly counted as drugs. There weren't enough of them to warrant a slap on the wrist, at least not in Travis County.

Unless they tied someone to murder. Had the questions I'd been asking over the past day or two been enough to get someone very worried? Beside the folks I'd annoyed, I'd spoken to Stan the Parking Nazi and to Maria Santos in the front office. Pat Carver had overheard everything I'd said to Maria, and, of course, any of them might have talked about me to anyone else. Had something I'd asked or said frightened a murderer?

Colin had stopped pacing and now stood with his arms crossed. "I wish you could see the expressions going across your face. What are you thinking about? Did you hear my question?"

"I don't have enemies. A few people might not send me a Christmas card this year, but that's it."

"Okay, well, I'm going. You get some sleep, and I'll talk to you tomorrow."

"Thanks," I said.

Giving me a searching look, he left with an awkward little wave. I sat motionless as the door closed behind him with a quiet click, not quite shutting out the constant drone of hospital noises, dormant now at 3:00 A.M., but never quite still. Somewhere in the building, machines hummed without pause, nurses padded down halls in rubber-soled shoes, and janitors pushed floor polishers between yellow warning cones. I couldn't help feeling a little bit sorry for myself. The worst part of being single always came at moments like these when it became very clear that no one minded that I wasn't at home in my own bed. Kyla had taken care of Belle, but other than my fat, curly-haired poodle, no one was lying alone in the dark wishing I was beside him.

I wondered what Colin Gallagher was like when he wasn't working. There was something very attractive about the man, and more than just his looks, which were pretty darned okay all by themselves. I liked the flashes of humor I'd seen and had a feeling he'd be fun and funny when he was off duty. And I liked the way he focused on what was being said. Even when nothing important was happening, he gave the impression that he was paying attention. Of course, the unending stream of questions and his ability to track me down could get annoying. Which reminded me, I was supposed to be mad at him still for spreading rumors about drugs and Fred. And he still had Fred's key. My key. I would ask for it tomorrow.

I fiddled with the control of the bed, lowering it a couple of inches and trying to get more comfortable. Despite the drip, my injuries were making themselves felt now that I had no other distraction. Glancing at the clock, which seemed to be moving in slow motion, I wondered what Alan was doing right now. It was Saturday morning in Italy, the final day of his tour, which meant he would be coming home tomorrow. His home, not mine. I wondered what would happen, or rather, I wondered how it would happen. Knowing Alan, breaking up wouldn't be nasty at all. Just a few kinds words, a laugh or two, and a gentle "let's be friends" speech. And of course I'd agree. And who knows, we might even exchange those Christmas cards that I wouldn't be getting from Gary Richards, at least for a few years. That was the problem about dating someone I genuinely liked. Lose the boyfriend, lose the friend.

Thankfully, a moment later the nurse bustled in, checking the pulse in my wrist, taking my temperature, asking if I wanted ice chips. She had a kind face, ridiculously alert for three in the morning. I thought about asking for a mirror so I could see my bruises, but a wave of tiredness swept over me again, and I let her turn out my light instead.

Chapter 11

BURGLARY AND BODYGUARDS

I left the hospital in the morning, glad it was Labor Day weekend and I didn't have to try to go to school. I'd left a stack of homework that needed grading on the desk in my classroom, but that could wait. Colin had not exaggerated—I had an impressive black eye. The swelling at my temple had subsided, leaving a graze that was little more than a raised red welt, but the bruising was a glorious purple and black, splashed across the eye socket and pooling under the corner of my eye as though I wept inky tears. After the initial shock wore off, I decided I felt no worse than I had the day after my first college party, when for some reason I had thought it would be a good idea to pour alternating layers of vodka and coke, beer, and fraternity punch into my stomach, like a mad scientist mixing a particularly vile potion. The resulting explosion had been inevitable and spectacular, although no villagers had come after me with pitchforks and torches. This was like that, minus most of the nausea, and I figured I would live.

Kyla arrived bearing a Louis Vuitton duffle bag filled with some of her own clothes, which were a little snug and low-cut for my taste, but better than the bloodstained rags I'd been wearing. She then walked me out, attempting to fuss over me and not doing a great job. She had never been particularly maternal. She did hold the door of her little red convertible open for me and held my things when I slid into the front seat. It was not yet nine o'clock, and the black seats were already hot enough to draw a yelp from me as my thighs met leather.

"I'll get Sherman to come and pick up your car," she said, pulling out of the hospital parking lot and accelerating quickly enough to press me back into my seat.

"Sherman?" I asked, for a moment not remembering who she meant. Then the image of the guy at Artz Rib House popped up, the one she'd wanted to set me up with.

"He's a good guy. He won't mind."

"That's nice of him," I said doubtfully. "You know, Kyla, I hate to break it to you, but he was not interested in me at all. And that's not just me being modest."

"I know," she said, unperturbed. "I'm pretty sure he's interested in someone else. Hope you're not upset." She wove in and out of the surrounding traffic, the motor of her car a deep purr that I could feel in my chest. I made an effort not to clutch the sides of my seat.

I felt immensely relieved, but I wasn't sure how tactful it would be to say so. "Not at all. I have interests in other directions anyway."

"Colin Gallagher," she said with a knowing smirk.

"Alan Stratton," I countered.

"Yeah, whatever. The guy is never here though. Doesn't that get old?"

I didn't answer right away. "Maybe. A little."

She lifted her eyebrows.

"Okay, yes a lot. I admit I don't have a good feeling about it." Saying it out loud hurt more than it should have considering how much I'd been thinking about it.

Uncharacteristically, she left it alone. A few minutes later, she pulled into a neat little neighborhood, full of tiny and all but identical houses, all neatly maintained, and gleaming in the sun. Preceding me to my front door, she unlocked and opened it while I followed gingerly, still not quite sure my head wasn't going to explode.

Kyla's gasp was my first indication something was wrong. Without a word, she backed away from the door, pulling it closed behind her. With one hand she dug in her purse for her phone, and with the other she grabbed my arm and tried to pull me away.

I dug in my heels, too slow and confused to understand what was going on.

"What are you doing?" I asked.

Her eyes met mine. "I need to report a break-in," she said into the phone.

Even then, it took a minute before her words clicked into place. I tore my arm from her grasp and rushed to the door.

My little living room looked like the Pamplonans had decided to hold the running of the bulls at my house this year. My floral sofa, a hand-me-down from my parents, had been overturned and every cushion slashed. Chunks of yellow foam rubber littered the floor. My coffee table was on its side, the tempered glass shattered but still intact. Bookcases were toppled, books scattered, spines broken like crows caught in a jet engine then spit out on the asphalt. My television lay smashed, thrown from its stand, and the floor was littered with my small DVD collection. Each case had been opened, the silvery disks stomped into fragments. Photographs and pictures had been snatched from walls or off shelves and thrown with force to the ground or against walls. Beyond the living room, the kitchen had received the same treatment. Drawers opened, contents strewn over the floor.

I felt as though I'd been punched in the gut. Even drawing breath took an effort. Then I remembered my dog.

"Belle?" I shouted. There was no response. "Belle!"

I raced through the rooms, my headache forgotten in my terror, only vaguely aware that Kyla was trying to hold me back. She said later that going in had been stupid, that we didn't know whether anyone was still in the house, but none of that occurred to me at the time. My only thought was for my fat poodle. In the distance, the wail of sirens started low, then grew steadily louder. Kyla was still on the phone with the 911 operator, repeating the address, giving her own name, then mine. In my bedroom, the devastation was, if anything, more complete. Nothing breakable was unbroken, nothing standing was left upright. The king-sized mattress had been ripped from my bed and tossed into a corner, a feat that must have required a good deal of strength or quite a bit of rage. But there was no sign of Belle. I stopped and called her name again.

This time, I was rewarded with a small sound, a faint thumping sound. I turned, unable to pinpoint it for a moment, then I dropped to my knees and peered under the gap left between mattress and floor. From the dark shadows, a pair of beady watery eyes stared back at me, ringed white with fear. As my eyes adjusted, I could see a mass of trembling black curls and the movement of a short tail thumping uncertainly against the wall.

She wouldn't come out. As the police entered the house, I was lying flat on my stomach trying to wriggle forward far enough to reach her.

"Ma'am, this is a crime scene. You need to get up, please," a woman's voice ordered.

"My dog's under here. I can't leave her," I answered.

"Ma'am, you need to get up now."

I ignored her. "Come on, Belle. Come here," I pleaded with the dog. I don't know why I thought that would work. She never came when called, even when she wasn't terrified.

"Did you find her?" asked Kyla.

"Yeah, she's hiding under here," I called over my shoulder, voice muffled under the mattress.

"Ma'am, you can't be in here," the policewoman said, again, exasperated.

"She needs to get her dog," Kyla protested.

"She can get the dog later. And I'm going to have to ask you to step outside, too, ma'am."

There was the sound of footsteps on the wood floor in the hallway, then a familiar voice called "Jocelyn?"

"Colin!" cried Kyla. "In here."

"What's going on? What's she doing? Is she hurt?"

"Poodle," said Kyla succinctly.

I was halfway under the mattress by now, squirming forward another inch. I was suddenly extremely conscious that my rear end was all Colin could see of me, but my fingers were just brushing against curls. I couldn't pull back now. A pink tongue hesitantly swiped against my fingertips.

"Oh, for God's sake," said Colin. And to my surprise, he lifted the mattress off me. I blinked in the light, then made a grab for Belle and sat up.

"Now why didn't we think of that?" asked Kyla, smiling at him through long eyelashes.

In spite of her glowing admiration, Colin was staring only at me, although that wasn't actually so surprising. Between my puffy black eye and my hair, which had come out of my ponytail and was spilling around my face, I'm sure I made an attractive picture. Plus, I had a poodle who was burrowing into my neck and trying to clean my face at the same time. He reached out a hand. I took it, and he pulled me to my feet.

Glancing at Belle, he said, "I thought you said you were looking for a dog."

I managed a wobbly grin. "Well, she has a lot of doglike attributes. She fulfills almost all of my carpet-staining requirements."

Then I looked around my bedroom and felt my eyes fill with angry tears. A muscle in his jaw tightened.

"All right, let's get you two out of here and let the officers do their job."

He let us sit in the back seat of his Crown Vic with the air conditioner running until the crime scene investigators were finished with the kitchen. Then he went back inside. When he was gone, Kyla turned to me.

"What the hell is going on?" she asked.

A very good question. I put a hand up to my eye, which was beginning to throb, and wished I'd had an ice pack.

"First you're attacked in the park, then your house is robbed. But why?" she went on.

Something about her words struck a chord with me.

"No," I said, sitting up straighter. "No. The first thing that happened was Coach Fred getting murdered. Then the other stuff happened."

"You think all this has something to do with Coach Fred? But you didn't have anything to do with him," she protested.

"He was a teacher at my school. I worked with him."

"So what? There's lots of teachers at your school. None of them are sitting in a cop car with a trashed house, a concussion, and a black eye. Why you?"

Another very good question. I didn't answer. Kyla had been watching the police officers come and go through my front door. My silence caught her attention.

"Jocelyn, why you?" she repeated.

I sat motionless, thinking. "Maybe because no one else has been asking any questions."

"What kind of questions? And who have you been asking?"

"Well, that's what doesn't make sense. It wasn't anything important. I was just trying to find out two things: whether anyone had noticed anything unusual the night Fred was killed or if anyone knew anything about the marijuana in his desk. And no one did. No one told me anything important. In fact, I actually feel like I know less about it now than when I started. But maybe I missed something. Maybe what we should be asking is what do I know that has someone worried?"

She threw me a concerned glance. "You need a gun."

I laughed, but she shook a finger at me.

"I'm serious. You need to be able to protect yourself."

"Yes, and that worked out so well for you," I said pointedly.

She had the grace to blush, but she went on doggedly. "You know guns. After all those summers on Uncle Herman's ranch, you're a better shot than I am. I don't understand why you're so resistant."

"I work in a school. It is specifically illegal to carry a weapon on school grounds."

"Well at least you could have it here."

"If I'd owned a gun, whoever broke into my house would have taken it and now they would be able to shoot me with it."

"So get a floor safe like Grandpa had. Keep the gun in there during the day, but leave it by your pillow at night."

I stared at her. Something she'd just said had sparked a thought, but it was gone as quickly as it had come, like water slipping through a sieve. I tried to think, but my brain seemed to be stuffed with cotton balls.

Colin returned at that moment, opening the car door for us and retrieving the keys from the Crown Vic.

"We've cleared an area. You can come back in."

We followed him to my kitchen. He had restored my breakfast table and chairs to the upright position, and, except for a couple of new scratches, they seemed to be undamaged. I wish I could say the same for the rest of my possessions. Police officers were going over every inch of my house, taking photographs, dusting for fingerprints, and examining the damage. Colin sat with us.

"Are you going to take our fingerprints for elimination purposes?" asked Kyla, interested.

"We hardly ever do that. We take the prints we find here and if they're viable, we run them through the criminal database to see if there's a match. If there is one, then I'll be asking you if there's a reason someone in that database would be in your house."

Kyla squirmed a little. "My prints are probably in here," she said with a sidelong glance at me.

He gave her a grin. "I already know all about you. Anyone else?"

"My boyfriend," I answered.

His eyes sharpened, brows drawing together in a frown. "Boyfriend? What's his name? Are you on good terms with him? Would he have a criminal record?"

"Alan Stratton," I answered. "No, he doesn't have a criminal record. And yes, we're on good terms."

"Any chance he's ticked off at you right now?"

"What?" I asked completely confused.

Kyla spoke up, amused. "He's asking you if there's any chance that Alan trashed your house."

"What? No! No way. And even in the unlikely event that I would date someone who would do something like this, Alan could not have done it. He's in Italy."

"Hmm," Colin said, jotting something in his notebook. "And how long have you been seeing this person?"

"About four months. No, more like six now, I guess," I said, counting back the months to March when we'd first met. "Anyway, what difference does that make?"

"It's not a real six months, though," Kyla pointed out, "since you only see each other about every other weekend. Long-distance relationship," she added for Colin's benefit.

Was it my imagination, or did he look pleased by that?

"Could we get back to the break-in?" I asked. "Do you know how they got in?"

"Looks like the entry was through the back door." Colin stood and went to the door in question. The wood around the lock and frame was splintered. "Probably used a crowbar."

"I thought a dead bolt was supposed to keep someone from doing that."

"Yeah, but a dead bolt's only as good as the frame it's in. It took quite a bit of strength, and it would have made noise. We've got people out talking to your neighbors. Still, behind the privacy fence, it's not likely anyone saw anything."

A single loud noise in the middle of the night. I thought about it. Even if someone had been awakened, there would be no way for them to know what it was if the burglar had kept quiet afterward. And once inside with the door closed, he could make all the noise he wanted.

"Can you tell if anything's been taken?" Colin asked.

I looked around at the devastation. Oddly, I hadn't even considered that something might have been stolen. For one thing, everything that I thought of as valuable was here, even if scattered over a wide area. My television, my computer, my iPod station—all still very much here, even if they were in pieces. How would I be able to tell if something was missing? And what would someone who was not interested in my somewhat outdated electronics collection be seeking?

Hours later, the police, the insurance adjusters, and the neighbors had all come and gone. A couple of Jehovah's Witnesses stopped by wanting to pray for my soul but left rather quickly at Kyla's suggestion that they perform an unnatural act on each other. Colin restored my mattress, thankfully unharmed, to the bed frame, and Kyla found fresh sheets and made the bed for me. It was now calling my name, but I was doing my best to ignore it, instead helping Kyla and Colin clean up the last of the broken glass. The sun was well on its way to the western horizon.

The sound of the doorbell made me start, and Kyla gave me a sharp look before going to answer it. A kid stood there with a couple of pizzas, and she paid him and returned with the boxes. I relaxed and breathed in the smell of melted cheese and pepperoni. My stomach grumbled.

We sat at the kitchen table to eat. Belle, who'd been sleeping curled up on one of the slashed cushions of the couch, hopped down and waddled over to beg halfheartedly from Colin. I noticed he slipped her a pepperoni when he thought I wasn't looking.

"You know," said Kyla, her mouth full of food, "you should come stay with me tonight."

Colin nodded. "That's a good idea."

I frowned. "Why? Do you think these assholes are going to be coming back?"

"No, not really, but I just figured you'd sleep better if you didn't have to worry about it," said Kyla.

I looked at Colin.

He shrugged. "She's right. I doubt they'd come back. They had plenty of time, and they've done a pretty thorough job. I wouldn't think they'd have any reason to return."

"So I'll just stay here. This is my house, and I've got Belle. We'll be fine."

"Belle isn't exactly what I'd call protection."

"She barks, though. No one could slip in without me knowing. And, like Colin said, if they were looking for something, they had time to find it. They must have known I wasn't here and chose that time to break in, so they aren't after me personally. There's no reason that I can't stay here."

Kyla didn't like it, but she couldn't find a flaw in my logic. She pulled out her phone to check the time.

"I'm supposed to go out tonight," she said. "I'll cancel and stay here with you. We can watch a chick flick." Then she looked over at my smashed television. "Or maybe not."

"No, no movies tonight," I said, feeling a pang of disappointment. That would have been a perfect diversion. "But there's no reason for you to cancel your plans. I'm exhausted. I'll probably just read for a while and go to bed early. You have fun," I added by way of encouragement.

Shaking her head, Kyla rose and collected her purse. "I don't see how, since I'll be thinking about you the whole time.

Keep your phone close. You can call me if you need anything or if you start feeling bad again."

I nodded and rose. We were halfway to the door when I realized Colin was still sitting at the table. I looked at him inquiringly.

"Oh, I'm not leaving. I'll sleep on your couch."

I frowned, but Kyla gave a broad grin. "Now I'll be able to have fun." She gave a relieved laugh and was gone.

I locked the door behind her and returned to the table.

"You can't stay here," I said, sinking into a chair.

Taking a stand would have been more impressive if done standing, but I felt like three-day-old roadkill. All I wanted was a hot shower and my bed.

He grinned and rose, carrying the plates to the sink. "No need to thank me," he said with a little wave of his hand.

"I'm not thanking you. I'm telling you to get out."

He did not seem bothered. "Now is that any way to talk to your own personal police protection?"

"I don't need personal police protection. I need privacy. And sleep. Especially sleep. So why don't you scamper off and do whatever it is you do on a Saturday night. But thank you," I added belatedly. "I appreciate everything you've done for me. Really."

"Nice try. I'm still not leaving."

Perplexed, I considered my options. It wasn't as though I could physically eject him, although the image of his splayed body catapulting through the door with a high-pitched squeal was oddly soothing. I decided to try reason one more time.

"You can't possibly do this for all your cases."

"Don't usually need to. By the time I'm called in, the victims are usually deceased."

"But I'm not a victim," I protested.

He blinked, his expressive eyebrows shooting upward. "Perhaps we need to work on your grasp of English. What do you think the word 'victim' means? You've been attacked, your house has been all but destroyed, and . . ." here he searched for a third item ". . . your poodle was terrorized."

A victim? Me? I glared at him. The term annoyed me because it made me feel helpless and powerless, which I definitely wasn't. Little old ladies were victims, not me. "Look, I'm not happy about all this, but I have insurance, a dog, and a baseball bat. I am not a victim."

He stared at me in exasperation, running a hand through his curling hair, which made it stand up in wavy spikes. "And if whoever did this comes back tonight, what are you going to do then?"

I reached for my baseball bat, which I'd pulled from my closet and left by the front door. "I will pound the everlasting shit out of him. In fact, I hope he does come back."

Silence hung in the air between us. From the kitchen Belle's tags jingled as she scratched an ear with great enthusiasm. A moment later, she waddled between us, bounced a few times, and at last made the leap onto the couch. Our eyes followed her, both of us glad to have something other than each other to watch.

At last Colin drew a deep breath and spoke slowly, as

though to someone very dense. "For several reasons, I think that we, the police, need to keep surveillance on your house for the next night or two. Because this is my case, tonight I've drawn that duty. Now, I can watch from my car, but that is a damn uncomfortable way to spend a night. However, with your permission," he said with exaggerated politeness, "I could fulfill my duties from the comfort of your sofa and possibly be able to get a few hours sleep. I was up fairly late last night."

A vision of him at my hospital bedside at 3:00 A.M. flitted through my brain, followed closely by one of him reassembling my bed, cleaning up broken glass, and generally being just about the greatest guy anyone could ask for. Also the most stubborn. I was being incredibly ungrateful and rude, two things that I didn't normally consider myself to be.

"I'm sorry," I said at last, though the words stung a bit. "I'm very thankful for everything you've done. I don't think you need to stay because I think everything that's going to happen to me has already happened, but if you are going to watch my house anyway, I'd be very happy for you to stay here."

He smiled. It was probably my imagination, but I thought he looked a little smug, having successfully handled a difficult member of the public.

"On one condition," I added.

His black brows drew together. "And what would that be?"

"I want my key back."

He looked blank for an instant, then the brows went up. "Fred's key? That key is evidence."

"Of what?"

"I'm not sure yet."

"It wasn't at the crime scene, you don't know what it's for, and it had my name on it. It's mine."

"It doesn't have your name on it."

"It was left for me. That makes it mine. And you can't tell me you still consider me to be a suspect in Fred's death."

He frowned at me. "Do you know what the key is for?"

"No."

"Then it's no good to you."

"I want it," I insisted. "What if I find whatever it is that it opens?"

"Then you can call me. Look," he raised his hands as I was about to protest, "it's logged into evidence. I can't get it back to you right now, even if I wanted to. You find what it's for, and I promise you can be there when we open it."

It would have to do, although I was pretty sure I'd just been outmaneuvered on all counts. I found blankets and pillows for him. I even offered the use of the spare room, but he said he'd rather be in a central location. I took Belle and went to my own room, oddly comforted by his presence, though I would never have admitted it. I fell asleep listening to the sound of his footsteps on the wood floors as he checked the doors and went for something in my refrigerator.

Chapter 12

SHOPPING AND SURVEILLANCE

Sunday started off better than the day before, although admittedly that bar was not very high. I awoke to find Colin already gone and was surprised by a feeling of deep disappointment. What did I expect? That we'd sit together over bacon and eggs, chatting about the day?

I took my time getting dressed. My head felt much better, but my muscles were picking up the slack, leaving me stiff and sore. The bruising on the left side of my face, though no longer swollen, had blossomed like violets in April and now included an impressive range of greens and yellows in addition to the original blues and purples. I started to pull my hair into a ponytail, then changed my mind. Leaving it down masked some of the injury.

By the time my coffee was ready and Belle was outside patrolling the perimeter of the yard for squirrels, Kyla was knocking at the door. I admit the sound made me jump, even more so when she almost immediately used her key to let herself in. I froze halfway to the living room, heart pounding, as the door opened. We stared at each other, both startled for a second, then Kyla entered the rest of the way and closed the door behind her.

"Sorry," she said. "I wasn't sure you'd be up yet. Didn't think about scaring the socks off you."

"Guess I'm a little nervous," I admitted. "Stupid." I returned to the coffeemaker and poured myself a mug. I offered it to her, but she shook her head.

"Had a latte on my way over." She looked around. "Where's Colin?"

I shrugged. "He was gone before I got up." I hoped she didn't hear the sulky disappointment in my voice.

"I hope you were nice to him. He was pretty damn awesome yesterday."

"Yes, he was," I agreed.

She looked me up and down, frowning. "I wish I knew what they saw in you," she muttered under her breath, as she pulled out a kitchen chair and sat down.

"What? Who?" I asked, as I poured cereal into a bowl and added milk.

Outside, the golden sunlight began pouring over the fence and into the yard, sparkling on the dewy grass like tiny jewels. The paths where Belle had trodden and removed the moisture crisscrossed the yard, showing dark green trails in the silver glitter. The raucous call of a grackle sounded clearly through the window, as much a sign of summer in Austin as the whirring of the cicadas.

She snorted. "Exactly. You are so clueless. Colin for starters. You aren't even trying, and he can't take his eyes off you."

"Don't be stupid. He's investigating a case. Not that I'm not completely fascinating of course," I added.

"I suppose you think he sticks around and helps everyone this way. You do realize that he was off duty yesterday."

"No, he wasn't. He said he was assigned to surveillance detail."

She just shook her head in disgust. "My God, you would believe anything. I'd put it down to your head injury, but you're always like this."

I paused as her words sank in. Had Colin really been off duty? And if so, why would he bother to lie about it?

I realized that Kyla was still watching for my reaction to her insult, so I shot her a glare and the finger.

"All right, all right," she held up her hands in surrender. "I'll drop it. For now."

I carried my cereal bowl and coffee cup to the sink. "Not that I'm not glad to see you, but what's up?"

"I'm taking you shopping," she grinned at me. "Labor Day weekend—everything is on sale, and every store is open early."

I felt a spark of interest. Shopping with Kyla is like watching a great master at work. She's extremely successful in her career, so money is seldom an object, and she has an eye for style and bargains that makes every expedition an adventure. Besides, it would be nice to get out of my wrecked house for a while and think about something else.

"I'm in," I said with pleasure. "What are you shopping for?"

"You," she said, gesturing around the room. "We're getting your stuff back."

I bit my lip. "We can't. It will be weeks before the insurance check comes."

She just laughed. "Monsieur MasterCard and I don't give a crap. I'm buying." She held up a hand before I could protest. "You can pay me back when you get the check. Now, get your purse. We're going."

And we went. Within one hour, I had a new TV, a PlayStation, which Kyla assured me was the best DVD player, and a computer monitor so large that astronauts would be able to read my e-mail from space. Within a second hour, I had a new sofa, which Kyla negotiated to less than one third the original price and somehow got free delivery and removal of the old sofa thrown in. After that, we stopped by my house to off-load the electronics, then drove to north Austin to The Domain, the snootiest luxury shopping available in central Texas.

As we turned onto Braker Lane and I realized where we were going, I finally protested. "I can't shop here. In fact, I don't think you can shop here. Don't you need to show your trophy-wife card to get into the parking garage?"

She just laughed. "Perhaps. But today is a magic day, and we have the keys to the royal enclave. All the summer stuff is on sale even though it's still ninety-five degrees out, and you and I need a few things."

I followed her along the tree-lined sidewalks, popping into one designer shop after another and marveling at her self-assurance and taste. My bruised face received far less attention than I anticipated, and I started feeling somewhat less self-conscious about it.

I mentioned it to Kyla, and she considered.

"They probably assume that either your sugar-daddy husband beats you or that you've just had a bad round of Botox. Bet they see worse every day."

She pulled three dresses from a rack in quick succession and pushed them into my arms. "Try those on," she ordered.

I'd lost the will to fight her three stores ago, so I obediently entered a large, carpeted dressing room and started stripping. After all, there was no harm in trying something on. I didn't need to buy it. I heard her enter the dressing room next to me.

"Alan gets back today," I said, suddenly remembering.

"Does he know about all this?" she asked, after a pause.

"No, not yet. I could have tried to call him, but there wouldn't have been any point. And the time difference makes it hard."

"Not that hard," she said. "You could have called if you'd wanted him."

"Yeah, but he couldn't have done anything."

"Because he's never here. What kind of a boyfriend is that? You guys aren't any closer to a real relationship than you were back in March when you each thought the other was involved in a murder."

I flinched, but I couldn't really argue. "I really like him, Kyla," I said finally.

She was silent for a moment. When she spoke, her voice was more gentle than usual. "Sometimes that's just not enough.

You had a bad experience with that asshole you married, but there are other good guys out there, you know."

I thought I knew what this was about. "I hate to break this to you, but I'm just not interested in that Sherman guy. Much as I appreciate the thought," I said.

There was another moment of silence from the next room. Removing one dress that did nothing at all for my figure, I slid on a shimmery blue wisp of silk and drew in a delighted breath as I looked into the mirror. It was gorgeous. I turned, admiring at the way it slimmed my waist before falling in soft folds to my knee. Then I turned again, struggling to reach the price tag. I hadn't had the nerve to look at a single tag since we'd arrived at The Domain, but now I needed to know.

Kyla cleared her throat. "About Sherman," she said.

"You have to see this dress," I interrupted, opening my door.

"Just a sec." I heard the sound of a zipper, then her door opened and she leaned out.

I turned, showing her all angles.

"It's perfect. It could have been made for you. You have to get it."

"Maybe. It goes really well with my bruise. Brings out the indigo hues," I said, catching sight of my reflection in a three-way mirror at the end of the corridor. "But where would I wear it?"

"Anywhere. It's just a casual dress. Exceptionally pretty, but still casual. You could wear it on a date for example."

Not the kind of dates I usually went on, which involved beer and food I could pick up with my fingers.

"Or a school banquet," Kyla added, as though reading my mind.

I brightened. "Good point. I'll take it."

I was about to step back into my dressing room, and Kyla was just shutting her door, when I remembered something she'd said.

"Hey, what were you going to tell me about Sherman?"

I heard the sound of a zipper again. She was trying on another dress. "It's not important."

"Tell."

There was a moment of silence, then the door opened again and she stepped out wearing a yellow sundress that made her look as slender and pretty as a teenage debutante.

"What do you think?" she asked.

"That I hate you and everything you stand for."

"Okay then. I'll take it," she said, looking satisfied. Then she added, "I might have gone out with him last night."

"What?"

"Sherman. I sort of went out with him."

"On a date?"

"Maybe." She'd slipped back into the dressing room. "You don't mind, do you?"

"Mind? What . . . no! No, I've already told you I'm not interested in him. But I didn't think you were either. Weren't you trying to set him up with me?"

I could visualize the shrug. "Yeah, it's not smart dating a coworker. He'd flirted a little, and I'd cut him off. But it didn't seem like he should go to waste, so I was going to give him to you."

"You are aware that he's a man, and not the last slice of pizza in the box?"

Ignoring me, she went on, "However, seeing him with that fat cow at Artz drove me crazy, so I reopened negotiations."

"I don't know, he looked like he was pretty into her. Or parts of her," I teased.

"Trying to make me jealous," she said. "Which it did. So now we're dating, and we'll see how it goes. I figured you wouldn't mind, what with having two men making goggle eyes at you." She said this last with the all too obvious intention of diverting the topic of conversation.

It almost worked. I was opening my mouth to protest but sidestepped at the last minute. "So, is he going to change his name?" I asked.

"He refuses. But I think I'm starting to like it. It's unique."

"Sherman. Yes, it has a nice ring to it. Sherman the German. No, too World War II. Sherman the Merman. No, too wet. Oooh, I know. Sherman the Vermin."

"Please, please, I'm begging you. Shut the fuck up," she said. But without heat.

She must really like this guy.

Kyla and I spent the rest of the afternoon setting up my new equipment, and then she took herself off, probably to slip into her new yellow dress for another date with Sherman. I decided not to tease her about it anymore, in part because of her kindness during the day, but mostly because I was too tired. Besides, there would be plenty of time for that later.

After she left I turned on the television, stretched out on my sofa to watch an old black-and-white movie that happened to come up while I flipped through the channels, and fell asleep without meaning to.

When I woke up, it was dark and Belle was standing on my chest, which was her subtle way of letting me know it was time to go outside. Feeling a little groggy, I felt my way to the back door and opened it without turning on any lights. Outside, the air was warm and a breath of breeze stirred through the branches of the trees like a sigh. The glow from the city lights in the distance and the half moon riding high in the night sky gave off enough light to verify there were no snakes in the immediate vicinity. I stepped onto the porch, feeling the warm concrete on my bare feet. A movement from the right caught my eye and my heart jumped, but it was only a possum making its way along the top of the fence, its hairless tail swinging from side to side as it concentrated on setting its tiny handlike feet on the tops of the narrow boards. I glanced over at Belle, hoping she wouldn't notice it and start barking. Although I wasn't sure what time it was, the lack of lights in the neighbors' houses meant it was late enough that high-pitched yapping would not be appreciated.

I stayed outside, breathing in the clean night air and looking at the stars for ten minutes, until Belle returned of her own accord. Going in, I carefully locked the back door, then made the rounds, checking other doors and thinking how very quiet and dark everything was. Now that I had my wish and was alone in my house, I was suddenly nervous. Maybe Kyla had a point about keeping a pistol. Not that I wanted to carry one in my purse, but having one in the house tonight would have been comforting. I peered out the front window to reassure myself that no one was waiting on the front lawn. And saw a strange car.

I looked again. It was parked in the darkest part of the street, lurking in between the circles of light cast by the nearest two streetlights. On any other night, I wouldn't have thought twice about it. But tonight, bruises still livid on my face and foam still oozing from a torn sofa, I was understandably alert. Besides, I knew most of my neighbors' cars. I was the only person on the street who used her garage for her car. Everyone else parked in their driveways or in front of their homes. Garages in Austin took the place that basements held everywhere else, and were used to hold everything from tools to artificial Christmas trees. The car waiting in the shadows was unfamiliar and menacing, a crocodile floating motionless in the water, waiting for its prey. I was suddenly glad I hadn't turned on any lights.

I watched for what seemed like a long time, but was probably no more than three or four minutes. Then I began to relax a little. There was no sign of anyone creeping through yards or slinking from bush to bush like Wile E. Coyote in pursuit of the Road Runner. And after all, what was a strange car? One of my neighbors probably had a guest staying for the holiday weekend. The street slept, a quiet short street in a safe neighborhood in the suburbs. I told myself to quit being so jittery and to go to bed.

Then I saw it. A movement in the car, as though someone sitting in the driver's seat had just shifted position. The hair rose on the back of my neck. So they had come back after all.

I thought of my little house all but destroyed, of my little dog terrorized and hiding under a mattress. Fear gave way to rage. I went for my baseball bat.

It was a good baseball bat. None of that new lightweight aluminum for me. I'd found it at a garage sale, a solid wood beauty that weighed almost five pounds and must have been intended for use by a giant. Right now I wished it weighed twice as much and had spikes embedded in it.

Knowing that the creep in the car could see my front door, I slipped out the back and crept around to the gate, trying not to think what could be waiting for an unwary foot in the grass. In Texas, even well-tended suburban lawns were havens for scorpions and snakes of all types. I wished I'd taken the time to put on my shoes. If I was lucky, I would find nothing worse than a dog pile.

With care I pushed open the gate and moved stealthily behind the shrubs to a position where I could see without being seen and considered my options. Unfortunately, there was no way I would be able to make it across the street undetected. I told myself the most important thing was to discover the identity of the occupant. Beating that person senseless would be a stretch goal. I hesitated only briefly.

I raced across the street as fast as my bare feet would take me, bat held at the ready position. If nothing else, I would leave some dents in that smooth fender. As I drew closer, I could see the shape of a man. A big man. I didn't care. I would pound him first and scream for help later.

I was just lifting my bat to shatter the front headlight, when the driver's door opened and the interior light spilled across the startled face of Colin Gallagher.

I froze, bat raised over my right ear. I could hear the pounding of my own heart.

Colin stepped out and closed the door quietly behind him. I lowered the bat slightly and straightened up. He walked around the car, then leaned one hip on the hood.

"Whatcha doing?" he asked in a bright tone.

My mouth opened, but no sound came out. I quivered, the adrenaline pumping hard, my knuckles still white on the bat.

He looked up and down the quiet street. "Do you want to get in the car?" he asked.

I shook my head.

"Can we go inside then?"

"Okay," I said after a pause.

I turned on my heel and stalked back across the street, then led the way through my backyard to the patio door. Belle waited on the other side, short tail wagging. Seeing Colin, she yapped a few times on principle.

The door closed behind us and I whirled on him. "What the hell were you doing out there? You scared the crap out of me!" My voice squeaked out a good octave higher than I intended.

"First, give me the bat. I don't want my head bashed in." He held out a hand, and I reluctantly relinquished it, my fingers stiff from clutching it so hard. He set it in a corner.

"Second," he went on, "the real question is what the hell

were you doing out there? If you thought I was the bad guy, why didn't you call 911?"

I looked at him blankly and then sank into a chair. "I wanted to know who it was," I said finally. "Who it was who did all this to me. And who maybe killed Fred."

"You should have called for help. I mean, look at you. You're barefoot, for Christ's sake. You weigh about as much as a cat. What the hell did you think you were going to do?"

The barefoot thing I couldn't argue with. The cat comment wasn't true, but I was hardly going to argue with that either.

"I was going to make a statement with my bat," I said with great dignity. "And I was going to find out what was going on."

"It was stupid," he said coldly, and I suddenly realized that he was very angry. "Stupid and risky. Maybe you've forgotten, but a man has been killed, and you were damn near killed."

"I haven't forgotten," I said through clenched teeth, angry in my turn. "The stupid thing was you—camping out there without letting me know. How did you think I'd feel about seeing a stranger sitting outside my house after everything that's happened?"

"I didn't think you were home. You didn't have any lights on."

"I fell asleep on the couch."

We glared at each other, angry because we'd both been given a fright. Looking at him a little more closely, I finally noticed that he wasn't wearing what I'd come to think of as his detective outfit—the pressed shirt, tie, and slacks that I'd seen him in before. Tonight, he was wearing a pair of faded jeans and a plain black T-shirt. His gun, black and heavy, rested in a holster on his belt. His jaw, though clean shaven, was showing the shadow of his dark beard.

"Are you off duty?" I asked.

"I'm never off duty," he answered shortly.

I rolled my eyes at that. "That's not true. You weren't assigned to watch my house, were you? You're just doing it in your free time."

He looked almost guilty, like one of my students caught doing extra-credit work by his friends. He didn't answer.

I looked at him thoughtfully for a moment, considering.

"Thank you," I said at last. "I'm sorry I almost pounded your car."

He glared at me, still not willing to let it go. "You know how stupid that was? You won't do anything like that again, right?"

"We really need to work on your personal skills," I said, as though thinking aloud. "After making your point with a lady and receiving an apology, a gentleman should never use the word 'stupid.' You should also offer an apology of your own," I added.

He looked outraged. "For what?"

"For scaring me and for being an ass."

His lips pressed together, and I could have sworn I saw his eye twitch. He held out a hand to me.

It seemed an odd moment to high-five, but men are strange. I slapped his palm gently and turned mine up for the return.

Instead, with an exasperated laugh, he grabbed my hand and pulled me to my feet. I found myself inches from his chest, looking up into his face with a startled gasp. He wrapped one arm around my shoulders and pulled me tightly against him so I could feel the whole warm length of him pressed against my body. With his free hand he gently smoothed my hair away from my bruised face and then bent his head to kiss me.

And yes, I kissed him back. Without thought I slid my arms around his hard body and melted against him. He smelled wonderful, of shaving cream and warm skin and man. He felt wonderful, too, his size and the hard muscles under his shirt making me feel small and feminine and sexy. His lips moved over mine with surprising gentleness before he raised his head to take a breath and gaze into my eyes.

Breathless, I gazed back, wanting more, wanting his lips back on mine. Then my brain returned from whatever little holiday it had been on and started waving giant red flags.

"Oh, no!" I said, breaking out of the circle of his arms and clamping a hand over my mouth.

His head snapped up with a jerk, stiff-necked and affronted, as well he might be at my reaction to what had been one of the top ten kisses of all time. I could still feel his lips and the warm, seductive languor that had flowed through my muscles like honey. I stamped my foot to make the desire go away. It went, but not far. Every part of me wanted to return to his embrace.

Appalled at my own feelings, I moved around the table so the polished oak could act as the barrier I seemed unable to create on my own.

"I'm seeing someone," I whispered. "What is wrong with me?"

At this his tight expression relaxed, the narrowed blue eyes softening again. My God, he was gorgeous.

"So, this boyfriend of yours. I haven't seen him around."

The observation, though lightly made, had a judgmental quality to it. The same one I'd been hearing in Kyla's voice recently.

I swallowed, trying to conjure up an image of Alan.

"It's not his fault. He's been out of the country, but he's due back soon. Today, in fact," I said, suddenly realizing that Alan should be home by now. And that he hadn't called.

Of course, there were lots of explanations for that, the most likely being that his plane had been delayed. I would certainly be hearing from him tomorrow. Or rather today. The clock on the microwave behind Colin's shoulder showed that it was already after midnight. The day wasn't even an hour old, and I'd already made one hell of a mistake. What was I going to do?

I must have asked the last question out loud.

"Well, for starters you can quit looking like I've soiled your honor," he said, half-joking, half-irked. "It was one kiss."

But what a kiss.

And it wasn't about Colin at all; it was about me. Me and my reaction to another man, when I was sure that I was still in love with Alan Stratton, regardless of whether Alan still felt the same about me. And it did not help to think that if I were not dating Alan, I would be naked and moaning under Colin at this moment.

I turned away, hoping he had not read my thoughts in my eyes.

Whether he could or not, he no longer sounded angry.

After a long pause, he said, "Look, it's late. I doubt anything is going to happen tonight, but I'd feel better staying. Is it okay if I take your sofa again?"

I hoped he was talking about the burglar and not about us. I nodded. "I'll get a blanket and pillow for you."

I lay awake a very long time, alternately burning with desire and shame, straining to try to hear the sound of breathing or of movement through the door. I wondered if he were as disturbed as I. Eventually I must have dropped off to sleep, because the next thing I knew, I was waking up to the chime of the doorbell followed by the sound of angry male voices.

Chapter 13

TRIALS AND TRIANGLES

Since I sleep in an oversized T-shirt with a picture of Tweety Bird on it when I'm alone, I took the time to pull on the jeans that I'd left in a crumpled pile on the floor before running out into the living room. I still had Tweety on my chest, my eyes were puffy from sleep, and my hair was waving around like a bad imitation of Medusa, but at least I was wearing pants.

I mention my appearance because I believe it had a lot to do with the fact that my entrance cut off a heated argument in midsentence as Colin and Alan turned to stare at me. Alan had obviously just entered the room and was bristling like a Doberman spotting a cat near its food dish. He carried a sheaf of bright flowers, which he was now holding upside down at his side like a weapon. Colin had returned to the sofa on which he'd slept and was leaning against the back, arms folded across his chest.

As I entered, Colin's eyes darted to me then went immediately back to Alan. Alan, however, stopped and goggled, his expression slack-jawed and horrified. Instinctively, I tried to smooth down my hair.

"What happened to you?" he gasped.

And only then did I remember that, in addition to my other early-morning attributes, I also had the purple and green remains of a truly world-class black eye.

"She was assaulted and robbed while you were halfway around the world," said Colin in the same tone he might have used to talk about the weather.

Alan's eyes, green and dilated, widened in alarm.

I hastened to explain. "Assaulted like a mugging, nothing worse. And I'm fine, nothing to worry about."

"Absolutely," said Colin. "Of course, a man is dead and someone is targeting her. But except for those two things, she's fine."

"Well, when you say it that way, yeah, it sounds pretty bad," I said, making soothing gestures with my hands. "But let's not get carried away."

"No, let's not," Colin agreed. He didn't look as though he'd slept very well. Unshaven, with dark circles under his eyes and his wavy black hair disheveled, he looked both vulnerable and dangerous.

Beside him Alan looked neat and civilized, but a great deal more hostile. My flowers, still upside down, quivered in his hand. I half expected him to slap them across Colin's face like a gauntlet.

Instead, he asked, "Who are you anyway? What are you doing here?"

"Your job, if you really are her boyfriend." The stress on

the word "if" was unmistakable, as was the contemptuous expression on Colin's face as he looked Alan up and down. He picked up the gun in its holster from the coffee table where it had been resting. Alan's eyes widened at the sight of it.

"I'll call you later," he said to me, then gave Alan one last cold glance and went out the front door, pulling it shut with a quiet click.

In the silence that followed, Alan and I stared at each other, neither one knowing what to say.

Explanations were going to take a long time. I went into the kitchen and began making coffee, opening the back door to let Belle out. Uncharacteristically, she hadn't barked at either the doorbell or at Alan, instead looking both subdued and glad to get out of the house. I knew how she felt. Alan watched me, trying to gauge whether it was safe to speak or maybe just trying to decide where to begin. I was mildly interested myself to see just which of the many possible topics he would choose.

"Are you really all right?" he asked at last, proving again that he was one of the nicest people I know. And one of the most attractive. He was close to six feet tall, athletic and lean. His hair was a rich golden brown and his eyes a changeable gray green. Right now they glittered almost emerald.

I tried to sound reassuring. "I really am. I know it looks bad, but it doesn't even hurt anymore." Not much, anyway. "And are those for me?"

With surprise he glanced down at the forgotten flowers, then righted the bouquet and offered it to me. The yellow tissue paper was crushed around the stems, and I suspected a few of the stems were crushed as well.

"Thank you very much. They're beautiful," I said, taking them from him and opening a cupboard for a vase. "How was your trip?"

He frowned. "I don't want to talk about my trip. I want to know what has been going on here. And who the hell was that guy?"

Where should I start? "He's a detective. He was keeping watch on the house last night." I gestured around the room, "Someone broke in and trashed my things. Kyla helped with the clean up, but look at my poor couch." I pointed sadly. "Colin wasn't convinced that whoever it was found what they were looking for."

"And why does this . . . Colin think that?" asked Alan, unable to say the name in a normal tone. "What does he think they were looking for?" He stood stiff and tense, close to pacing or possibly throwing something.

I shrugged. "Both very good questions. I wish I knew the answers."

The coffeepot was half full by now, and I poured two cups, then added a little more water to the top. Sinking into a chair, I pushed a second one out with my foot.

"You might as well sit down. This is a long story."

He hesitated a minute, then finally sat down gingerly, as though afraid the chair was going to break or that he was going to hear something really bad. I marshaled my thoughts, trying to decide where to begin, and then finally launched into the whole confusing tale. I didn't tell it very well, hopping back and forth in time as I remembered details. To give him credit, Alan didn't interrupt me other than to ask one or two questions when my explanations became unclear. When I was done, he sat in silence for a few moments, cradling his cooling coffee cup between both hands, staring into the dark liquid as though into a crystal ball.

"So," he said at last, "the bottom line is that this coach . . ."

"Coach Fred," I supplied.

". . . that this Coach Fred had an argument with a violent parent, that he also had some kind of connection with drugs or with someone who had access to drugs, and that he knew a secret that he planned to share with you and that he kept locked up somewhere. And someone killed him for one of those reasons."

I frowned. "It doesn't sound right when you say it like that. You don't understand what he was like."

"It doesn't matter what he was like. You have to concentrate on the facts," said Alan.

But it did matter. It mattered who Coach Fred had been, how he'd spent his life, what he'd accomplished. Colin and now Alan seemed to think that Coach Fred had done something very wrong, which had somehow led to his death. I did not agree. I frowned at Alan.

He went on without noticing. "What if he'd gotten in too deep with these drug dealers and he was going to leave you their names as insurance? Or maybe not their names—just the key so that you could find their names if something happened to him. That would explain what it was that he had locked up. Only they killed him before he could get it to you."

"No!" I protested. "What the hell? This wasn't a hit. Fred worked with kids, not the Corleone family. And it's not like it was bags of cocaine—it was a few ounces of marijuana. Willie Nelson keeps more than that in his sock drawer."

Affronted, he held up his hands. "Well, you explain it then."

I sighed. "I can't. Not yet anyway," I said, thinking about my options. There were still things I could do.

For one thing I hadn't spoken to everyone at the school yet. And I still needed to figure out why someone had attacked me. Had I unknowingly frightened one of the people I'd questioned, frightened them badly enough to make them act? If so, who could it be? And why the heck ransack my house? Unless, of course, it was to look for the key I no longer had?

"What do you mean 'not yet'?" asked Alan. "You can't seriously be thinking about pursuing this on your own."

"I'm not on my own," I said, thinking of Colin and Kyla and all they'd done for me. And there was Laura Esperanza, too, who'd promised to ask questions for me.

I frowned at that thought. I should call her today to let her know what had happened and to tell her not to ask those questions after all. "And it's not a matter of pursuing it," I went on. "I'm involved whether I want to be or not, and I need to figure out what's going on."

"No, you don't. This is a job for the police. You can't go around putting yourself in danger. In fact, you should get away for a while."

His concern was touching, but his suggestion was impossible.

"I can't do that. I have a job."

"After what's happened, I'm sure you could get a leave of absence for a few weeks."

"Yeah, right."

I thought about the school, wondering if there was someplace there that Fred might have hidden a lockbox or a little safe. I'd searched the tennis shed thoroughly, but maybe he had a hiding place in his classroom. Or somewhere at his home. Even if his wife hadn't known about it, maybe she'd be willing to search or to let me search.

Alan slapped his palm on the table, and I jumped. "You're not listening to me."

"I'm sorry, what did you say?"

"I said you need to leave here."

"I heard you. I just didn't think you were serious. I can't leave."

"Yes, you can. You were injured at a school-sanctioned event. They'll be so happy that you aren't suing them that they'll probably beg you to take some time off. You could come to Dallas," he added quietly and reached out to take my hand.

I looked at him, really looked at him, for the first time since he'd arrived, taking in the furrowed brows and lines of tension around his mouth. I had no doubt that he was really worried for me. But was it anything more than the concern of the moment, of one human being for another? Feeling his warm hand around mine, I realized this was the first time we'd touched in weeks. And as much as I'd missed it, it no longer felt the same.

I squeezed his hand, then pulled away, rising to get more coffee, and tried not to notice the hurt look on his face.

"I can't leave. I have students and classes and now the tennis team. And regardless of how it looks, I don't think I'm in any real danger anymore. Whatever is going to happen has already happened. Plus, I'll be watching more carefully. Coffee?" I asked, holding up the pot.

He watched me through narrowed eyes, as though he was trying to figure out a particularly complicated puzzle.

Leaning back in his chair, he said, "So tell me more about this cop."

Chapter 14

STAGES AND STOOGES

On Monday night I met Kyla at the Hyde Park Bar & Grill on Westgate, which had a small outdoor patio where you could get a reasonably priced dinner and happy-hour priced drinks. It was true that the patio was basically in a mall parking lot, but it was enclosed by walls and potted plants, which masked the lack of scenery, and it was fun sitting outside in the twilight in the warm evening air. It was only seven o'clock, but already the clear summer sky was aflame with vivid orange and gold, fading into pearly grays. Autumn was undoubtedly on the way, even if the central Texas temperatures hadn't received the memo yet.

I sipped on a Brazilian merlot in a long-stemmed glass, while Kyla took a long deep draft of a Bombay Sapphire martini, which came with its own frosty shaker. She gave a great sigh of satisfaction.

"These are so good here. You really need to try one. Here, you want a sip?"

I declined. "Infidel. It would war with the fruity nose and exuberant plumminess of my merlot."

She laughed. "That would be more impressive if you knew what it meant. I want to be a wine snot."

"We should take a class. It would be fun."

"So how did things go yesterday with your boys?"

"They aren't my boys. And it was awful. No, wait. Awful is at least two steps above what it was. What is worse than awful?"

"Catastrophic? Horrific?" she suggested.

"Yeah. Both of those." I stared into the burgundy liquid in my glass, feeling deeply depressed. "What am I going to do?"

Kyla gave me a measuring look. "So Alan walked in on you and Colin?"

"You make it sound like something was going on. Which it wasn't. But yeah. He finally came right out and asked if Colin was sleeping with me."

"What did you say?"

I frowned at her. "I told him no. Because he's not. But I was mad at him for asking."

"I don't see why. Seems like a reasonable question to me. A blind monkey could tell Colin wants to."

"What? Why a monkey?" I asked, diverted for a moment.

"Why not? They seem stupid and unobservant. Pick another animal, I don't care. The point is, wait . . . what's my point?" She took another sip of her martini, which was apparently already working.

"God only knows."

"Oh, I know. The point is that Colin is interested, and

there's definitely some major chemistry going on between you two. Alan isn't stupid. Well, he's stupid about the way he's been acting, but he's not stupid about that. And let's face it, he walks into your house early in the morning and Colin is there. What's he supposed to think?"

"He's supposed to trust me."

"Yeah, well that gets back to the stupid bit. But come on. If the situation was turned around, you'd be having some questions."

"What, you mean if Colin answered Alan's door early in the morning? Yeah, I guess I would have some major questions. About both of them."

She grinned. "That's a good one. But you know what I mean."

"I guess so."

The waitress arrived, a young woman with a pierced nose and an intricate band of tattoos running from shoulder to wrist. "Y'all ready to order?" she asked.

"Sonora salad, chipotle ranch on the side," said Kyla.

"Chicken fried steak with extra gravy, please," I said.

"And your side?"

"Macaroni and cheese," I said, ignoring Kyla's expression of outrage and poorly disguised envy.

The waitress went off to place our order.

"Wonder if her mom hates the nose ring or the tattoos more," I said.

"I don't know, Grandma," said Kyla. "So where are your two men now?"

I shrugged, taking a sip of wine to stall. I finally answered,

"Alan went back to Dallas. He didn't seem very happy. And I haven't seen Colin since he left after meeting Alan."

"Have you and Alan broken up?"

"I'm not sure. Not formally, anyway."

"And just how depressed are you?"

"What do you mean?"

"You just ordered enough comfort food for a football team." I began to protest, but she held up her hands. "Never mind," she said. "You're entitled. So what are you going to do? And I'm talking about your two boyfriends, so don't pretend you don't know what I mean."

"If I knew that, I wouldn't be sitting here drinking with you, now would I?"

On Tuesday morning, I got to school early and went in search of Laura, finding her, as expected, in her classroom bent over a stack of papers, reading glasses perched on the end of her nose. Today, her waist-length brown hair was falling loose around her shoulders in a shining soft curtain. She looked up as I opened the door.

"*Queso paso,*" I called by way of greeting.

She jumped to her feet. "God, I'm glad you're here!" she said, then did a double take. "Whoa—what happened to you?"

I put a hand to my face. The bruises were fading to yellow and green, which was a good sign, but they were actually getting larger and uglier if that was possible. And apparently my makeup, which I'd practically applied with a spatula, was not doing a very good job of concealment.

"I'll tell you later," I said. "What's up?"

She grabbed my arm and pulled me out the door. "Come on. You are never going to believe this."

She hurried down the halls, out the doors, and across the courtyard to Building A, which held the gym, cafeteria, and theater. Her short legs meant she was taking two steps to each one of mine, her high-heeled sandals tapping out an allegro rhythm on the concrete floors. And still I found myself panting to keep up with her.

"You are not going to believe this one. You know how I told you I'd check with Roland about that night Coach Fred died? I came up here yesterday near lunchtime to pick up some homework to grade, and I saw the drama kids were having rehearsal. So I figured, what the heck, it was probably a good time to have a chat with him, right?"

"Well, maybe, but about that, Laura. I don't want you asking any more questions," I said, suddenly worried. I should have called her the day I was attacked. I hadn't anticipated that she might come up to the school over the weekend.

She cut me off. "Never mind about that. You aren't going to believe what I saw. I still don't believe it."

"What was it? And look, Laura, did you talk with Roland? Or anybody?"

"I did, but it wasn't super helpful. He's such a douche."

We had reached the entrance to the theater, and she looked up at me. "Are you ready?" she asked, eyes sparkling.

"For what?"

"For this." She grinned, and slowly pushed open the heavy door.

I peered around her. We stood at the back of the dark

auditorium. Before us, the empty rows of theater chairs sloped downward toward the stage where a single set of soft lights illuminated a couple of kids who were rehearsing lines. It was what shared the stage with them that riveted my attention and had my jaw dropping in shock.

The stage set was spectacular. Glittering gold-sequined curtains covered the back wall, twinkling and sparkling with a thousand colors as they swayed in response to an unseen air current. Large platforms, painted blue and rose and lavender, stood at varying heights, all on wheels, capable of being moved and turned as the scenes required. Lavish furnishings filled the nooks: a plush red chaise longue that looked as though it were a real French period piece, a massive gentleman's chest carved with cherubs and scrollwork, a delicate claw-foot table with two matching chairs. From the ceiling, a gilded trapeze swing cushioned with scarlet velvet hung suspended above the lights.

It was a set that was about a hundred times grander than the normal high school theater production. But the crowning glory stood just left of center, a fourth platform carved to look like an enameled and bejeweled elephant. On its back perched a flat dais made to look like a maharajah's howdah, with golden posts supporting a silk awning dripping with tassels and gemstones the size of my fist.

I just stared.

Laura poked me in the ribs. "Come on," she whispered, and we backed out of the theater, holding the door to keep it from making a noise as it swung shut.

Kids were starting to fill the halls, so we walked back toward our classrooms, keeping our voices low.

"What was that?" I asked.

"Yeah."

"No, really. What was that?"

"Yeah, I know." Laura was almost beside herself with suppressed excitement. "They've done it this time. I've always thought they were funneling funds away from somewhere, and now we've got proof. I don't care how many concessions they sell or raffles they hold, you can't tell me the booster club earned that much."

"No. There's no way. That must be fifty thousand dollars worth of stuff."

"And that's not even the half of it. They had the costumes on a rack behind the stage when I was here yesterday. We're talking real costumes, not just stuff the moms have sewn in their spare time. Even if they rented those, they're still costing a small fortune."

"And the elephant," I said in awe.

"Yup. The elephant. It's something else, right? I'm so excited. That bitch Nancy Wales will never get out of this one. I'm going to get Pat Carver to go over their books with a fine-tooth comb. That money came from somewhere."

I was thinking hard. "They can't possibly think that no one is going to notice."

Indeed, the posters in the halls were already proclaiming the musical as "visually stunning" and urging students to get their tickets early for what were sure to be sellout performances. Until now, I'd thought this was the typical hyperbole of advertising.

Laura rubbed her hands together. "I wonder how they got

the money," she mused. "I can't imagine them slipping anything by Pat. She's like a pit bull. Last year, she wouldn't even let the lacrosse team buy Windbreakers." Her eyes widened. "Ooh, maybe it's not even paid for. Maybe they charged it all, and the shit's going to hit the fan after the performances."

"Why are they doing all this? And why now?" I asked out loud, though I knew Laura had no way of knowing. "Nancy's been the drama coach since the school opened. In fact, I'm pretty sure mammoths still roamed the earth when she started. Why would she suddenly put on a blowout performance? This isn't even the normal time of year for the musical—they usually do it in the spring."

"Who knows? Maybe she's dying, and she wants to go out with a bang. Do you think she's dying?" she asked, a little wistfully.

"No. Remember, only the good die young. Which means Nancy is immortal."

We'd reached my classroom, and I stopped at the door. "One way or another, the money for that stage set will have to be explained. If you want to pursue it with Pat, go ahead, although I don't think it's necessary. Something like that is definitely going to come out. But, Laura, please don't ask any more questions about the night Fred died. Not of Roland, not of anybody."

She turned to face me. "Why? What's this about?"

I pointed to my face. "Someone mugged me and trashed my house, and I can't think of any other reason than because I was poking around about Fred. I don't want the same thing to happen to you."

Her eyes widened. "That's crazy," she said at last, but without conviction. "You think that whoever killed Fred is still hanging around here?"

She looked up and down the corridors uneasily, as though expecting to see a shadowy figure lurking in some corner like Snidely Whiplash.

"It's a possibility," I said. "I definitely think it's someone connected with the school. Someone who thought that he was safe from suspicion until I started asking questions."

"So, what did you find out?"

I sighed. "Nothing at all. That's the weird thing. I haven't learned one single thing that I thought was important. But I must have. Something I said or heard must have worried someone. I wish I knew what it was. But I don't want you accidentally doing the same thing."

She pressed her lips together, looking stubborn. "Are you sure it's not just a coincidence and doesn't really have anything to do with Fred?"

"I'm not sure about anything anymore, but please don't take the risk. Besides," I added as a distraction, "you have bigger worries now."

"What do you mean?"

"Nancy is never going to move that elephant off the stage so that you can have the FLS recital."

Her eyes widened, and a dull red flush slowly rose from her neck and suffused her cheeks like a rosy sunset. Her teeth clicked together with a snap.

"We'll just see about that," she said, and then tapped off toward her classroom.

• • •

At lunchtime, I sat at my desk as the kids filed out, trying to decide what to do. I'd been prying into something that was undoubtedly better left to the police, and I'd had my fingers burned pretty severely. I knew that Colin, if he was still speaking to me at all, would tell me to do my job, keep my head down, and watch my back until the police solved the case. Alan had told me exactly the same thing after I'd refused to take a leave of absence and hide in Dallas until it blew over. My own inner voice of reason told me that my advice to Laura was golden and that I should take it myself. Head down. Eyes lowered. Hear no evil. Stay safe.

With a sigh I rose and went looking for Ed Jones.

He wasn't in his classroom or the teachers' lounge. After a prolonged search, I found him standing behind one of the portable buildings at the back of the school, sneaking a cigarette in a furtive manner usually seen only in teenage boys. I looked hard at the cigarette as I approached, suspicious that it might be hand rolled and maybe not even tobacco. He looked up guiltily when he heard my steps and quickly put his hand down to his side, cupping the lit cigarette in the curve of his palm.

"Hi Ed," I said. "What are you doing out here?"

"Oh, you know. Just taking a break, getting some sun. I'm an outdoor person, hate being cooped up indoors."

He must use one hell of a sunblock then, I thought, noting the pale skin and buggy blue eyes. Judging by the pile of butts on the ground, either he came here frequently or he smoked more than one at a time. He noticed my glance and scattered a few of them with his foot.

"How's the tennis team doing?" he said, his voice an odd mixture of scorn and eagerness.

He probably hoped that I was here for his help.

"They are doing great. We have our first tournament this week in fact."

"Well, you really need someone who knows the ins and outs of the game. It's not enough to know how to play, you have to strategize, pick and choose your battles, motivate the players. Maybe you don't know it, but I was an assistant coach this past summer at a tennis camp in Wimberley. I have a lot of experience."

I ignored this, watching him carefully. Petulant, yes, and maybe bitter. But was there anything more dangerous than that lurking in Ed Jones? I still didn't see it.

"I was chatting with some folks last week, Ed. One of them mentioned that you'd been talking with Coach Fred about the team recently."

After a moment of silence in which he was obviously trying to decide whether or not to lie, Ed answered, "Maybe. Yeah, I supposed I talked with him sometimes."

"I was sure this person had misunderstood, but they seemed to think you had quite the argument with Coach Fred."

He paled visibly, which I wouldn't have thought possible considering how pasty he was already. His eyes darted to my face, then to the ground, then off to the horizon as if he were looking for an escape route. He half raised the hand holding his cigarette as though he wanted to take a drag, then seemed to remember he was hiding it from me and lowered it again.

"They misunderstood. I never argued with Coach."

"I didn't think so," I said promptly. He looked relieved, and his shoulders relaxed somewhat. I waited a long moment, aware of the sun beating down on the baked earth at our feet. Then I asked, "Why do you think someone might have thought you were arguing?"

"I just said we weren't arguing," he protested.

"Of course. But you must have been discussing something. What was it?"

"That's none of your business," he snapped, his resemblance to a bad-tempered Chihuahua becoming more pronounced.

I raised one eyebrow and stared coldly. It was as effective with him as it was with my students. He shifted from one foot to another, an awkward move that made the too-thin fabric of his shirt slide over his man-boobs.

"It didn't have anything to do with his death," he blurted finally, as though succumbing to a last twist of the thumbscrews.

"Did you get mad enough to hit him, Ed?"

"No!" He looked appalled at the thought.

I pressed on, using my most reasonable voice. "Maybe it was an accident. He was an old man, maybe frailer than we knew. You lost your temper and punched him. You didn't mean for him to die."

"No!" he said again, his voice rising a full octave. "I never touched him. Yes, we had words, but I never hit him. I'd never hit anyone," he added, aggrieved.

Looking at the sweat rolling off his forehead, it was hard not to believe this.

When I didn't say anything, he went on. "Look, we argued about my taking over as tennis coach. I want that job," he said defiantly, glaring at me, "and I told him so. So what? He'd been doing it too long, he was soft. The team wasn't going anywhere, and they weren't winning. He let anyone play, for God's sake."

"Yes, he did. It was the best thing about the team. Any kid could participate."

"You're never going to win with that attitude!" he said with sudden venom. "I could have turned things around, shaped those kids into champions. I even offered to take on a select few of the players and make them an elite squad. The old man could have kept his hobby team going." Ed's eyes filled with sudden angry tears, and his voice broke as he added, "He laughed at me."

Ah, there it was. Coach Fred had laughed and poor, ambitious, vulnerable Ed had exploded. A small man in every way, and no match for a man of Fred's experience and confidence. Ed had no way of knowing that Fred's laughter only showed how bad a day Fred had been having. The argument with Gary Richards, the infighting with Nancy Wales, the pressure that he must have felt regarding whatever that mysterious key was about. Being confronted by Ed Jones at the end of a long miserable day must have been just about the final straw, because Coach Fred would never have intentionally humiliated another human being. On any other day, he would have tried to convert Ed to his way of thinking about teaching and about life.

But could Ed have struck Coach Fred? And hard enough to kill? That didn't seem likely, I thought, looking at the spindly arms protruding like knobby sticks from the sleeves of his shirt. Now, if it had been a death by slap fight, Ed would have been my number one candidate.

"Did you hit him, Ed?" I asked slowly and forcefully.

"No!" he wailed the word. "I never touched him. I yelled at him. That's all, I swear."

I believed him. I wished I didn't because it would have been an easy answer. It would have meant that no one had wanted to kill Coach Fred. A single blow in a moment of anger, instantly regretted. It was an explanation, the only explanation that made any sense to me. Although of course it didn't explain everything else that had been happening ever since. But I believed Ed Jones was telling the truth.

I sighed and started to walk away. Then I stopped and turned. "You do know it's dangerous to smoke and wear a patch, right?" I asked.

"I . . . well, of course. It would be stupid to do both."

"Well you might tell that to your hand. I can see the smoke, Ed."

He glanced down at the thin stream of smoke curling around his cupped palm, glared at me, then sighed. He raised the cigarette to his lips, taking a long grateful drag. I noted it was commercially made, filter tip and all. So much for the notion it might be a special version like those that Colin had found in Fred's desk.

"Well, the patch isn't exactly cutting it," he said defensively.

• • •

Laura Esperanza made another appearance just as sixth period was ending and the kids in my last class were jostling and shoving their way into the halls like overeager salmon making their way upstream. Over the indistinct babble of voices, the sound of hundreds of feet slapping on concrete, and the clanging of lockers, I heard the staccato tapping of Laura's shoes. She pushed her way through the knot of kids, not afraid to use elbows, and stormed up to my desk.

With a loud bang, she slapped a flier onto the surface in front of me and all but shouted, "Look what that bitch Nancy Wales has done now!"

Half a dozen heads turned to look our way, and a couple of kids went so far as to halt and watch. This was way more interesting than making it to seventh period. I waved my hand as though flicking them away.

"Go on, you don't want to be late for your next class."

They left reluctantly, dragging their feet and craning chins over shoulders until the last minute. I suspected they might wait outside the door to try to hear something more.

I lowered my voice. "What is this?"

"Just look!"

I looked. It was a flier for the musical, brilliantly printed on heavy glossy paper in full color. The elephant featured prominently in the middle, with a couple dressed in evening wear singing into each other's faces on its broad back. The words *Moulin Rouge—A Stage Spectacular* floated above their heads. Below their feet, in golden script, another line proclaimed, "Original Stage Adaptation by Roland Wilding."

"Wow," I said, impressed in spite of myself. "This must have cost a fortune to print. Where do you think they're getting the money?"

"No, no. That's not the point! Look at the picture!"

I looked more closely. The girl, long fair hair falling in shiny curls about her shoulders was McKenzie Mills. The boy . . . I blinked, trying to clear my vision. It didn't help. The picture did not change. The boy was no boy at all.

"That's Roland Wilding," I said.

"Exactly."

"But . . ."

"Yes!"

"He can't . . ."

"He is."

I lifted my eyes from the picture. "Maybe this is just a publicity shot. The real kid wasn't available that day and Roland subbed for him."

"Nope. I already checked on that. He's got the lead."

"Please tell me you're kidding."

"Nope. According to my kids, that bitch Nancy Wales told them there wasn't a boy with a strong enough presence to carry the role."

I was speechless for a moment.

Laura paced back and forth in front of my desk, looking exactly like a wild panther, if that panther was wearing four-inch-high gladiator sandals.

"They can't do this. It's outrageous to cast Roland in a school play. He's not a student. He's not even a human. What the hell are they thinking?" I asked.

"She must be banging him, and she needs to keep him happy."

Behind Laura, kids for my French III class were hovering uneasily by the door, not sure whether to interrupt or not. Exasperated, I waved them in.

"I'll have to talk to you about this later," I said to Laura.

"Don't worry," she said. "This is not going to happen. I'm going straight to Larry, and if he won't stop it, I'll go to the school board. My cousin is a board member."

She tapped off down the hallway, small shoulders squared and stiff with rage. I thought about calling her back to tell her I'd go with her, but I had a class to teach, and I decided it could wait. She could go see Larry on her own, and I'd return with her for a follow-up visit if it became necessary. As a plan, it made perfect sense. I just wished I knew why I felt so uneasy.

Chapter 15

CASH AND CLOCKS

Tennis practice was almost over when Michael Dupre and Carl strolled over from the area behind the school where the movie trailers were parked. Cigarette dangling from his bottom lip, Carl carried a clipboard in one hand, while the other was busy scratching at something under his greasy blond hair. Beside him, Michael Dupre seemed like an advertisement for cleanliness and personal grooming. I went to meet them, conscious that I'd pulled my hair back into a ponytail of my own without using a brush or looking in a mirror and that a trickle of sweat was running down the side of my face.

"Hi guys. What can I do for you?" I asked.

Michael Dupre cocked his head to one side, looking at me. "You look a lot better than when I saw you last."

"Always the ladies' man," I responded with a grin.

He smiled back, a flash of white teeth in his lean face. "I hope you are fully recovered."

"Yes, I am, thank you."

They continued to stare as though considering what camera angle to use on me, and the silence moved into the awkward zone.

"How did the shoot, or whatever you call it, turn out on Friday? Are you here for the kids again?" I asked.

Carl shifted from one foot to another and shot a sidelong glance at his boss.

Michael pondered for a long moment. "That is what we're here about. The shoot was perfect. Your kids did great, and in fact when we looked at the rushes, we realized it turned out far better than we'd planned. There's just one small problem."

I waited for him to elaborate, but he just stood there as though waiting for me to say something. I wondered how long the silence could continue and had a brief vision of darkness falling and we three still standing in the parking lot in the moonlight. I decided I didn't have that kind of time.

"What problem?" I asked.

"You, actually. You made it into frame near the end when you came up the path."

My memory of that event was blurry, but I had a vague recollection of seeing running, screaming kids and cameras on rails before I passed out.

"I'm sorry. Did it ruin the scene? Can't you cut that bit out?"

"Yes, we could," he admitted. "And I was going to. Until we saw the rushes. It was brilliant. Scariest thing in the entire scene. Changed the whole focus of the chase. See, it made it look like there was something even worse in front of the kids, like they were being herded forward. I loved it."

I looked at him uncomprehendingly.

He went on. "I've got writers working right now on the script. The thing is . . ." and here his voice trailed off.

Carl cleared his throat as though to speak, then thought better of it, and inhaled a long drag on his cigarette. The tip glowed orange.

Michael Dupre tried again. "The thing is, well, we'd sort of like to keep that scene."

"Well, okay, that's good news, right?"

Carl spoke. "We need your permission. We didn't have you signed on as an extra—we only had the tennis players."

Michael added quickly, "We'll pay you, of course. Double, in fact. We can even throw in a screen credit."

So that's what this was about. He didn't want to have to reshoot the scene. I gave a relieved laugh.

"Wow, I thought something was really wrong. No problem, I'll sign whatever. You don't have to pay me, and I definitely don't need credit. I can't imagine what I must have looked like, but I'm pretty sure I won't want anyone knowing it was me." I gave a little shudder at the thought.

Michael gave a whoop and threw his arms around me before Carl muscled him aside and thrust the clipboard into my hands.

"Sign here and here," he said, pointing as though worried I'd change my mind.

I heard the sound of running feet behind me, and turned my head in time to see Roland Wilding flying across the parking lot toward us. He really was very pretty, I thought dispassionately, with his golden hair aglow in the sunlight and his fine figure almost graceful in motion. Too bad he was such a worm.

"What's going on?" he cried, panic very near the surface. "Are you signing the tennis team for more work? I told you before, the drama department is ready and able to do whatever you need."

Michael lifted a hand. "No, it's nothing like that."

"Then what . . ." Roland's voice trailed off as he glanced from Michael to the clipboard in my hands.

I decided to take pity on him. "I accidentally made it into one of the shots, Roland, and they need my permission to use the footage. That's all."

"You? You made it into a shot?" he whispered, stricken. "In a Michael Dupre film?"

"Entirely by accident," I tried to reassure him.

Carl grunted. "Yeah, she got mugged. Bummer for her, but gold for us." He tapped the clipboard impatiently. "Here and here," he reminded me.

Roland went as white as it was possible to get under his spray-on tan. "Getting mugged got you into the film?"

"Yeah. Weird right? But I'm fine, thanks for asking," I said, signing the form with a flourish. I handed the pen and clipboard back to Carl.

Carl gave an unexpected grin.

"Told you she'd be cool about it," he said to Michael, and then slouched off, reaching behind as he walked to give his sagging pants an upward tweak.

Michael gave me a little nod. "Thank you," he said simply, turning to go.

"Wait!" Roland grabbed Michael's arm, then realized what he'd done and snatched his hand back. "Sorry," he mumbled.

"I'm very sorry, but I don't have any roles for your group," Michael said with some coldness.

"No, that's not why I came over here. Look!" Roland pulled out a handful of brightly colored theater tickets. "Tickets for our production. Opening night is Friday. It's going to be spectacular."

Spectacular, spectacular, I thought to myself, thinking of a song in the show.

Michael looked pained. "We're going to be extremely busy wrapping up our production here. That's our final week of shooting. I'm very sorry, but . . ."

Roland cut him off, something that probably didn't happen very often. "Don't say no! Look, you're known in the industry as a director with an eye for bright new talent. You've discovered dozens of new actors. I . . . we've got some serious talent this year. The best I've ever seen. Come. Just for half an hour if you can't manage more than that. You will be seriously impressed."

Michael hesitated, and Roland thrust the tickets at him again.

"Please. Half an hour. I'll reserve you seats in the back. Or the front. Whichever you prefer."

Michael reluctantly held out a hand, taking the tickets with the enthusiasm of someone receiving a religious pamphlet from a beaming swami in saffron robes. "The back. Near the door."

"You got it," said Roland. "You won't regret it."

Michael's expression said otherwise, but he managed a nod before walking back toward the set.

Roland watched him go, then turned back to me, eyes spiteful. He opened his mouth to spew out some kind of nonsense, but I held up a hand.

"Whatever you're going to say, save it. I didn't tell him you only want him to come so that he can see you perform as Christian. Or that the only reason the play is happening this week at all is because it's the last week he is here. But I will if you don't leave me the hell alone."

A lie. I was hardly likely to see Michael Dupre again, let alone talk to him about Roland Wilding of all subjects, but Roland didn't know that. He closed his mouth with a snap and scuttled off as quickly as possible.

I watched him go with a feeling of revulsion. I couldn't wait to tell Laura that I'd figured out the reason for all the expensive props, the killer rehearsal schedule, and the casting choices. All done to give Roland Wilding his chance to audition for director Michael Dupre. What a weasel.

Returning to my classroom to prepare for a quiz I planned to give the next day, I noticed the door to Coach Fred's classroom stood slightly ajar. Inexperienced substitutes had been known to trample a kid or two in their hurry to leave at the end of the day, so occasionally a door was left unlocked or even open. This door in particular required a good hard pull to make the latch click into place, and Fred used to bang it shut quite loudly. It was always my cue to go home. I crossed the hall to close it, thinking about poor Fred and how much had changed in such a short time.

As I put my hand on the doorknob, a sound caught my ear and I paused, listening. Inside, someone was rustling through various papers and opening and closing drawers in a hurry. Of course, it could have been the substitute, but that was unlikely so long after the school day had ended. I opened the door wide enough to peek around the corner.

Pat Carver sat in Fred's chair, busy going through his desk. I straightened, then entered the room, but Pat was completely absorbed in her search and didn't notice me. I watched her pull open the file drawer and start pawing through the folders, muttering to herself. I cleared my throat.

The effect was spectacular. She jumped an inch off the seat and slammed her own fingers in the drawer in her haste to close it. A brick red flush crept up her neck and into her cheeks, but she met my gaze defiantly.

"Hi, Pat," I said. "Looking for something?"

Her pale eyes darted down and sideways as though a reasonable answer might be skittering across the floor like a cockroach. Then she rose, pushing back the chair with a screech and drew herself up to her full height, which was fairly impressive. She topped me by a couple of inches and outweighed me by at least fifty pounds. I stepped back involuntarily.

"Yes, I needed the receipts for the new watercoolers Coach Argus purchased for the tennis team."

This threw me. "But the team doesn't have any new watercoolers. The ones we're using are older than most of the kids."

This flummoxed her for a moment, but she came back strong.

"Ah, well he submitted a purchase requisition that I approved. I assumed he followed through and actually bought them." She sniffed at this sign of incompetence, then gave me a sidelong look, and said, "In any case, the team has approval for two new coolers, so if you want to make the purchase, you can turn in the receipts to me."

"Okay," I said. "Are you sure there wasn't something else?"

"What else could there be?" she asked sharply.

Which was completely unanswerable. She waited a moment, but when I said nothing, she pushed past me and left.

I watched her go, thinking it was really a very good question. What else could there be? In this tangled and seemingly random series of events that had occurred since Fred's death, what was I missing? And here was Pat Carver, the school accountant, whom I had never seen anywhere near a classroom, rooting through Fred's desk. For what? Not receipts for coolers that had never been purchased. Especially not after the long pause she'd needed to come up with the lie. But if not that, then what? I sat down in Fred's chair to think.

Pat Carver. Unlikely though it seemed, if she was connected to this in some way, then school finances might be involved. It was the first whiff of money that I'd caught in the entire mess. Why did people kill or attack other people? If you ruled out cases of self-defense, it was always for personal gain. I supposed that gain could come in many forms, but in Austin, Texas, it usually meant drugs or money.

Drugs seemed unlikely, even counting the miniature stash

that Colin had found in the tennis shed. A few ounces of marijuana weren't worth enough to be a motive, and if it had been the cause of Fred's murder, why had it been left at the crime scene? But the accounts Pat Carver managed were something else. High school or not, Pat oversaw an enormous budget. Besides the funds allocated to the school by the state, which were substantial, Bonham had over thirty clubs, teams, and societies, and every one of them spent most of the year raising money. The senior class alone had already raised over sixty thousand dollars intended for prom. The French club was busy selling candy bars to fund next summer's trip to Paris. The lacrosse team had just finished selling coupon books. The list went on and on. And every dollar from every fund-raiser went through Pat Carver.

Coach Fred had managed the tennis team funds. Sure, the booster club parents had done much of the work, but Fred was very hands-on when it came to money. He'd mentioned a couple of times that having a new treasurer every year was just asking for trouble because the rules were confusing. After one of the parent volunteers had accepted a cash donation, which for some reason was forbidden and which had almost caused the team to be disqualified from competition, Fred had taken over the team accounts himself. What if he'd stumbled on an irregularity in the books?

Embezzling school funds was scarcely unknown. Just last year, a school employee in Iowa was accused of siphoning over five hundred thousand dollars from her school district accounts into her own. On a slightly smaller scale, a couple of mothers in California had stolen thirty thousand dollars from an elementary school fund intended to hire school counselors and teach handwriting skills. They'd been caught because they'd charged pedicures, Swiss massages, and tickets to a Peter Frampton concert to the fund account and someone at the bank had eventually noticed. They'd been stupid, but whatever else she was, Pat Carver was not. She was far too intelligent to ever make purchases directly from an official account, but how hard would it be for her to shuffle cash around? If she wasn't greedy, if she kept the individual amounts relatively small, would the typically unorganized and constantly changing club leaders notice? School regulations and requirements were complex—parent volunteers, no matter how competent, had a hard time keeping up. They had no choice but to believe what Pat told them. How often had I heard Laura complaining that Pat had refused to cut a check for something the FLS needed for two weeks or more? What if she delayed, not just to exercise her power but to give herself time to shuffle funds around?

I did not have much trouble believing that Pat might be an embezzler, but it was a big step from that to think that she might be a murderer. Creative accounting hardly seemed a likely bedfellow to the violence that had marred the beginning of this school year. Fred's death, the assault on me, the trashing of my house. Maybe she was physically capable of everything, but would she really have done those things?

A clock somewhere in the room quietly ticked away the seconds as I sat pondering this last question. Start at the start, I told myself. With Fred.

Fred was conscientious, meticulous, and honorable. I could safely say that he knew all the district fund-raising rules, that he followed those rules unerringly, and that he kept complete and accurate records of the tennis team's funds. If there had been any discrepancy at all, he would have noticed it. And he would have gone to Pat at once, not accusing, not suspicious, just wanting to correct what he would have considered an honest mistake. But what if it had not been an honest mistake? What if he'd realized that something criminal was occurring? Fred would never have let that go.

I thought about the key and the note Fred had left for me. "As we discussed, it's just a precaution," he'd written. What if he'd intended to talk to me about Pat, maybe providing proof of wrongdoing. And then never had the chance.

The clock continued to tick, still faint, but becoming louder now that the noises in the halls were dying down. The feeling of passing time made me glance at my own watch. Almost six o'clock. Students and teachers, even those participating in after-school meetings, were long gone by now. The sky outside the classroom windows deepened into the soft rich blue of twilight. On the other side of the building, the sun would be turning orange in the west. Time to be going home. Time. A thought occurred to me, and I looked around. Where was the clock I could hear so clearly? The obligatory classroom clock, mounted high on the wall was behind me, electronic and silent. I tipped my head listening, then rose, walking around the room. No other clock was in sight. I played an abbreviated game of Hot and Cold, and at last ended up back where I'd started—at Fred's desk.

I sat again, and pulled open the file drawer in the metal desk. Thumbing through the hanging files, I could see nothing, but I could still hear the faint ticking. Frustrated, I pulled the drawer all the way out, and got down on my knees to peer into the cavity. In the very back, duct-taped to the underside of the desktop, hung a fat manila envelope. I reached in and detached it carefully, finding it surprisingly heavy, and sat cross-legged on the floor to open it.

Inside was the source of the ticking—the miniature clock that Fred had always kept on the corner of his desk and that I'd assumed had been collected for his wife with his other things. Pulling it out of the folder, I turned it in my hands as I had done on the day of his death. On the back, the brass plaque read,

Fred Argus,
You'll make a hell of a teacher.
Congratulations from your friends at Tracor.
We'll miss you.

The clockworks were electric, the ticking sound made by the jerky movement of the second hand, and instead of a pendulum mechanism, the base below the clock face held a small drawer with a keyhole. A keyhole, but no key.

Clutching it in to my chest as though afraid it would fly away, I returned to my classroom, pulling the door to Fred's room shut behind me with a bang. Retrieving my purse, I slipped the little clock inside. My students would be getting a break tomorrow. I was certainly not going to come up with a quiz on French grammar this evening.

Chapter 16

PERFORMANCE AND PERFIDY

I was so eager to get home to look at the clock that I was practically trotting as I cut through Building A on my way back to my car. To my left, I could hear the hollow thump of basketballs on the wood floor of the gymnasium and the sharp blast of a coach's whistle. A small group of girls giggled together like conspirators while they waited just inside the doors for a parent to drive up, not wanting to leave the comfort of the air-conditioning until the last minute. Through the open doors of the hall that stretched along one side of the theater, I could see a flurry of bright color and movement and curiosity slowed my steps. A couple of dozen kids in full, glorious costume milled about, talking in stage whispers, their makeup more garish than any worn by the Parisian courtesans that they pretended to be. They were so excited that I couldn't help grinning. So sad that Nancy Wales and Roland Wilding were such incredible tools. These kids deserved better.

I had just started toward my car again, when Laura

Esperanza sprang from the theater doors like a Pop-Tart from a toaster. Catching sight of me, she rushed forward and grabbed my arm.

"Oh my God, I'm so glad you're here. You have to see this!" She tugged at me, trying to pull me after her. It was a little like a dachshund trying to move a fully loaded Yukon sled.

"What is it? I need to get going," I protested, my mind on the key and clock.

"No, you don't. You need to see this. Trust me, you'll thank me later."

I hesitated, then shrugged and followed her into the theater. She waved her hands at me in what I took to be a signal to be quiet. She held the door after we entered to make sure it closed silently, then peered around the corner, gesturing me to follow. I stood close behind her, easily able to see over the top of her head.

As before, we stood at the very back of the auditorium. Rows of darkened seats sloped downward along two aisles toward the stage, now lit up like a jewelry store by half a dozen high-intensity beams sweeping overhead. The magnificent elephant, huge and bejeweled, had been rolled to center stage, the massive glass gemstones glittering like the real thing. McKenzie Mills, blond hair swept up in a disheveled updo, stood atop its back, singing a haunting song. Her voice, rich and warm, filled the house. Hard to believe such a magnificent voice could come from such a slender little thing. No wonder Nancy had backed down and allowed McKenzie to stay on the tennis team rather than lose her altogether.

Then, ascending the stairs attached to the side of the elephant, Roland Wilding made his entrance. Much as I loathed him, I had to admit he looked spectacular in his tuxedo. His hair was an even richer gold than McKenzie's, his shoulders were broad, his face intent and finely chiseled. He looked like an old-time movie actor, intense and brilliant.

Then he stepped onto a platform beside the elephant's ear and joined McKenzie in song.

For a moment, what I was hearing did not compute. Then I clapped a hand over my mouth to keep from howling with laughter. Reedy and clear, Roland's voice was almost as high as McKenzie's. Worse, it was ever so subtly off-key. Not all the time, and not every note, but randomly, devastatingly flat. In fact, being consistently off would have been easier on the ear. As it was, the uncertainty had the same effect as fingernails on a chalkboard.

"Cut!" shouted Nancy.

Roland stopped, lips pressed together in annoyance. McKenzie lowered her arms, looking anxious.

Nancy rose from her seat in the front row, where she'd been watching the performance. She wore another of her many flowing dresses, this one bright pink and vaguely Hawaiian, having a random border of palm trees along the hem. Heavily, she walked around the edge of the stage and stomped up the stairs, surely making more noise than was actually necessary. She radiated displeasure and contempt. The knot of kids waiting in the wings for their cue to come on receded like a discreet outgoing tide.

She walked right up to the elephant and said something in a low voice to Roland. His voice rose in angry response.

"She came in too early. It threw me off." He shot McKenzie a hostile look from under gold lashes.

The girl flinched and looked away, but with a lack of emotion that told me she'd been subjected to the same complaint before and found it unjustified. And since Nancy would never have held back on publicly reaming out a kid, I felt sure that the trouble was in no way McKenzie's fault.

Nancy and Roland spoke together a few more minutes, and then Nancy waddled off the stage and returned to her seat. The rehearsal continued without interruption, although I could see no improvement.

After a couple of minutes, Laura and I slipped out the doors, and once in the hallway, Laura doubled over in laughter.

"That was so good," she said at last, breathless. "I'm just sorry you weren't here earlier. If you think his singing is bad, you should see his acting. I can't believe he lasted for a single week in New York, no matter what story he tells."

I grinned. "And get this. You know the rush to get this play done? All for Michael Dupre's benefit."

"Who?"

"The director. The one who's in charge of the movie they're filming here," I reminded her. "I was there when Roland fawned all over him and forced him to accept tickets to opening night."

"No! Oh my God, that's so pathetic. That's why he's playing the lead, too, isn't it?"

"I'd bet on it."

She shook her head. "It's outrageous. I'm writing to the school district to complain."

"Well, it'll all be over tomorrow. We'll know by then whether Roland becomes a star or a stinker."

"We already know that," she said.

At home I fed Belle and let her into the backyard, then took my tool kit and sat at my kitchen table with the clock. I tried everything. Screwdrivers, paper clips, hairpins, a pencil, a fingernail file, a nail, and finally the business end of a skewer. I thought about taking a hammer to it, but it was so pretty and it had belonged to Fred and now belonged to his widow. Destroying it would be wrong. In fact, just having taken it seemed a bit wrong, but I knew that Fred had meant for me to know where it was, even if he hadn't had a chance to tell me about it before he died. I considered my options, but didn't see any way around it. At last, I pulled out my cell phone and selected Colin's number from the list.

We hadn't spoken since the disastrous meeting with Alan. Of course, that had only been a day and half ago, but he'd said he'd call, and he hadn't. Not yet anyway. Maybe not ever. Who knew? But this was possibly police business, which made it Colin's business. I just had to make sure I handled it in such a way that it stayed my business as well.

I pushed the Call button. It rang four times, and I was deciding whether to leave a message or just hang up, when I heard his voice.

"Hi," he said, a wary note in his voice.

"Hi," I answered, trying to judge what his tone meant. In the background, I could hear restaurant noises, the clink of flatware on plates, the sound of voices and music. "Is this a good time?"

"For what?" he asked with a certain lack of warmth.

"Do you still have my key?" I asked.

"I've already told you, it's evidence. You can't have it back." Now his tone was dismissive, even impatient. "You could always make a written request for return. During office hours," he added.

I ground my teeth together but said nothing. The longer I waited, the more petty his words sounded. At last, I heard him sigh, and shift the phone.

He said more quietly, "Look, I don't have it on me, but I could get it if necessary. Why do you want to know? And why now?"

"Because," I said deliberately, "I now know where you can stick it."

There was a long pause. Finally, he asked, "Do you mean that in the literal or metaphorical sense?"

"Literal, although I'm happy to transition to metaphorical if you make me fill out a written request."

"Where are you?"

"Home."

"I'm on my way."

"Bring the key," I reminded him.

Colin arrived about an hour later, by which time I was pacing up and down and cursing him under my breath. I jerked the door open before his finger left the bell and pulled him inside. Belle waddled out and yapped at him a couple of times, then returned to her blanket on the couch.

He looked around the room, eyes narrowed. "Where's your boyfriend?" he asked, managing to inject an impressive amount of scorn into the last word.

"Gone back to Dallas," I answered.

He looked pleased. "He seemed like kind of a wuss. You dump him?"

"What? No! He has a job and he had to go home. He lives there."

The smug look faded. "Your call," he said with a shrug.

"Yeah. Did you bring the key?"

He nodded, then scanned the room. "So what does it unlock?"

I'd hidden the clock. Not that I didn't trust him, but . . . no, that wasn't true. I didn't trust him. I had visions of him taking the clock and leaving and my being unable to stop him.

"You said if I found what it went to, I could see what was inside," I reminded him.

"Yes," he agreed warily. "I said we'd open it together."

"And whatever is inside is mine. Meant for me."

Frowning, he again nodded slowly. "Okay. To a point, anyway. But I still have to consider it evidence in the case. I'll have to take it with me."

"Not before I get to look at it. And I mean really look at it."

"You don't even know what it is," he protested.

"I think I do," I said thoughtfully. "If I'm right, it might be the reason Fred was killed."

He looked at me sharply, his blue eyes suddenly intense. "What do you know?"

"I don't *know* anything," I said. "I've only got suspicions. But I think Fred knew, and the proof might be in the clock."

"Clock? What do you mean, clock?"

I pressed my lips together.

He shook his head in exasperation. "You know, we're on the same side here," he pointed out.

"Exactly," I said.

"Fine, we'll look at it together."

I looked at him with narrowed eyes.

He threw up his hands. "Really! I said we will look at it together. What, do you want me to pinkie-swear?"

"Fine," I said at last. Anyway, it wasn't like I had much choice now that he was here.

I removed the clock from its hiding place behind the flour canister in my pantry and set it on the kitchen table. Colin picked it up, turning it over in his hands, reading the inscription on the back, then he produced the key from his pocket.

I frowned.

"That key's not even in an evidence envelope," I pointed out. "You've had it with you this whole time."

He had the grace to look embarrassed, but only slightly. "I might not have had a chance to enter it into evidence. Yet."

"Uh-huh. You would have been up a creek if I'd actually filled out that request form."

"It seemed a remote possibility at best," he said, then shot me a quick grin.

My heart did a little flip, and I felt a warm glow creep into my cheeks. I looked away quickly. Annoying or not, he was far too attractive for my peace of mind.

"Gimme," I said, holding out my hand.

"Why are you the one who gets to open it?" he asked, holding the key just out of reach.

"Because I'm the brilliant detective who found it," I answered.

He tilted his head to one side. "Where did you find it, anyway?"

I told him.

He nodded, but then said with a grin, "So your brilliant detective move was to sit on your butt in a quiet room?"

"You didn't think of it," I pointed out.

"True. And it worked for you. Definitely brilliant."

I tried to stare coldly, but I couldn't help grinning a little, too. "You're not giving me credit for discovering Pat Carver rooting through the same desk."

"Yeah, actually that was pretty good. I'll run a background check on her, see if we can turn up anything. You said she was the school accountant?"

"Exactly. Evil overlord of all the money."

He snorted. "How much money can there be in a school? You guys are more strapped for cash than the police department. I bet every penny is already allocated for salaries and so on."

"Sure, the state funds. But you're not considering the private money. I'm talking thousands, if not hundreds of thousands of dollars," I said. "Think about the clubs, teams, and graduating classes, all spending every spare moment raising money for trips, for prom, for competitions. There are dozens of organizations at school, and every one of them is required to have an account managed by the school accounting office."

He gave a low whistle and a little nod. "Okay, Nancy Drew, open the damn clock. The suspense is killing me."

The key fit, the tumblers tumbled, and the drawer opened. We held our breath, our faces almost touching as we bent over the tiny drawer. With trembling fingers, I pulled out a folded square of white paper and, meeting Colin's eye with an eager glance, I opened it.

I've never been so let down in my life. Opened, the square revealed itself to be three pieces of paper. The smallest, a receipt for three new coolers, the second a requisition for new nets, and the third, an accounting spreadsheet with numbers in about twelve different columns.

We looked at it a long time, and finally Colin straightened, ran a hand through his wavy hair, and turned to me. "Is this what you expected?"

"No. I thought it was going to be a note accusing Pat of embezzling."

"So, do these receipts mean anything to you?"

"Not a thing."

Or did they? I reconsidered, then tapped the top slip. "Pat said she was looking for this. The thing is we don't have any new water coolers."

He picked it up. "This is for a grand total of one hundred and fifty dollars. Nice, big coolers, I'd assume, but not much of a motive."

Of course he was right. It was ridiculous. And yet, something was bothering me about it. I finally reached out for the purchase requisition for the nets. "This isn't Fred's handwriting, and I can't read the signature."

"Is he the only person who could ask for new nets? Isn't that something the booster club might have bought for him?"

"Technically, yes. Booster clubs can and do purchase new equipment and supplies all the time. But in this case . . . well, the school should buy new nets. That's considered part of the facilities, just like having goal posts on the football field. And this requisition doesn't look like it's for booster club funds anyway. It's a school form."

"Again, I'm not sure I see what the problem is."

"I don't either," I admitted. "But it's odd. And besides if there's nothing wrong, why would Fred hide it at all?"

"Look, I'll take all this stuff with me and get one of the guys who knows about financial crimes to go over it. Maybe he'll see what we're missing."

That made sense, although I was reluctant to lose possession of the clock and the papers. If only Fred had been able to tell me what it was all about. I was somehow not clever enough to see what had apparently been clear to him.

Feeling let down, I followed Colin to the door. He turned abruptly, and I had to stop and sidestep to avoid running into him. I found myself inches from his broad chest, looking up into blue eyes. He raised his free hand as though to touch me, then let it drop.

"I like things out in the open, where I can see them even if I don't like them," he said, his West Texas accent becoming more pronounced. "And right now, I think I'm seeing something I don't much like."

I felt the heat rise in my cheeks, but I met his eyes squarely and said nothing, not sure what he was getting at.

He gazed back, searching my face, his expression unreadable. "The thing is," he said finally, "it looks like you have a boyfriend, but I can't tell for sure. I can't tell if I should walk away while I still can."

A sudden pressure filled my chest, a mixture of longing and pain. I thought of Alan and our last words before he'd driven away, nothing resolved. He hadn't called since that day, and I hadn't called him. There had been a few moments when we'd laughed, but the meeting had ended so awkwardly. I knew he'd felt it, too, and that he'd wondered about Colin, about how things stood between Colin and me. Worst of all, I'd wondered, too.

"Two months ago, I would have been able to tell you that. Now . . ." I swallowed hard to push back the lump in my throat. "I'll have to let you know when I know."

A muscle worked in his cheek, then he gave a curt nod. "I guess that will have to do."

Chapter 17

FRIENDS AND FAREWELLS

I did not sleep well that night. I tossed for so long that Belle, who normally slept at the foot of the bed, gave me a watery, reproachful look and took herself off to the sofa, small shoulders hunched with resignation. When the eastern sky finally lightened into a pearly gray and a single mockingbird began its trill in the oaks, I gave up. I rose, took a hot shower, and got myself dressed, feeling exhausted and headachy. The circles under my eyes were almost as dark as the fading bruises at my temple, giving me the countenance of a raccoon who'd spent a hard night on the tiles. My biggest worry was that my students would think I was hung over, which was completely unfair. Looking and feeling this bad should at least be the result of something more fun and exciting than stewing by myself. Briefly, I considered calling in sick, but I had too much to do. I hadn't graded anything the previous evening, and another day off would put me even further behind.

I arrived at school even earlier than usual. Parking by the

tennis courts, I cut through Building A to reach the courtyard and then the academic building. Halfway down the darkened hallway that ran between the theater and the gymnasium, I skidded into something wet and slick, my arms flailing wildly to regain my balance.

What the hell, I thought, startled and outraged. What idiot would spill water all over a floor without bothering to clean it up? The fluorescent lights overhead had not yet been turned on and the only illumination came from the faint morning light streaming in through narrow windows above and beside the big double doors. As my eyes grew accustomed to the dimness, I could see that this wasn't the result of an overturned cup or a dropped can of soda. A shallow pool had spread across much of the hall and appeared to be growing. Stepping gingerly, I traced it back to its source and saw a slow steady flow coming from the girls' bathroom.

I groaned. The Bonham bathrooms strike again. Every month or so, at least one toilet overflowed, sometimes helped along by idiocy (flushing something patently unflushable) or intent (flushing a cherry bomb). The janitors could amaze and disgust with their tales of the items they regularly found jammed inside the school toilets.

I looked around, trying to decide what to do. Finding the janitors was the best option, but it was unlikely they were here yet. A large part of me wanted to avert my eyes and scamper on to my classroom as quickly as I could. "Oh my goodness," I could picture myself saying, "I must have walked right by without noticing." But the next person might fall and really hurt themselves. I would have to do the responsible thing, I thought with reluctance, which meant going into the bathroom and attempting to shut off the water before the lake on the floor grew any larger.

Stepping gingerly through the puddle, trying not to splash it on my clothes, I pushed open the door. The sickly white fluorescent lights flickered and hummed overhead. Inside, I could hear the sound of softly trickling water more clearly. I set my purse in the relative safety of a sink, then waded forward, checking each stall for the source.

Without knowing why, I hesitated at the door of the last stall, as though part of me did not want to see whatever was in there. Then, giving myself a shake, I squared my shoulders and opened the door. And gave a sharp cry.

A figure was kneeling in front of the toilet. I jumped back, startled, part of me thinking that maybe she was sick and that I'd intruded. But a smaller part of me knew that couldn't be true. Heart pounding in my chest as though it wanted to escape, I opened the door again, more widely this time. Someone was there all right. A woman's form, head tipped forward into the bowl, her long hair soaked and streaming forward over the rim and down her back. Her arms hung limply from the shoulders, palms up, heedless of the water running over them, her feet twisted askew by enormous platform sandals.

Everything around me seemed to grow dim, out of focus, as I stared at those shoes. Frozen, I couldn't draw air into my lungs. For a moment it seemed as though even my heart had stopped its frantic pounding. I opened my mouth to scream, but no sound came out, because who wore shoes like that except Laura?

With superhuman effort I drew in a great gasping breath and leaped forward to wrench the figure out of the toilet. She was lighter than I expected, and we crashed over backward together, slipping in the water on the tiles, her limp cold form half on top of me. Panicking, I scrabbled out from under her, catching my head with a painful thump on a sink. Then, kneeling beside her, I pushed the long streaming hair from her face.

It was Laura. Yet it wasn't. Her poor face was reddish blue, the eyes open and glistening sightlessly as water trickled from her parted lips. The clothes were hers, the long beautiful hair was hers, but Laura was no longer there. She was dead. And had been for some time. Beyond the reach of any CPR skills, beyond the reach of anyone. Laura Esperanza. My friend. The toilet, free of her long hair, ceased to flow, and silence filled the cold room, broken only by my ragged breathing and a soft dripping. I sat beside her for a long moment, then slowly got to my feet and dug through my purse for my cell phone.

I called 911 first. I spoke calmly and reasonably, although something must have been wrong with the connection because the operator kept asking me to slow down, saying that she couldn't understand me. Stupid woman. I finally got her to understand enough to come to Bonham High, then I hung up on her despite her protests and called Colin.

He didn't understand much of what I said either, but it didn't matter.

"On my way," he said, and must have meant it because he arrived with the paramedics, following them through the doors. I had never been so glad to see anyone in my life. I rushed to him and gripped his arm.

"In there. She's in there," I said, pointing.

He patted my hand. The paramedics hurried past us into the bathroom, only to reappear a second later.

"Nothing for us here," said the taller one. He looked a little sick.

Colin glanced at me and beckoned to the paramedics.

"Here," he said. "Need some help. This one's in shock. Can you stay with her?"

He disengaged my grip on his arm and vanished into the bathroom. I kept my eyes fixed on the door until one paramedic wrapped a red blanket around my shoulders and the other started waving a small flashlight in my eyes. I winced away from the glare.

Colin reappeared, looking grim. He stalked past, speaking into a radio as he went. Patrol officers began arriving and he went to them, giving directions, gesturing. One of them stood outside the doors I had entered to begin directing people away from the building, while the others fanned out through the building, going down halls, checking doors. Colin returned carrying a plastic chair from one of the rooms.

He put it down around a corner, away from the puddle and out of sight of the bathroom, then returned and, putting an arm around my shoulders, led me to it and sat me down gently. I was trembling so hard by now my teeth were chattering and my fingers clutching the edges of the blanket were a bluish color. One of the paramedics gently loosened my fingers from their grip on the blanket and slipped a blood pressure cuff around my arm. I couldn't take my eyes from Colin.

For some reason, he was the only thing that seemed clear and solid. Everything else was growing oddly hazy. The second paramedic pulled out an oxygen mask and tried to slip it over my face. I pushed him away with a frown.

"Ma'am, this is just oxygen. We want you to keep it on just for a few minutes."

"No," I said. I was sure I had a good reason, although I was unable to find the words to express it.

"But, ma'am," he started to protest.

Colin said something to the paramedic that I couldn't hear and then took the oxygen mask.

"Jocelyn," he said gently, squatting down beside my chair.

"Hi," I answered in a small voice.

"You've had a pretty bad shock, you know. We'd like you to have some oxygen just to clear your head. So, do you think you could breathe through this? Just for a minute or two?"

His face was only inches from mine, but he seemed to be talking from a great distance. I stared into the blue of his eyes, thinking the color was remarkable. A deep midnight blue. If I tilted my head just right, I could see myself reflected in them.

He raised the mask to my face, and I leaned away from him. What was he doing?

"Sweetheart, you need to breathe through this."

Well, if he was going to call me sweetheart. I let him put the mask over my face.

He waited patiently beside me. More people had arrived: even more patrol officers, a photographer with a camera, and a plainclothes cop who was probably another detective. The latter two vanished inside the ladies' restroom, wading gingerly through the water. A moment later, Alonzo, the school janitor, arrived with a bucket on wheels and a mop, and began cleaning up the water in the hall. He mopped quickly, his movements jerky, sneaking glances at the cops from under half-lowered lids.

I finally drew in a deeper breath, feeling somewhat less cold and a little more alert. Colin noticed. He knelt beside me again, looking into my eyes and taking one of my hands in his. The warmth of his big hands made me aware that mine were little more than hand-shaped ice cubes. I flexed my fingers, puzzled.

"Feeling a bit better?"

I gave a small nod.

"I need to ask you some questions, then."

I sat up a little straighter, trying to clear my head. Of course he needed to ask questions. Someone had done this to Laura. Someone we needed to find.

"Okay, I've seen the bathroom. Can you tell me exactly how you found her?"

"I got here early and slipped in the water. I figured one of the toilets was overflowing, and I thought I'd try to shut off the water at least."

"Uh-huh. And when you walked in the bathroom, was she lying on the floor like that?"

My eyes filled with tears. "No," I whispered.

"Where was she?"

A hot tear spilled down my cheek. I could not find my voice.

"Was she in one of the toilets?" he asked.

I closed my eyes and nodded.

"Do you know who she is?"

"Her name is Laura Esperanza," I whispered. "She's a Spanish teacher here." I swallowed, tears now coursing down my cheeks. "She's . . . she's my friend. My best friend. We eat lunch together, we go shopping. She's . . ."

"Oh my God," he said, appalled. "Oh, Jocelyn."

He wrapped an arm around my shoulder, and I buried my face against his chest, sobs wracking my body.

"Look, we'll get you home. I'll call your cousin. Just . . . is there anything else you can tell us that would be important right now?"

I raised my head a little. "She's tiny. And someone stuffed her head in a toilet. Some bastard. I want you to find him, and I want to kill him."

"Yes," said Colin.

"I mean it," I said fiercely.

"I know."

I don't remember much about the next few hours. Colin called Kyla, then drove me home himself in my car. He waited with me until she arrived and a patrol officer came to take him back to the school. It was only later that I thought that he probably should have stayed at the scene instead of babysitting me, but I was grateful.

Kyla was perfect. Instead of fussing or asking questions, while I showered and scrubbed my skin until it was pink, she turned on the television and mixed drinks. She settled me on the sofa with a blanket and a box of tissues.

I took the glass she handed me and took a big gulp, thinking it was orange juice. I sputtered for a few minutes as the warm glow of the alcohol burned a path to my stomach, and then settled back to sip the rest down.

In the middle of the afternoon, the phone rang, and I answered it without looking at the caller ID. You'd think I'd learn not to do that.

"What the hell is going on at that school of yours?"

My ex-husband, Mike Karawski. Oh joy.

"I called over there, and they said you'd gone home. Something about you finding the body. Did you?"

"Did I what?"

"Did you find the body?

"What do you want, Mike?"

Kyla had been listening intently and at that name, her puzzled expression cleared. "Gimme that," she said, trying to take the phone from me.

I fended her off.

"Murder in our public schools," Mike was saying. "It's a fucking publicity nightmare. My phone here is ringing off the hook, news stations, the public. Every jackass in the city has pulled his finger out of his ass and is using it to dial me! And I don't know a goddamned thing. Who is the principal there? Obviously his security is not up to snuff. Who is the investigating detective? And what do you know about the woman who was killed? No one is saying anything."

He finally had to pause to draw in a breath.

"How nice of you to call."

"Ah. Um," he floundered at this.

"I'm afraid you'll have to pull your own finger from wherever you keep it and call someone else. Don't call me again, Mike. I would hate to have to get a restraining order," I added, and hung up.

"Nicely played," said Kyla.

I shrugged. I felt exhausted and a little drunk. "I hope he doesn't really run for judge or whatever it is he's going for. Seeing that smug face on television would just about make me sick."

"Judge? Mike? Oh, Jesus."

"Yeah. Can you imagine having anything important decided by that man?"

"Makes me want to yack. But even if he is running for judge, why do you think he's calling you?"

"That's just what he does. He networks. Anyone he's ever known is just someone he might be able to use at a later time."

Colin came over at about four o'clock. He had showered and changed his clothes. His dark hair still curled damply along the nape of his neck. I felt a warm rush of gratitude toward him. For coming so quickly, for taking care of me, for his consideration.

Kyla let him in, and I tried to straighten myself on the sofa.

"Don't get up," he said quickly. "I can't stay. I just thought I'd drop by and see how you were doing. Well, that and ask a couple of questions. If you're up to it."

I braced myself, but nodded.

"Do you know a guy named Mike Karawski?"

Not what I expected. "Unfortunately, yes." I wished I

could leave it at that, but with a sigh, I added, "I was married to him for almost a year."

Now it was his turn to be surprised. "You're kidding. The guy's a giant . . ." He hesitated.

"Douche bag" I supplied. "Yeah, I know. What's he doing now?"

"Mostly trying to pry confidential information out of anyone who will talk to him. He's saying that he's a relative of yours and has the right to know."

"Neither one of those is true."

"I thought so."

Kyla broke in at this point. "You on duty, Colin? I make a killer screwdriver or we have beer."

"Better not. I need to get back soon."

"Tea, then?"

"Sure, thanks."

Kyla went into the kitchen, and Colin slanted an odd look at me. "Married? Really?"

Some mistakes haunt you forever. I shrugged. "I was young and stupid. And although it's not obvious now, he can be both funny and charming. When it suits him."

Colin made a sound very near a snort. "Well, I'll put the word out that we can safely ignore him."

"I don't know how safe it is," I cautioned. "When he was trying to get information out of me, he let slip that he's going to be running for judge."

"Super."

I laughed a little at that, then grew serious. "What have you found out?"

"Off the record?"

Kyla returned with tea and a sugar pot. "Record? Who the hell would we be on record with?"

"He's worried we'll talk to Mike," I said, trying not to feel hurt.

Colin hastily busied himself with the sugar bowl, dumping three large spoonfuls into the amber liquid and giving a quick stir. Sugar crystals swirled and settled at the bottom.

The look on Kyla's face said, "Want some tea with that sugar?" but before the words had a chance to come out, I said, "Of course off the record. I wouldn't give Mike directions to a Dairy Queen, much less tell him anything important. And neither of us will talk to anyone else, either."

"Yeah," agreed Kyla.

He said, "It's not that much anyway. We've been going over the security cameras. Unfortunately, the ones at Bonham are old-style. Probably been there since the school was built."

"Meaning?"

"Meaning half of them are fakes and the other half produce terrible quality video. There's only one working camera in that hallway, and it doesn't include the bathrooms or even the doors to the bathrooms."

"You're kidding."

"Nope. Privacy concerns, according to your principal, along with practicality. There's not much worth stealing down that hall, and nothing other than the bathrooms to vandalize. And again, taping kids going to the bathroom gets pretty close to invasion of privacy, so Dr. Gonzales and the school board felt a prominent but fake security camera would be enough of a deterrent."

"But surely the cameras near the doors work?" said Kyla, then held up her hands. "I know, I know. Don't call me Shirley."

He laughed. "Yeah, they work. Or rather, the ones on the doors that lead to the parking lots work. Anyone could enter or exit by the courtyard doors, and from there, they wouldn't necessarily have to pass another camera, not if they were smart and knew about the cameras. Even if they didn't do that, the school is like Grand Central Station. The cameras caught kids, parents, and teachers coming and going until after eleven o'clock."

"So even if you caught the right person on tape, you'd never know it because you don't know if they were in the hallway."

"Exactly. And the quality of the video is too poor to tell if anyone had wet clothes."

"Wet clothes?"

Colin hesitated, looking at me. "Ms. Esperanza put up a gallant fight. The killer would have been soaked."

His words dropped into a pool of silence. A single tear spilled down my cheek, and I wiped it away angrily.

"What time?" I asked when I could control my voice. "Do you know what time it happened?"

"Not exactly. The initial estimate is between eight and midnight."

"See, that's wrong. She had no reason to be at the school so late."

"We've spoken with her husband. Apparently, she told

him she had to work late and wouldn't see him that evening. He works the night shift at St. David's Medical Center—seven to seven. He only noticed she was missing when he got home this morning, and he called it in right away. But you'd already found her by then."

"She had no reason to be there," I repeated.

Kyla was thinking hard. "It was a terrible risk for the killer, wasn't it? A girls' bathroom. Pretty busy spot."

"Yeah," Colin agreed. "We figure it had to have been closer to midnight for that reason. Any earlier and someone would have noticed the water if not the body."

I swallowed. "It wasn't flowing that much, though."

"What?"

"I mean, the amount of water. It wasn't just pouring out. It was more of a steady trickle. It had only made it to the hall because it had been running for so long."

"Yeah, the mechanism couldn't quite close, probably because of her hair. When you pulled her out, it stopped," said Colin, then winced at my expression. "Sorry."

I swallowed hard, but kept going. "So, since the stall door was closed, I don't think anyone would think much of a trickle of water."

"They'd report it, wouldn't they?"

"An adult would report it. But a kid? At Bonham? Water and worse on the floors in the bathrooms isn't anything new. You should ask the drama kids. I'm assuming they were the ones up there until eleven?"

"Yeah. Seriously, you think it's possible that a kid could have gone into that bathroom and not noticed anything?"

I closed my eyes, not so much to remember, but to get the vision out of my head. "Other than the water, there wasn't anything to notice. She . . . she was in the last stall. The door was closed. If you used one of the first two stalls, you wouldn't see a thing. And why would you go closer to a running toilet?"

"We'll check," he said, his face alert, the hunting instinct kicking in. He rose to his feet.

He started to carry his glass to the kitchen, but Kyla stood and took it from his hands. I stood as well, a little stiff from being curled on the sofa so long. Ridiculous or not, his presence was comforting, and a big part of me didn't want him to leave. It was all I could do not to clutch at him and pull him back.

He must have seen something of my emotion in my face, because he turned back and took me into his arms, holding me close, resting his cheek against my hair. I buried my face against his shirt, feeling his warmth through the thin fabric, aware of how solid and comforting his body felt. I felt him patting my back, soothing me as he might have soothed a child. I could have stayed just like that forever, but it was feeling a little too good. I straightened, sniffing and rubbing my eyes with the back of my hand. He released me, opened his mouth to say something, then closed it again. With a flash of blue from his eyes more intimate than a caress, he turned and left without a word.

Kyla followed him to the door and locked it after him. Then she turned to me.

"Damn," she said.

Chapter 18

GRIEF AND GUNS

There had been talk of closing the school for a few days, but the massive wheels of the Austin Independent School District turned quickly for once and the powers that be decided that 2,800 kids need their education, and, more importantly, the district needed the federal funding.

Kyla protested, but I sent her home after Colin left and somehow rose the next day and went back to school. I did not, however, cut through Building A, and instead parked in front and walked through the main entrance beside the administration building. A glance through the windows showed the office was overflowing with strangers, all talking at the same time. Larry Gonzales stood in the middle of them, looking harried and grim.

Curious, I went in, sidled past the group, and slipped behind the front desk. At the sight of me, Maria Santos jumped to her feet and rushed to throw her arms around me.

"Oh, Jocelyn, I didn't think you'd be here today. How are you? How are you holding up?"

I patted her shoulder awkwardly. Over her head I could see Pat Carver sitting stiff and disapproving behind her computer monitor. She gave me a sour look and turned her attention to the screen in front of her.

"I'm fine," I said, which was precariously close to being an outright lie. However, I was upright, so I thought I could get away with it. "What's going on? Who are all these people?"

She released me and stepped back, pulling me down into the chair beside her desk. Lowering her voice, she said, "Grief counselors."

I looked at the group again. "Seriously? There can't be this many in the entire city. They must have imported some from out of state."

"Yeah, basically. They figure the kids are going to be really upset. Teachers and staff, too. They're going to have grief-counseling sessions and then let everyone who wants to sign up for one-on-one meetings."

"Waste of money and time, if you ask me," said Pat grimly, continuing to type.

"No one did," retorted Maria. She leaned closer to me, lowering her voice. "All she cares about is who is getting charged."

"Someone has to care," snapped Pat, again proving the efficiency of her hearing.

I looked over at Pat, taking in the large shoulders and grim set of her jaw. A new thought niggled in the back of my mind, nebulous and just out of reach. I thought about the papers

Colin and I had found in the clock. Did they mean something? Was Pat cooking the books in some way, maybe embezzling money? And if so, what did that mean regarding Fred? Or Laura? I looked at Pat again. She was taller than I was, a big woman who looked like she was in fairly decent shape. Physically, could she have killed someone? I looked at the hands flying over the keys. Large for a woman, which didn't mean they had been used to hold Laura's head under water until she'd drowned. It only meant they could have been.

"I found those receipts you were looking for, Pat," I said.

She jerked as though I'd given her a jolt with a cattle prod, then said stiffly. "Well, fine. Please turn them in as soon as you can."

"They were with some of Fred's things, so I turned them in to the police."

This time she went absolutely white. "That's extremely inconvenient. I'll need to request copies from the merchant now." With a malevolent glare at me, she rose and walked away.

Well, that touched a nerve anyway, I thought with some satisfaction. I just didn't know how a few fifty-dollar coolers could be involved with anything criminal.

I realized Maria had said something and was now looking at me with sympathy. I drew myself together. "Sorry, what did you say?"

"Nothing. Are you sure you should be here today? Everyone knows you and Laura were close. Even Larry would give you time off if you needed it."

I shook my head. "Better to be working than sitting at home doing nothing."

She considered this, and then nodded. "Okay. But if you do want to talk to one of the counselors, just give me a call. I'll make sure you get priority."

I walked to my classroom still wondering about Pat. How did she fit into this mess? And how did Laura's death relate to Fred's? Or were they entirely separate things? I didn't think so. I didn't see how they could be connected, but the likelihood of two murders in the same small community not being related had to be miniscule.

A small group of kids was sitting on the floor in the hallway outside my door. McKenzie Mills, Dillon Andrews, Eric Richards, and Brittany Smith hopped up as I approached and rushed me, McKenzie and Brittany hugging me in a death grip. Dillon hung back, probably worried that someone else might see them fraternizing with a teacher, then finally managed an awkward pat on my shoulder as though I were a dog. Kids. No one on earth could be more generous, open, and loyal than teenagers. The good ones, anyway. These kids were the reason I loved teaching and the reason I put up with the kids who weren't so good. I hugged them back and then extricated myself as gently as I could.

"Stop it, you all. You're going to make me cry."

"You should cry, Coach J. It's good for you. It releases endorphins," said McKenzie earnestly.

That was all I needed. One tear and the flood would start again. I said firmly, "It also releases my mascara, and I don't want to look like a raccoon all day. Now let me unlock my door."

Inside the room they hovered around my desk instead of taking their seats as usual and working on the homework that they should have completed the night before. I put my purse inside my desk drawer, locked it, and raised my eyes.

"What?" I asked them.

Brittany asked in a hesitant voice, "We were wondering if we're still playing today. You know, the match?"

The match. Our first match of the season. I'd completely forgotten about it. Wildly, I went over everything that would have to be done today, and then realized with relief that I couldn't think of a thing. I'd made all the preparations days ago.

I kept my face calm. "Of course," I said, then added, "unless you really don't want to. I think the very best thing all of us can do is continue our normal schedules and stay busy."

Brittany looked at me so doubtfully I had a hard time suppressing a smile. I knew the teenage mind. She would have been much more comfortable if I'd instructed them to rend their clothes and cover their heads in ashes. Carrying on seemed so . . . dull.

I gave her a reassuring pat on the shoulder. "Don't worry. If your game is off, well that's just the way it is. After everything that's happened, it's a victory just to show up. I know Senora Esperanza would do the same for me."

And saying it made me realized that I actually believed it. Which was a tiny, and very cold, drop of comfort.

McKenzie spoke up with a voice that quavered just a little. "Do you think it's safe to be here? At school, I mean?"

Safe. What did that mean anymore? But I looked into their anxious faces and realized they were only asking what 2,800 other kids and their families were probably asking. Larry Gonzales had made all kinds of statements and promised to increase security, but even if they had listened to his droning, long-winded speech, they hadn't quite believed him. So they had come to me. A teacher they trusted. I considered my words carefully.

"No one knows why this happened to Señora Esperanza, but I do not believe that we have a madman running through the halls looking for random people to attack. I think we are all safe enough, especially during the school day. Those of us who have after-school activities when there are less people around . . . well, I think maybe we should go to the bathroom in pairs, at least until the police figure this out. There's no harm in being cautious for a few days, even if it's just for our own peace of mind."

"I don't think I'll ever go to the bathroom again," said McKenzie sadly.

Eric gave a hoot of laughter. "Good luck with that."

"Yeah, what are you going to do, wear diapers?" chimed in Dillon.

"Astronaut pants!" agreed Eric.

"Yeah, the PTA could sell them in the Tiger's Den. They'd make a fortune."

"Okay, enough," I broke in. "I think we all know what McKenzie meant."

"Yeah. You turds," said McKenzie, glaring at them and turning red.

"It isn't funny," chimed in Brittany, although her lips twitched just a little.

Funny or not, the boys had definitely lightened the mood.

My cell phone rang from within the depths of my desk

drawer. I normally silenced it while I was in the classroom, but today I'd forgotten. I pulled it out and glanced at the number.

It was Alan. With a glance at the kids, I answered.

"Jocelyn. Are you all right?" his voice came over the phone, tight with anxiety.

"Yes," I said, moving to the door. Four pairs of eyes, bright and curious, followed me. I walked into the hall, pulling the door closed behind me.

"I just saw on the news. A teacher was killed at your school? They didn't give a name," he added, an echo of the desperation he had felt in his voice.

Oh dear Lord. I hadn't thought about the news. I needed to call my parents to reassure them. I wondered if Kyla had thought to do that yesterday.

"Yes, it was horrible," I said, the words true enough, but seeming unreal even as I spoke them. "I'm sorry I didn't call. I . . . wasn't thinking very clearly."

"Where are you now?"

"At school," I answered. "I can't really talk very well, but everything is fine. Well . . . no, not fine, but . . ." I struggled to find words.

"I understand. Well, as long as you're all right, that's all I need to know. But Jocelyn, we need to talk. Really talk."

I swallowed. Here it came. My thoughts flashed to Colin, then back to Alan. I was so confused. I didn't even know what I wanted. But a really big part of me did not want to let this man out of my life.

He continued, "How about me coming down there on

Friday night after work? I'll leave early, beat the rush hour. I could be at your place by seven o'clock. Maybe we could go to dinner. Someplace nice."

Dinner. That sounded promising. That didn't sound like a breakup, which could be done in my living room even if he was too much of a gentleman to do it over the phone.

"I could make us reservations at Olivia," I suggested tentatively.

"Great, Olivia. But I'll take care of the reservations. Leave it to me. Jocelyn," he said my name again with tenderness, "I'm . . . very relieved to hear your voice. I'll see you Friday."

"See you then," I said. We disconnected, and I stood in the hall a moment, thinking of all the things we'd said and left unsaid. Then I dialed my parents.

The bell rang, indicating the end of fourth period, and as the kids filed out, I remained at my desk feeling exhausted and depressed. And hungry. I'd forgotten to pack my lunch this morning, which meant either facing the crowd in the cafeteria or leaving school and driving to the nearest fast food restaurant. However, going hungry was not an option, and I was beginning to succumb to the siren call of burgers and cheese tots, when the door to my classroom opened. For one instant I expected to see Laura's face peer around the corner, to hear her cheerful call of "*queso paso.*" My breath caught in my throat.

Kyla entered, carrying a couple of white bags and two Styrofoam cups.

I sagged back, acid disappointment rising like bile in my throat.

Her face softened. "I know. That's the reason I'm here. I remember you saying you guys ate together a lot."

Her kindness was almost overwhelming. I kept my face hidden, fighting back tears.

In the tone of someone coaxing a toddler to take a spoonful of cough syrup, she said, "Look, it's your favorite. Number two burger, large tater tots with cheese, and a cherry limeade."

Maybe none of us ever grows up. Her tone and the smell of the food made me sniff and sit up a little straighter as Kyla spread our greasy little feast on my desk. She even unwrapped my straw and stuck it in my cup for me.

Wiping my eyes with the back of my hand, I popped a crisp tot into my mouth and mumbled around its squishy goodness. "New purse?"

Her face lit up. "Yeah. Look at this baby."

She plopped it down in front of me with a desk-rattling thud that told me it was loaded to the brim. Loaded. Oh no.

"Don't tell me . . ." I began, but she cut me off.

"It's a gun purse. Or rather, a concealed-carry accessory." She opened the top gleefully. Look, there's an inner pouch that holds your gun upright. You just casually slip your hand into this little slot and your gun is right there, ready to go. You don't even have to draw it—you can fire right through the side of the purse. And if you do? They replace the purse. For free. You just can't beat that kind of guaranty."

I just stared at her. "Are you out of your mind?"

"What?" she asked defensively. "I have a permit now. I can carry."

"Not on school property, you can't. You know that. And

today, of all days. When you can't swing a dead cat without hitting a policeman."

"Why do people swing cats?" she asked, distracted. "I mean, when does that ever happen? Under what circumstances would you ever pick up a cat and swing it to measure crowd density?"

"Okay, no one swings cats," I said. "Focus, here. You have to leave and take this gun with you. Now."

Her lower lip jutted out ominously. "I don't see why. No one is going to know. That's the definition of 'concealed.'"

It was like arguing with a post. I let it drop and returned my attention to my food. I could tell she was miffed but was making a pretty good effort to suppress it for my sake. Sulkily, she pried off the top of her cup and fished one manicured finger through the ice until she found the maraschino cherry. I wiped one hand on a napkin and did the same.

"This is really good. Thanks," I said.

Her face softened. "Yeah, no problem. Hey, have you heard anything from Colin? Does he have any idea who did it?"

"I haven't talked to him today, but I don't think so. I just can't get it out of my head that this is related in some way to Fred's death."

She frowned at this. "Why, did they have something in common? I mean besides both working here? And being dead?"

"No, not a thing. It just seems so unlikely that we would have two killers on the loose. This is a nice school, in a nice area. We might have some peripheral gang activity, maybe a few kids who take some drugs or think they're tough, but not many. It's not like it's downtown Detroit. It's not even east Austin."

"So something specifically to do with Fred and Laura. Was there someone they were both having problems with?"

"I don't think so. I mean, both of them were having minor issues with Nancy Wales, the drama teacher, but in Laura's case that was just about getting to use the theater and not working the kids to death. And Fred wanted her to let one of his students keep her role in the play and still play tennis. Not anything serious. Besides, if Nancy started killing everyone in the school who pissed her off, we'd all be dead."

"So what else do we know?"

I took a breath and blew it out slowly, thinking back. "It all started with Fred having a fight with Gary Richards."

"The asshole parent from the tennis team?"

"Yeah. At the time, I thought that Gary might have lost his temper and attacked Fred. Maybe he didn't even mean to kill him, just hit him a bit too hard. And he was pretty mad at me for not doing what he wanted with the team. I even considered whether he might have followed the team to the park and took the chance to jump me."

"That part seems pretty weak."

"Exactly. And if he had somehow accidentally killed Fred, I think he'd be scared. It seems like he would want to keep a low profile, not show up at the courts and try to bully me. That would just draw attention to himself. Plus, what good would attacking me do for him?"

"Well, what good would it do anyone?"

"A very good point and something I've been thinking about a lot, believe me. It brings us back to Fred's note. Fred had found out something that he intended to tell me before he died.

Something important and delicate, because otherwise, he would just have e-mailed me or mentioned it between classes."

"I don't get what you mean."

"Say Fred found out that our school accountant, Pat Carver, had been skimming money out of school funds. He had some receipts and a spreadsheet hidden in a clock he kept on his desk, which must have been important or he wouldn't have bothered to hide them. That might be enough to make her want to kill him."

"That's stupid. If he'd found that out, he would just have reported her."

But at this I shook my head. "You didn't know Fred. He was the most truly decent guy I've ever met. He would never have turned her in without giving her the chance to explain the discrepancy. And if she pretended that it was an honest mistake, he would have given her the chance to fix it. Even if he knew she'd been stealing on purpose, he still might have given her a break rather than ruin her life. Something like that would mean losing her job at best, and fines and prison time at worst."

"So why write the note to you?"

"Who knows? Fred was the kind of guy who backed up his hard drive daily. He reviewed his will every year. He might have wanted to make absolutely sure that she didn't get away with it if something happened to him. Which doesn't necessarily mean he thought she would kill him. He was just like that."

Kyla was thinking hard. "Say that's all true. Say this Pat person was embezzling money, Fred finds out, so she kills him. But he's also told her that he's given the proof to you. So, she follows you to the park on the day of the movie shoot."

"Yeah, but she can't have planned that. For one thing, she couldn't have counted on my being off by myself like that."

"A crime of opportunity then. She's lurking around just waiting for any chance to get you. Then, seizing the opportunity, she kicks the shit out of you and goes to your house and trashes it while looking for the receipts or whatever they are. But how'd she know where you live? I thought you kept that stuff private."

"There is no privacy anymore. Besides, my address is in the school files, and she works in the office. That part would be easy," I answered absently, still thinking hard.

Kyla was looking excited. "I'm liking her for this. It sounds right."

"Yeah," I said doubtfully. "All except mugging me. I still don't get that part."

"She had to make sure you wouldn't walk in on her when she was searching your house. Anyway, put that aside for now. How does she tie in with Laura?"

"She doesn't."

"What?"

I held up empty hands. "I can't think of a thing. Laura ran the Foreign Language Studies cultural recital. She would have had a few very minor expenses to file with Pat, but that's it. Oh, and she mentioned she was going to check with Pat about the theater budget," I added, remembering Laura's feverish excitement at the thought that Nancy Wales might have made a misstep at last.

"Theater budget?" Kyla drained the last of her cherry limeade with a short slurping sound.

I popped the last cheese-covered tot into my mouth. It was cold by now, but still good. I looked longingly at the cheese that coated the paper container, but decided Kyla would judge me if I used my finger to scrape it off and eat it.

"Yeah, Laura thought the set was outrageously expensive. Too expensive for them to afford in any legitimate way."

"And is it?"

"Yeah, I'm pretty sure it is. But so what? That wouldn't have been anything against Pat."

"Unless she was passing stolen funds to the drama department."

I gave her a withering look. "Yeah, it's common for criminals to embezzle funds and risk jail time to support their local high school theater productions. I remember Al Capone was accused of the same thing, but the Feds couldn't make it stick."

"Fine. Then you explain it."

I glanced again at the empty paper carton and discreetly picked a little cheese off the side. "I can't explain it. None of it makes any sense to me at all."

"How about you? You've been battered pretty hard. Who have you pissed off?"

I laughed mirthlessly at that. "You name them, I've pissed them off. Mr. Richards, Pat Carver, Nancy Wales, her toady Roland Wilding. I don't know what's going on this year. I usually get along with everyone."

Kyla snorted, but it wasn't that far from the truth. Normally, my interactions with the other teachers, the kids, and their parents were pleasant and reasonable. Minor conflicts occurred over things like lesson plans or grades and were generally friendly, or at least civil. But this year, everything and everyone had been out of kilter starting from the day before school began. What had changed?

We gathered the trash from lunch and stuffed it into my trash can.

"Look, what are you doing tonight? Want to hang out, maybe go see a movie?" Kyla asked, glancing at her watch. "I have to be back up here this afternoon to teach the computer-science girls again. We could go right after that."

"Ordinarily yes, but today's our first tennis match. I'm driving the kids over to Westlake High at three."

"Seriously?"

"Yeah, I have to run to pick up the short bus in about an hour."

"You drive a short bus?" She laughed out loud.

I grinned back. "You know, some days I really think I do."

I didn't expect to see Kyla again that day, but she popped in, slightly out of breath and wild-eyed, just as I was gathering my things to leave for the tennis match.

"What's wrong?" I asked, alarmed. Surely no one else had been attacked.

"They've called me down to the office! They're interviewing all the teachers, one at a time."

"They who?"

"The police!"

I drew a relieved breath and closed my desk drawer. "So what? They're probably just interviewing witnesses, trying to narrow the window for when the crime might have occurred. Just go down there."

"How can I?" she asked, voice squeaking a little. She waved her purse in the air.

"Oh." I looked at the new bag, realization dawning.

"Yeah, oh. What if they scan me or something and find the gun?"

"They aren't going to do that. That's just a guilty conscience talking."

She glared. "I'm not guilty, and I'm not doing any more time. They can't take me back."

I grinned at that. "Why don't you just run it out to your car?"

"Because you were right. This place is swarming with cops. It would look so suspicious."

I sighed. "Fine. Look, take out your wallet and your keys. You can leave the purse locked in my desk here. I'll take it home with me tonight after I get back from the match. And let this be a lesson to you."

Chapter 19

MATCHES AND MAYHEM

The tennis team did better than I expected. Eric won his first two singles matches. Then his father showed up, his grim bulk throwing a shadow of gloom over his son if not over everyone else. I could see the tension in Eric's shoulder when he tossed the ball for the first serve, and I knew he'd already lost. By the time the score reached four games to zero, his father was shouting obscenities at the opposing players, accusing them of cheating and worse. In interscholastic matches we had no referees, and players kept score themselves. The other coach and I finally demanded that he either keep silent or leave, at which point it looked like he was going to explode. I was about two heartbeats from calling the police, but then Eric lost the final game of the set, and his father stomped off in disgust without a word to his son. Something was going to have to be done about that man. The rest of the match went pretty well, at least by my admittedly low standards. We didn't win overall, but Dillon won his match and the rest of the kids won a respectable percentage of their games. More importantly, as far as I was concerned, the team rallied around Eric, refusing to allow him to withdraw in embarrassment, gently teasing and cajoling until he regained his spirits and joined the rest of them in cheering on the final players.

Back at the school, the parking lot was empty, and I parked the bus directly in front of the tennis shed to unload the gear. The evening drew in around us, the sky turning pearly gray above the brilliant orange glow in the west. The air seemed almost cool after the scorching afternoon heat, and a swirl of brown leaves skittered along the sidewalk, the first hint of the coming autumn born along a gentle breeze. Daytime heat aside, fall was upon us and already the days were growing shorter. I gave a melancholy little shiver.

"Dang, I wish McKenzie could have been here," Dillon said, taking one of the now empty orange coolers from Travis, who handed it down through the bus door.

"Yeah, we could have used her for that second match. Playing two matches in a row is too much, Coach J," said Brittany.

"You played really well anyway. And the musical will be over this week, and we'll have her back full-time," I reassured her.

The kids were still standing beside the bus rehashing each stroke of the final boys' doubles match, and Dillon was vowing to win the next time we played Westlake, when my phone rang and made me jump.

Colin, his voice low but excited, said, "We've made an arrest."

My heart leaped. "What? Who?"

"Pat Carver. We're holding her on embezzlement charges, but they're interrogating her now about the murders."

I rose and moved away from the kids. Their eyes followed me with the unblinking intensity of dogs watching a hot dog turning on a grill.

"What is she saying?"

"Nothing. She lawyered up pretty damn quick," he added with disgust. "She denied any wrongdoing, of course. Then, the minute we brought up the deaths, she shut up completely. She's scared."

I thought about my talk with Kyla, our conclusions and questions. "Are you sure she's the one?" I asked doubtfully.

"We're sure about the embezzlement. And that gives her motive for killing Coach Argus."

"But what about Laura?"

"We don't know yet."

I frowned, feeling I was still missing something. "It doesn't make sense."

"No. But that's the way it is sometimes. It's hard to accept, but sometimes murderers are motivated by things a normal person would consider trivial or incomprehensible. It's not always possible to wrap everything up in a neat, logical package. If they were normal, they would never resort to murder."

"No, I guess not."

"How are you holding up? I thought you'd be relieved by the news."

"Oh, I am," I reassured him. "And I'm doing okay. And . . . yeah, that's really good news. You all did a great job."

An awkward silence followed. I felt it but did not know what to say.

"Could I see you tonight?" he asked abruptly.

"I . . . I'm going out with Alan tomorrow night." Which wasn't an answer to his question at all.

The silence that followed was even worse than the first. I felt a sinking in my chest, sure he would now tell me to go to hell. And quite rightly.

He broke it, his voice fierce and low. "I don't care. I don't give a shit about him. I want to see you."

For a moment my breath caught in my throat, then I found my voice. "Yes. Okay. I'd like to see you, too."

"Good. I'll come by your place about eight."

Glancing at my watch, I said, "Make it nine. I need to finish up here and then drop the bus off." Plus I needed to shower and change, but he didn't need to know that.

"What? What bus? Where are you?"

"Right now, I'm in the school parking lot with sixteen teens. We just finished a tennis match. I need to wait for parents to pick up the ones who don't have their own cars."

"Right. Nine it is."

I hung up feeling absurdly pleased considering that this complicated my life exponentially. But somehow I didn't think I could bear to let Colin go. But what did that mean in terms of my relationship with Alan? I didn't want to lose him either, but was it because I valued his friendship or did I want his love? It wasn't as though I could go out with both of them. And honestly, what the hell was wrong with me? What kind of woman didn't know which one of two men she was interested in?

We finished putting away our equipment, and the kids who could drive rolled out of the parking lot with waves and shouts. I sat with the remaining kids on the bench beside the shed. Finally, the last minivan pulled out of the parking lot, and I carefully locked the shed and returned to the bus, my mind on my coming meeting with Colin. Then I remembered Kyla's purse.

I was tempted to leave without it, but I really didn't like having a gun in my desk. Plus Kyla would throw a fit if she didn't get it back tonight. Cursing under my breath, I headed back toward the school, by habit heading for the shortcut through Building A. I had my hand on the door when memory returned, and I veered sharply to my left, walking the long way around. Halfway along the path, I wished I hadn't. The distance was twice as long as my shortcut, and I felt exposed and alone in the twilight gloom, every little sound making me twitch nervously. I hurried into the academic building, relieved at first to be safely indoors, but the empty building wasn't much better. The wide halls, the concrete, the metal lockers all conspired to magnify every small noise, from the quiet tread of my tennis shoes to the ordinary clicks and sighs of individual classroom air conditioners. Shadows filled the vaulted ceiling overhead and lurked in corners and behind the stairs. Foolish or not, my heart began beating faster, and I quickened my pace as I headed up the stairs to my room, wishing I could just break into a run. I tightened my grip on my keys, holding them as though they were a weapon. Which was ridiculous. If anyone jumped out at me, I most likely would drop the keys, wet my pants, and bolt like a jackrabbit spotting a snake.

I made it to my room without incident, grabbed Kyla's purse, practically grunting under the weight of it, and exited the building. The shadows in the courtyard were now merging with plain darkness, and this time I decided to take the shortcut after all. I could see a faint glow of lights in Building A and, bad memories or not, it seemed safer than walking all the way around the campus again. Besides, if I didn't hurry, I was going to be late to meet Colin.

I opened the door cautiously, holding it so it wouldn't slam behind me. After the exposed darkness of the courtyard, the lighting here seemed safe and welcoming. Not that there was much of it—only the minimum dim glow that the security staff left on at all times. Even the theater hall was mostly dark.

Which was odd. My steps slowed as I became aware of the stillness. No late practice this evening, even though tomorrow was the opening night? I wondered if the principal or some parents had finally forced Nancy into giving the kids an early evening. Well, it wasn't any of my concern, at least not tonight. I walked quietly, trying to hurry, trying not to glance at the door to the women's restroom. But there was no sign that anything had happened. No police tape, no remaining water, no sign at all that a woman's life had ended here only the day before. I gave a shiver.

I was almost out the door leading to the parking lot when a scream from the theater ripped through the silence.

Chapter 20

STAGES AND STANDOFFS

For an instant I froze, flinching as though from a blow. Then it rang out again, rising high, then trailing off into a wrenching moan. Heart in my throat, I listened intently, but heard nothing more.

It must be the play, I told myself. They're rehearsing after all. I told myself to keep going, that everything was fine, that this was nothing to be concerned about. I should hurry away, return the bus, get myself home so I could get a hot shower before Colin arrived. But I knew I couldn't. Not without making sure. After all, what if someone had heard noises from the bathroom yesterday and had ignored them, thinking it only kids horsing around. I'd just pop my head in the back of the theater and make sure everything was in order. Calling 911 seemed premature. I would feel like an idiot if I summoned the emergency squad and it turned out to be a dramatic scene from the play.

I crept through the theater doors on tiptoe and poked my head around the corner. The auditorium was mostly dark, illuminated only by two spotlights beaming on the closed red curtains, casting a golden glow along the scarlet folds. I hesitated. It was unusual to see the curtains closed. Moreover, they swayed gently in response to some unseen movement behind them. I could hear the sound of feet, quiet but distinct in the eerie stillness that filled the empty room. Silently, I moved forward until I was almost in front of the stage. The feet continued to pace back and forth.

I drew breath. "Hello? Is anyone there?" I called, thinking at the time I was being stupid.

Just how stupid was revealed all in a flash. I heard a muffled oath, then with a motorized whirring sound, the heavy swaying curtains parted, revealing the lavish set of *Moulin Rouge*. The large rolling platforms were now adorned with brilliant silks in turquoise, magenta, cerulean, and lavender. The gems on the elephant winked and twinkled in the lights and overhead a pink feather boa hung quivering from a bejeweled trapeze. A set that shouted to be noticed, yet I was only dimly aware of the gaudy backdrop. My attention was completely and totally focused on the figure of Roland Wilding and the knife he was holding to the throat of McKenzie Mills.

He looked like a madman, golden hair disheveled, light eyes gleaming wildly, face distorted with rage. I glanced at McKenzie. Tears ran down her cheeks, but she seemed otherwise unharmed. Behind the pair the figure of Nancy Wales lay unmoving on the stage floor, her enormous pink-clad bulk unnervingly still. I turned my eyes back to Roland and pivoted slightly away, trying to conceal that I was slipping my hand into my purse, reaching for a cell phone.

Only it wasn't my purse, I realized as my fingers brushed against the unfamiliar clasp. Mine was still stuffed under a seat in the school bus parked beside the tennis courts, and my cell phone and keys were in the pocket of my pants. This was Kyla's purse. And its secret compartment held a 9mm Glock 19, upright and ready to fire.

"No, no! Stop right there," called Roland. "Keep your hands where I can see them, or I swear I'll cut her throat." The blade of the knife pressed just under McKenzie's jaw, turning the pale skin white along the length of the blade.

McKenzie choked back a sob as I quickly lifted my hands. "Roland, no! Look, I'm not doing anything. Just standing here." I waved frantically to show both hands were empty.

He relaxed a little, lowering the knife a miniscule amount. His hand was white on McKenzie's small shoulder, fingers digging into her flesh.

Eyes wild, he glared at me. "You're always butting in, fucking up my chances, doing your best to make sure I fail."

I swallowed. "No, that's not true, Roland . . ."

"Shut up!" he shouted.

I shut up, closing my mouth with a snap. I could feel my heart pounding in my chest.

"You've been trying to sabotage me all year," he went on. "Interfering with our rehearsal schedule. Stealing movie roles. MY movie roles. For your goddamned tennis players who don't even know what acting is. You just swooped in and took over."

"That was just an accident. I didn't . . ."

"Shut up!" he screamed, spittle flying from his lips, briefly caught in the stage lights. "You! You're going to be in a Michael Dupre movie. Deny it!"

I quivered, but didn't speak.

The hand holding the knife swept away from McKenzie's throat as he pointed it at me. "That's called irony," he said in a more controlled voice. "Irony of the gods. You would never have had that part except for me. Did you know that?"

I shook my head, afraid to say anything more. He still had a death grip on McKenzie's shoulder, and she looked paralyzed, a mouse caught in the talons of a hawk. Even if I could get to the gun, I could hardly shoot while he held McKenzie in front of him like a shield.

"You're so goddamned stupid," he said. "You never even knew what hit you that day at the park. I could have killed you, and you couldn't have stopped me. God, I wish I had."

"That was you?" I asked to keep him talking. My voice shook.

"Of course it was me! Or do you have other people who want to kill you?" He gave a horrible laugh at that. "Actually, you probably do. People lining up to put you out of their misery. And then I find out that my hitting you got you into the movie. A Michael Dupre movie." There was wonder in his tone.

"I'm sorry, Roland. I never meant for any of that to happen."

"You think that makes it better? You stuck your nose in

where it didn't belong. That means anything that happened is your fault. Your fault!" He shouted the last words. McKenzie whimpered.

I held out placating hands, willing him to calm down. "I'm sure we can fix it, Roland. Michael Dupre is still here. We can talk to him."

"Yes, he's still here. But this bitch has ruined everything!" He gestured wildly at the immobile form of Nancy Wales, the knife glinting in the light. "In one minute she gave away everything I've been working for. Everything."

"What did she do?" I asked, taking a small step forward. He didn't appear to notice.

"She canceled the show. Canceled it! Behind my back, too. She went to Larry and told him we couldn't possibly perform this week."

"But why?" I asked. Although maybe a second murder and an assistant who was completely insane might have had something to do with it.

He looked confused for an instant, his blue eyes darting from side to side as though watching a Ping-Pong match. An unexpected blush suffused his face, turning his cheeks as pink as a girl's. "Never mind that. She thought we weren't ready, that's all. And this one," he turned the knife back under McKenzie's chin, "this one kept fucking up her lines. Fucking up my lines."

I thought McKenzie was going to faint. At his words her face, always fair, drained of the last vestiges of color, bleached as lace. Her eyelids fluttered briefly, then drooped over unfocused eyes.

Hastily, I tried to turn Roland's attention away from the girl. "Canceling the performance. Wow—that was very wrong of Nancy. Very wrong. She can't do that, not after all your work. The show must go on, right?"

"It was wrong," he agreed. "Completely unjustified."

"Exactly! Unjustified. But you can still fix this. You can make Larry understand that Nancy doesn't have the authority to cancel anything. It's not too late. Larry hasn't made the announcement yet. All you have to do is catch him in the morning and explain that you're in charge now. I know him, he'll support that one hundred percent. You know, Larry admires a take-charge kind of man, the kind of man who gets the job done."

Roland blinked and twitched like an addict in withdrawal. I wondered if that was indeed the case, but at least he lowered the knife away from McKenzie's throat.

"Not cancel?" he asked at length. "Perform anyway?"

"Right! You can override Nancy. Everyone would support that."

"She already told the kids," he said slowly.

"So what? You can untell them in the morning. You're in charge now."

Without meaning to, my eyes flew to Nancy, still lying motionless on the stage, like a walrus on the sand. What had he done to her? I couldn't tell if she was still breathing.

He followed my gaze, glancing at Nancy's bulk with something like annoyance in his glance. "She'll try to interfere."

Maybe she was alive after all. If so, I didn't want his attention turning that way.

"No, she won't. Half the school has been trying to get her fired for years. And canceling the show at the last minute—that just proves she's not up to the job anymore. Everyone will be glad that you're stepping in."

"She'll be mad," he said, looking like a small boy worried that he was going to be in trouble with Mom.

"So what? Nothing you can't handle, right? When you show her how well you can run things, she'll probably be grateful to you. She'd probably be happy, knowing she can leave everything to you."

"Nothing I can't handle," he repeated under his breath, brightening a little. "Yeah. She can't talk anyway. Not with what I know about her. She has to do what I want."

I hesitated, not knowing how best to support this statement.

He gave me an odd sidelong glance, half-fearful, half-triumphant. "I bet you have no idea what I'm talking about."

"I don't," I admitted readily, trying to sound admiring, anything to keep him talking. "You've been one step ahead of me, of everyone, from the start."

"Yes," he agreed, blue eyes glinting in the spotlight. He pointed the knife toward Nancy again, a decided improvement as far as McKenzie was concerned.

"She started it all. Her and her temper. Bet you didn't know she's been attending anger-management classes."

"They don't seem to be working very well," I said, which was the first thing I'd said to him that I'd really meant.

He laughed at that, too loudly. McKenzie quaked under

his hand. "No, they sure aren't. She's the one who killed that idiot Coach Fred. Entirely by accident. He was in her office demanding something or other and wouldn't take no for an answer. She hauled off and hit him. I was standing right outside her office. Saw the whole thing through the glass. The old guy spun around and cracked his head on her desk. Dead before he hit the ground." He laughed at the memory.

My jaw hung open slightly, mouth dry as sand. Waves of horror washed over me as my fingers itched to slap his face. Keep him talking, I reminded myself.

"What did you do?" I managed to grate out, unable to maintain the admiring tone I'd been trying to use. He didn't seem to notice.

"Oh, it was perfect for me. I saw that right away. The stupid bitch should have called for help right away, but she panicked. I helped her hide him until it was dark, then we rolled him out to the shed on one of the AV carts." He grinned at the memory. "Old guy was heavy."

"But why? Why move him?"

He looked at me with contempt. "You really are stupid, too, aren't you?"

Apparently, since I had absolutely no idea where this was going. I simply waited.

"She was terrified that she'd be found out. Which meant," he added as though explaining something to a particularly slow three-year-old, "that she had to do whatever I wanted."

Blackmail. A few things clicked into place. "The show," I said without thinking.

He nodded with satisfaction. "Now you understand. She just couldn't understand that we had to have the show ready while Michael Dupre was here. It was my chance. I knew that once he saw me perform, he'd want me for his movies, especially when he found out I'd written the script myself, too. Actor, writer, singer. I'd be on my way to Hollywood at last."

"And so you got her to agree to move the show up to September and to buy the professional costumes. And the set," I added, looking at the extravagant props, the gem-encrusted elephant towering sightlessly behind him.

"Anything I wanted," he crowed. "She could hardly refuse me, now could she? And what I wanted wasn't unreasonable, not really. She should have wanted all those things for the department anyway."

"It was very clever. A production that will never be forgotten. You will be a star." I tried to sound enthusiastic and admiring. It wasn't easy. I drew a breath and said in a bright tone, "So, look, Roland, why don't you let McKenzie come with me? I'll run her home before her parents start getting worried, and then you can tell Larry in the morning that the show is back on."

For a moment, I thought he considered it, but then he shook his head a little sadly. "No, that's just not going to work."

"But why? You've got everything under control. Michael Dupre will be here tomorrow, the show will go on, and he'll see you. Everything will be perfect."

"You're not only stupid, you think I'm stupid, too," he

said, sounding more regretful than outraged. "I know the three of you would never let that happen."

Something in his tone made my hands break out in a cold sweat. I swallowed, trying desperately to think of anything to say that would sound convincing.

At that moment the phone in my pocket rang, its cheerful little ringtone slicing through the strained silence.

Roland brought the knife back to McKenzie's throat in one swift motion. "Answer it and I'll kill her," he shouted at me.

I kept my hands where he could see them. "It's my boyfriend in Dallas," I said quickly. "He's worried because I haven't checked in with him, and he'll call the cops if he can't get hold of me. Just let me tell him I'm all right."

Roland hesitated, while the ringtone continued. Then he gave a sharp nod. "Tell him you're safe at home. If you say anything else . . ." He gave McKenzie's shoulder a painful squeeze, and the girl gave a pitiful cry.

"I won't!" I snapped open the phone. "Alan, hi," I said, hoping to God it wasn't really Alan.

Colin's voice sounded both hurt and annoyed. "It's Colin," he said.

I could feel Roland's eyes on me, could see the terror in McKenzie's face. I struggled to control my voice.

"No, I'm fine," I went on, trying desperately to sound natural. "At home, doing homework. Sorry I didn't call."

"What the . . . Are you in trouble?"

His quick comprehension filled me with gratitude.

"That's right," I said with a nod and a smile. Or as much of a smile as I could manage with frozen lips. "Look, I'm completely swamped here. Can I call you tomorrow? Okay. No, love you, too. Bye sweetie."

I closed the phone and looked at Roland. He seemed to be considering, then gave a curt nod. "That was good. Now toss it here. I don't want you trying anything."

From my position in the aisle, I was five feet below stage level and some fifteen feet back. I swung underhand and let the phone fly, intending to have it land somewhere near Roland's feet. Instead, it left my hand late and flew high and wide, whizzing past Roland's ear and landing with a thump on Nancy Wales's inert form. Specifically, in the right eye, which would have been painful if she could feel anything. And to my enormous relief, it seemed she could. Against all expectation, she stirred and gave a shuddering moan.

She was still alive.

Roland half turned, distracted by this new threat. He took a step toward Nancy, dragging McKenzie with him. I didn't know what he had in mind, but it couldn't be good. I prayed Colin would hurry, and that he would have the sense not to come with sirens blaring. In the meantime, I had to do something to distract Roland.

I took several steps closer to the stage and called his name.

He stopped. "Stay right there," he said sharply.

I stopped, holding out my hands desperately. "So Roland, how about it? Why don't you let us go home? We can sort out the play tomorrow. In fact, I'll come help you talk to Larry."

The look he gave me was colder than anything I'd ever seen before. I saw his eyes flash from me to Nancy, from Nancy to the top of McKenzie's golden head. He was considering his options. I had to distract him before he realized he had none.

Desperately, I said, "So what happened with Laura, Roland? How did you get Pat Carver involved? Or was that something entirely different?"

For a moment, I didn't think he'd heard me. Then he gave a bark of laughter and turned back to me, Nancy now forgotten. I prayed if she was conscious she would have the sense to hold still.

"Pat Carver. What a godsend."

"So why'd she kill Laura?" I asked. "Did it have something to do with the money for the show?"

He gave me a scathing look. "Do you really think Pat, Fat Pat, killed anybody? She wouldn't have the balls for it. Or the strength. It wasn't easy, you know."

A tear slid down my cheek. "No, I guess not."

"But as long as the police think she did it, everything is just fine."

"Did it have to be in the toilet, Roland?" I asked, not to keep him talking but because I needed to know.

"She walked in here and told me she was going to make sure I didn't perform. That the part of Christian should go to a student, as though a student could handle a part like that. She said it was pathetic that I should have a part in a high school play. Pathetic. Me." His voice quivered with rage. "I was perfect in the role. And Michael Dupre would have seen that."

"But Roland, Laura couldn't do anything. Nancy wouldn't have let her stop you," I said.

"Nancy wasn't here. She'd gone home with a headache."

"That doesn't matter. Laura might even have tried to talk to Larry, but she couldn't have done anything. Not really."

"She called me pathetic," he said sullenly. "She said I was a terrible actor, and she walked away from me. Like I was nothing."

His words hung heavy in the air, like a faint echo of a bad dream. I thought of how Laura and I had giggled together about Roland's ridiculous performance, of our scathing comments, of our outrage that this grown man had usurped a part in a high school theater production. Unlike me, Laura had possessed the courage to repeat those comments to his face, and now Laura was dead. Behind my paralyzing fear and sorrow, a slow rage began filling my veins.

"So you followed her out of here? And then what? Dragged her into the ladies' room? She was half your size, Roland."

For a moment he looked confused, then his face hardened. "Enough of this. Get up here on the stage. Now."

The knife pressed again into McKenzie's throat. I could see the skin turning whiter under the pressure of the long blade. Where was Colin? What if he hadn't understood me after all? Or what if he couldn't figure out where I was?

I moved as slowly as I dared, walking in front of the stage, then up the stairs on the right. Kyla's bag slipped from my shoulder and fell heavily, the strap catching in the crook of my arm. Automatically, I lifted it back into position, a gesture every woman wearing a shoulder bag performs half a dozen times a day. As I slowly mounted the stairs, I slipped my hand into the hidden pouch that Kyla had bragged about. Sure enough, the gun was held upright in a deep pocket, heavy and cold against my flesh. I slid my fingers around the grip, searching for the safety catch with my thumb.

Roland looked from me to Nancy Wales. "I think we're about to have a tragedy in three parts. Here, you come over here," he gestured at me with the knife, keeping a death grip on McKenzie.

I moved as slowly as I dared, trying to catch the girl's eye as I did so. If I could just get her to move, even to fall to the floor and give me a clear target. Unfortunately, she seemed dazed, her eyes unfocused and blank.

"Let's see, should Nancy attack you first? No, maybe you should attack. You see Nancy bending over this kid's body and you strike her. She stabs you, but you're able to wrench it out and kill her. Then you both die together before help can arrive."

I stared at him. "That's insane."

"Don't call me that!" he shouted, his voice rising suddenly to a high-pitched scream.

"No one will believe that story, Roland. You'll have to do better."

"They'll believe it. Now get over here."

I took one step closer to appease him, then stopped again. "Seriously, Roland. Why would Nancy stab one of her students?

The police will arrest you and then you'll never get to audition for Michael Dupre. You need a better story."

He hesitated, the dramatist in him considering the possibilities.

I stared again at McKenzie, willing her to read my mind. Her glazed eyes slid past my face, then suddenly returned. At last, she seemed to realize I was trying to tell her something.

I went on. "You have to let us go. This has just gone too far."

Roland blinked, then his handsome face crumpled like a child's. "It has gone too far. I'll never get to audition now. The play is canceled. There's nothing I can do."

Was he going to see reason? Maybe this thing was going to end without any further violence. Where was Colin?

His face hardened again, now with a hopeless despair, as though he had nothing left to lose. "You come over this way now," he said quietly. "You're going to sit in that chair."

I didn't like that. Looking into his eyes, I knew that he was going to kill us all.

"Let me take McKenzie home," I pleaded again.

"No. You sit down."

The hand holding the knife had stopped shaking. He'd reached a decision, and he was not going to be deterred by any words of mine.

I kept talking anyway. "Let the girl go."

"Do what I say, or I'll kill her right now," he countered.

I flashed McKenzie one frantic look. From her position on the stage floor, Nancy Wales let out a loud snorting groan that made us all jump. For an instant, the blade of the knife wavered, and McKenzie acted at last. Striking his arm away from her throat, she dropped to the floor, her sudden dead weight wrenching her loose from the hand that gripped her shoulder. Roland staggered, caught off balance.

I raised Kyla's purse and shot him in the chest.

Chapter 21

RECOUPING AND REGROUPING

Roland Wilding died on the stage he'd loved. He was dead before he hit the boards, the neat little round from the Glock stopping his heart on its way through, leaving only an expression of startled wonder in his blue eyes before the light went out of them forever. He even managed to collapse gracefully, the long wicked knife dropping from his fingers to clatter harmlessly to the floor. In all it was not the worst ending he might have expected, and if he could have done it in front of Michael Dupre, he might almost have been content.

The cavalry arrived only moments too late, Colin bursting in just ahead of a SWAT team and followed closely by a platoon of patrol officers, emergency technicians, and firemen. He'd been wonderful and wonderfully efficient, but I didn't have more than two words with him before official forces swept us apart, leaving him to handle the new unattended death and me to somehow answer for it.

The next few days passed in a mind-numbing blur of bureaucratic procedure; I probably would have spent them rotting in jail if it hadn't been for the tireless efforts of two unexpected advocates. McKenzie Mills's mother turned out to be one of the top divorce attorneys in the state. After she heard what had happened on the stage, she used every connection she had to obtain the services of a top-notch criminal defense lawyer for me. And, though it burned worse than a fat man's hemorrhoids to admit it, my ex-husband Mike Karawski came through for me and swooped in like a weasel-faced avenging angel to turn the avalanche of media coverage in my favor. I didn't even mind knowing that he did it only to protect his own reputation and to advance his tough-on-crime political platform. I spent the next two weeks on some kind of unofficial administrative suspension, at first hiding at Kyla's place to avoid the constant phone calls and media visitors, and then when the worst was past, eventually moving back home.

My own role preyed on my mind less than I feared. If I awoke crying in the middle of the night, I let my tears spill unheeded into the short black curls of my sleepy and bewildered poodle and never told another soul. In the end Roland had left me no choice at all. For McKenzie Mills, for Nancy Wales, and for myself, I'd done the best and only thing I could have done. I had to content myself with that.

The tennis kids came to visit me a week later. McKenzie Mills, bearing a huge armful of flowers, Brittany Smith carrying a box of Godiva chocolates, and Dillon Andrews and Eric Richards both looking shy and uncertain as though they'd never seen me before. I was glad to see them and told them so.

"So how is practice going?" I asked, realizing to my shame

that I hadn't given a thought to what they were doing in my absence.

Dillon rolled his eyes. "You've got to come back soon, Coach J. They've let Mr. Jones loose on us."

So Ed Jones had finally got his heart's desire, I thought, surprised at feeling an unwarranted pang of jealousy at the thought of him trying to take over my team.

"Yeah," said Eric with the expression of someone catching a whiff of dog poo. "He tried to get me to change my grip, my stance, and my racquet. He had me so messed up for a few days I couldn't hit a backhand to save my life."

Brittany chimed in, "And he's so grumpy. He's always yelling at us. We weren't even allowed to talk on the courts for the first week. You have to come back."

I was outraged on their behalf. "Have you complained to anyone about him? Maybe Principal Gonzales?"

"Eric did better than that," said Dillon with a grin, bumping Eric with his elbow.

Eric reddened and grinned at me sheepishly. "I told my dad."

"It was awesome, Coach J," said McKenzie, looking at Eric with adoring eyes, which boded well for his chances of having a date for homecoming. "Eric's dad made Mr. Jones cry."

I shouldn't have laughed, but I did.

Eric said, "The best part is that my dad went to Principal Gonzales and told him to get you back."

I was astonished. "He did?"

Four heads nodded in unison.

"He thinks you have guts," said Eric.

Dillon added, "And after that, all our parents e-mailed or called. We want you back."

I was pleased and deeply moved. "Well, I want to come back, so as soon as everything is settled, I will."

If the administration would let me, I thought glumly. I had no idea whether I would be allowed to keep my job, much less the coaching position.

Trying to shake off that thought, I asked, "So what else is going on?"

"We have a new theater teacher," said McKenzie. "She's really young and pretty, and she has a ton of new ideas. But *Moulin Rouge* was canceled. Ms. Clark says that Mr. Wilding didn't have the right to turn the movie into a play. We could actually have been in big legal trouble for performing it."

"Well, that's a shame in a way, but it's probably for the best."

"Definitely," said McKenzie with a shudder. "I don't ever want to think about that story again as long as I live."

I looked at her with concern. "I hope you won't let this sour you permanently on theater. You really do have an amazing voice, McKenzie."

She glanced down shyly, turning pink. "I didn't know you'd ever heard me."

I smiled. "I popped my head in once during a rehearsal," I said, recalling the way poor Laura had crowed with delight at the scene. "You have a serious talent. The worst thing you could do is let something like this get in your way."

"We'll see. Maybe. I don't know if I can go back in the theater."

"I'll go with you," I said, hoping that I'd be allowed to make good on that. "We'll go together."

"I'll go with you, too," offered Eric hesitantly. "If you want. If that would be okay."

"Yeah, we'll all go," said Dillon enthusiastically. "Make a party out of it. Set the demons to rest once and for all."

I was pretty sure this wasn't what Eric had in mind, but it wasn't such a bad idea. Strength in numbers, and from the look of things Eric would have plenty of opportunities to spend time alone with McKenzie. The kids stayed a little longer, chatting and devouring the contents of my snack cupboard like biblical locusts going through a wheat field. Then they were gone, leaving me feeling both cheered and oddly bereft. I wanted my job back.

I called Alan the day after the shooting and asked him to postpone his visit. He'd been reluctant, gallantly wanting to rush to my side, but he finally agreed after I told him I was planning to stay with Kyla. However, he insisted on coming the next weekend, and, like the kids, arrived bearing chocolates and flowers.

Opening the door and seeing the warm light in his eyes, I was glad I'd forced myself to make an effort for his sake, fixing my hair with care and putting on a sundress instead of my usual jeans. The sight of his face reminded me of the times we'd shared, of how nice he was, and how very good-looking. But I no longer knew what to say to him, and he must have felt the same because we greeted each other like strangers, and I found myself using the flowers as an excuse to move away from him rather than fly into his arms. He would have been an idiot not to sense it, and Alan had never been an idiot. He sat on the couch and waited for me to join him, showing no surprise at all when I took the chair opposite instead of snuggling in beside him as I once would have done.

We talked for a long while, or rather I talked, telling him about all that had happened as far as I knew it, up to and including my current legal woes and status in limbo.

I ended by saying, "I honestly don't know what will happen next. So far, my lawyer doesn't think they will prosecute me, but I don't have confirmation of that. And I don't know what's going to happen with my job. It might be that they're just waiting to see whether the charges are dropped or not, or they might be trying to figure out how best to fire me. I just don't know."

He sighed, leaning forward on the couch, arms resting on his knees, hands clasped almost as though in prayer.

"Would you be hurt if I told you that I almost wish they would let you go?" he asked.

"Why?" I asked, taken aback and indeed feeling somewhat hurt.

He lifted his eyes to mine at last, a flash of green from beneath long lashes. "Because then you might consider coming to Dallas," he said simply.

My lips parted but I could think of nothing to say.

"With me. I want you to come to Dallas and live with me. We could even get married," he offered, then quickly added, "or not. Whatever you want. However you want to work it. Live near me, live with me, marry me. Whatever you want to do. I don't want to lose you, Jocelyn."

The last sentence was almost a cry, more heartfelt than he could have intended, but though he paled, he continued to hold my gaze.

"Alan," I started, but he quickly held up a hand.

"Don't say no. Just think about it. I know things haven't been that great the last few months, but it's the distance, not us."

At least I knew he'd been feeling the strain, too. "Alan, I . . ."

He cut me off again. "Really, don't say no."

I managed a small laugh at that.

"We need more time. I need more time," I amended. "And you know I can't just pick up and move to Dallas, any more than you can move down here."

"Fine, so we'll do better. I'll come every weekend, and we'll talk more in between. We can arrange a trip together, maybe over your Christmas break, anywhere you want. Anywhere in the world. London, Paris, Tahiti, you name it."

I finally felt a grin tugging at the corners of my mouth. "You're trying to bribe me."

His answering smile lit up his face. "Exactly! Like I said, whatever it takes."

He leaned across the coffee table, reaching for my hand. After a small hesitation, I reached back, all too aware of his warm presence. He rose, pulling me to my feet, then stepped around the table, moving close to me. His eyes darkened to emerald as he reached up to touch my cheek.

In a spectacular display of bad timing, the doorbell rang.

Alan and I froze, listening in disbelief, only inches from each other's arms and embrace. I looked past his shoulder to the window, and Alan caressed my hair, gently trying to turn my head and attention back to him. The doorbell rang again, followed by insistent knocking.

With a sigh and an apologetic look, I disengaged myself. Alan said something under his breath that I didn't quite catch, which was probably just as well. He ran a hand through his chestnut hair, then turned, hands on hips, glaring at the door.

I opened it with a jerk, drawing breath to tell whoever it was to go away, and met the cool blue eyes of Colin Gallagher. He was dressed in his familiar detective clothes—tan slacks, maroon pressed shirt, and tie—but the look he gave me was that of a stranger. I could feel the disapproval flowing off him like an icy wind off a glacier.

As I gaped, he said, "Can I come in?" and pushed past me without waiting for an answer.

"Sure," I managed, and at least had the presence of mind to close the door. I was definitely going to have to work on my thinking-on-my-feet skills.

Colin faced Alan, stance wide, paper sack in one hand, the other hand on his hip, perilously close to where his gun rested heavy and black in its holster next to his badge. Frowning at this, I wondered if he knew how intimidating he looked, before it dawned on me that was his intention. I turned a disapproving stare on him, then realized neither one of them was paying any attention to me at all.

"Stratton," Colin said, by way of acknowledging Alan's presence.

"Still around?" Alan asked. "I thought the case was surely wrapped up by now."

"Just a few loose ends to tie up with your girlfriend here."

"Yes, my girlfriend here has had a very difficult time of it. You probably should have called before dropping by."

I wondered if either of them would notice if I just slipped out the front door and left them to their chest pounding.

I said, "Why don't you both just sit down? I'll pour us some iced tea. Or would you rather have a Coke?"

I walked between them, but I wasn't tall enough to make them break eye contact. They continued to glare at each other over my head.

"I'm sure the officer won't be staying long enough to need a drink," said Alan.

"I'd take a tea," responded Colin. "Sweet. Please," he added belatedly.

"I know," I said and flinched at the hurt look in Alan's eye.

Then I felt annoyed. It was hardly a betrayal to know that another man drank sweet tea. I hoped I wasn't going to have to knock their heads together like coconuts.

"Both of you, sit down and behave like gentlemen," I said, the exact words and tone my grandmother had used so often on my brothers popping out without thought.

By the time I returned with the glasses, they had at least withdrawn to opposite sides of the coffee table, although they were perching on the edge of their seats like sprinters on starting blocks. I handed Alan a glass of plain tea, then passed Colin a glass in which the sugar still whirled in little clouds beneath the ice cubes.

Colin accepted the glass, then thrust the brown sack he'd been carrying toward me. "Here, this is for you."

I took it with a questioning look, feeling its weight, then opened it cautiously. Inside was Coach Fred's little wooden clock, the key still in the keyhole in the miniature drawer beneath the face. Drawing it out, I turned it to read again the little brass plate on the back with its inscription of friendship and farewell.

Fred Argus,
You'll make a hell of a teacher.
Congratulations from your friends at Tracor.
We'll miss you.

He had made a hell of a teacher, and I missed him more than I could say.

"What's this for?" I asked.

"Mrs. Argus asked me to give it to you," said Colin. "She said she thought you might like to have something of her husband's."

I nodded, my throat tightening a little. She was right. I would treasure it.

Colin went on. "You should be hearing from your lawyer any minute. All charges are dismissed. Self-defense and defense of a child—they could hardly try to prosecute you for those. They'd look like idiots. You'll probably get a stiffly worded warning about carrying a gun on school property."

The relief was enormous. With a little whoop of delight,

I gave him a blinding smile and jumped up, wanting to dance around. Both men half rose as well. I quickly sat back down.

"Don't get up," I said, gesturing for them to sit, then adding, "Just think, now neither one of you will have to bake me a cake with a file in it."

"I'm guessing that means your job is safe, too," said Colin, his easy drawl returning as his face relaxed into a wintry smile at my small joke. "A friend of mine at one of the news stations says the school district is getting a flood of e-mails from parents, about ninety percent in your favor."

I wasn't as sure about my job as he was. "That might be good or it might not. I doubt the administration is all that pleased with the publicity. The sooner this is swept under the rug, the better."

"Oh, it will be. Pat Carver is being arraigned Monday on embezzlement charges. With the budget shortfalls in the headlines, her case is going to make everyone forget about you, especially when the amount is made public."

"How much did she take?" I asked.

"They're still investigating, but at this point, the running count is over half a million dollars."

My jaw dropped. "You're kidding me. How in the world?"

"She's been at it for a long time, and she apparently is exceptionally clever. She kept money moving around constantly, so it wasn't easy to see when a little fell through the cracks and into her own pocket. Still, the scandal will keep the press and the school board too busy to worry about you. Oh yeah, and she's the one who trashed your house, although I don't think they'll prosecute her for that. She's cooperating fully, so I imagine that will be one of the things they throw out."

I was outraged. "What! They should nail her to the wall for that. All my stuff! And for what? What could she possibly have had against me?"

"She was at Coach Fred's funeral and saw Mrs. Argus give you the envelope," said Colin. "Coach Fred had approached her about the discrepancies in the tennis team funds. He'd become suspicious for some reason and had obtained copies of receipts and payments that didn't match what she'd reported. His death was a gift from heaven for her. Then, when she saw the envelope, she figured that you were now the enemy. She had no way of knowing that Coach Fred was giving her the benefit of the doubt and hadn't actually told you anything, but she did think that if she could get those receipts and replace them with her doctored copies, then she would be able to 'prove' to you that Coach Fred had been mistaken."

"So, trashing my house was going to get me on her side?"

"Not exactly. She heard at the school that you'd been in an accident and were in the hospital, so she had a window of opportunity. She decided to break in to substitute the papers, and she was going to make it look like a burglary to cover her tracks. When she couldn't find what she was looking for, she took out her frustration. I doubt the destruction was part of the original plan."

"That cow. I hope she gets a life sentence." I fumed for a long moment, then thought of something else. "So was she funneling money into the drama department? I still can't figure out how they were paying for the set and costumes."

Colin snorted. "No way. In fact, the theater expenditures were causing Pat a lot of anxiety—she definitely didn't want anyone noticing and looking closely at the books. But she never spent a penny of the money she stole for herself as far as we can tell. It's another reason she was able to continue for so long. Most embezzlers start living beyond their legitimate means. She saved it all, and it may reduce her prison time since it sounds like she'll be able to repay it. No, the drama budget came out of Nancy Wales's retirement fund."

I hadn't expected that. "Really? Why would she use her own money?"

"Blackmail. She says Roland Wilding threatened to turn her in for the murder of Coach Fred unless she did what he wanted for the play, and that included the first-class sets as well as letting him play the lead."

I tried to absorb this. "I don't understand why she didn't just call 911 when Fred died."

"A bunch of reasons. She'd been taking anger-management classes and thought that would count against her, but basically she just panicked. Then Roland seized the opportunity and helped her hide the body in the tennis shed. You were right about the joints—they weren't Fred's. Roland planted them. He told Nancy they could make it look like a drug deal gone bad."

"I knew it!" I said with triumph.

Alan chimed in, interested in spite of the source. "What else did she say? Did he really do it all just to perform in front of that director, what's his name?"

"Michael Dupre. And yeah, if you can believe it, that's

what this whole thing has been about. Dupre has a reputation for discovering talent in unexpected places and making stars, and Roland Wilding wanted to be a star more than anything in the world. He was very bitter about his failure as an actor in New York and thought he'd never been given a fair break. When he found out Michael Dupre would be filming at the school, he decided he would try to get Dupre's attention.

"It's a long way from that to murder, though," said Alan doubtfully.

"That was never part of his plan, if he even had one at the start. Nancy's accidentally killing Coach Fred just fell into his lap. It gave him a hold over her, and he jumped on it to get his way about everything to do with the play. Without that, she would never have let him write the script or take the lead role. Also, she would never have paid for the set and costumes, which he thought were critical. He believed that only an over-the-top production would get Dupre into the theater."

I shook my head at my own stupidity. "I completely misread what was happening. I thought she must have a monumental crush on him and was doing it all to get him into the sack."

"That's my little cynic," said Alan, with an affectionate twinkle.

Colin gave him a sour stare at the possessive, then turned pointedly back to me. "Anyway, things started going south in a hurry. First, you turned up and forced them to cut back on the practice schedule, which from his point of view was catastrophic. The play had to be perfect, and they only had a couple of weeks before the film crew would be leaving. Then, you managed to swoop in and steal the extras roles from him."

"I didn't swoop," I protested.

"From his point of view, you swooped, and according to Nancy, it was eating him alive. The day at the park, he left the rehearsal and drove to the location with some vague idea that your kids wouldn't be any good, and he would be there to offer the services of trained actors. It was your bad luck that he was turned away at the main entrance and decided to sneak around through the woods. When he saw you talking on your phone with your back to the path, he attacked."

I shivered, remembering the violence and rage. "He must have been insane."

Colin shook his head. "Everyone says that when a criminal does something they don't understand. I disagree. He wanted something, and he did whatever it took to get what he wanted. You were in his way. He decided to remove you. It's a miracle he didn't finish the job. That's not insanity. That's pure evil."

Now both men were looking my way, Alan with deep sympathy in his eyes, Colin . . . well, Colin's expression was unreadable.

"And Laura? Was she in his way, too?"

"Nancy Wales says she didn't know anything about that. In the technical sense, she's probably telling the truth, but I think she knew Roland was to blame the minute she heard about the death. What we do know is that Ms. Esperanza—Laura—spent most of the evening on the phone, calling school board members and other district officials. According to them, she was outraged that a teacher was performing in a student play, although she also accused Nancy of mismanagement of department funds and violation of the rules surrounding extracurricular activities. It took a while, but she finally got them to agree to step in. All the calls were from her cell phone, so we can't be sure where she was when she made them, but we do know she made her last call at about eight o'clock. Her husband was working the night shift, so there was no one waiting for her, and she probably wasn't in any hurry to get home to an empty house. My guess is that she stayed at school to make the calls from her classroom, then couldn't resist the urge to stop by the theater on her way out."

I buried my face in my hands, feeling sick.

Alan's phone rang, its cheerful little melody a welcome interruption. Alan reached to silence it, but frowned as he glanced at the caller ID.

"It's my assistant, who knows not to call me this weekend unless it's an emergency. I probably should take it," he said apologetically.

"Yes, absolutely. You can go in my room if you need some privacy," I said.

He nodded, but instead of going to my room, he crossed through to the kitchen and out the sliding door to the back porch.

We sat in silence for a long moment, Colin's eyes on Alan, mine on him.

"How do you do it?" I asked him at last. It was something I'd been wondering about a lot lately. "Dealing with death and murder every day. I don't know how you bear it."

He rose and moved to the seat Alan had just vacated, leaning forward to take one of my hands in both of his. His touch was warm and unexpectedly comforting.

"It's not always like this, you know. For one thing I'm not usually emotionally involved with any of the suspects," he added, the corner of his mouth twitching into a wry grin.

"I was never a suspect," I protested.

"That's what you think. Although yes, I admit, I ruled you out pretty quickly."

He looked into my face, his blue eyes serious and intense. I was too aware of his touch, of the wave in the lock of hair resting on his forehead, of the long line of his jaw and set of his broad shoulders. I knew I should get up or at least lean away, but I couldn't move.

He went on. "My job helps people, people who find themselves in the worst situation of their lives. They need answers and my job is putting together the pieces of the puzzle for them. What exactly happened to my brother, my wife, my child? Was it an accident or suicide? If it's a case a murder, then it's trying to catch the murderer, to achieve some kind of justice. I won't lie—it can be damn hard at times, but it's important. And I love it."

He said the last almost in a tone of surprise, as though he'd never thought of it that way before.

His words and enthusiasm provided a new view of what he did, and my respect and liking for him increased. I wished I could separate that from the inconvenient attraction that also increased with each moment that I spent so near to him. I could actually feel the heat rising off my own skin.

"Jocelyn . . ."

"Colin . . ."

We spoke at the same time, then stopped. I tried to withdraw my hand. He tightened his clasp.

"Don't," he said, voice still quiet but urgent. "Don't say anything. I just want a chance with you. We haven't known each other long, but you can't say there isn't something between us. I don't want to let that go."

"But," I started, glancing toward the back door where Alan was now pacing back and forth, immersed in his phone call.

"I don't care." Colin cut me off again. "I don't care about him. I don't care who you're dating or who you were married to. I just don't care. I want you to give me a chance."

"You don't even know me," I whispered.

"I do. I know you're smart, you're funny, and you're kind. I know you're an amazing teacher, that your kids love you and would do anything for you. You're loyal to your friends, without reservation. And I know you're brave, stupidly brave, but God help me, I love that about you."

Slowly, as though afraid a sudden movement would startle me, he raised a hand to caress my cheek, then gently slid it under the fall of my hair to cup the nape of my neck. The warmth of his touch flowed downward through my whole body in a tide of desire. My lips parted, but no words came out.

He went on hoarsely. "Then there's this, whatever it is, between us."

I sat motionless, feeling, not thinking, for far too long. Then with a wrench, I came back to myself and jumped to my feet, almost knocking my chair over in the process. It rocked on its legs before settling back to the floor.

"No!" I said. "That's not . . . that doesn't matter."

He rose and stepped forward, now only inches from me.

I could feel the heat radiating from his body. Or was it from my own?

"It matters to me."

It mattered to me as well, not only for itself—and it was marvelous—but because of what I was afraid it meant about . . . well, everything. I wanted Colin Gallagher like I'd never wanted a man, but I'd been dating Alan for six months and I cared about him, too. And whether or not Colin was right about knowing me, I didn't really know him. Not the everyday stuff, the stuff that mattered in a relationship. Plus, Alan was standing in my backyard, and I was one tattered shred of willpower from throwing myself into Colin's arms and pulling him to my living room floor. All of which meant there was something deeply wrong with me. Surely I was not that woman, a woman who would sneak around behind a boyfriend's back, who would turn to a second man less than an hour after the first had proposed. A small annoying voice told me I might be, but I squashed it. I was not that woman, I told myself firmly. Really.

I stepped away from him, putting the chair between us, my fingers clutching the upholstery hard enough to leave impressions.

"More tea?" I asked brightly and too loudly and because I couldn't come up with anything else to say.

The hurt in Colin's eyes was harder to bear than the desire had been.

The sound of the sliding door made us both turn our heads. Alan returned, looking warily from me to Colin, taking note of the chair and of my white face.

"Sorry about that," he said to me, although his eyes were

again on Colin. "Riots have broken out in Cairo again, and I've got a tour group there. I don't think they're in danger at the Mena House, but, understandably, they're panicking and demanding to come home. If things don't calm down in the next few hours, I'll need to arrange an evacuation."

"Easier to do that from your office, don't you think?" asked Colin. "Dallas, right?"

"Shouldn't you be getting back to the station or wherever it is that you hang out?"

They glared at each other, Colin stepping past me away from the furniture and Alan turning to face him. To my disbelief, they looked like they were actually squaring off for a fight.

"Enough!" I said sharply.

They turned to me in surprise. I swear they'd both forgotten I was there.

"I mean it. Enough. I can't do this."

They still stared at me blankly. I collected my thoughts and made a lightning decision.

"Both of you need to go," I told them.

"What?" asked Alan in disbelief.

"No!" protested Colin at the same time.

"Yes. Both of you. I need some time. We all need some time. As of right now, I'm not dating either one of you. There, I've said it."

Alan looked stunned, Colin hopeful. At least they were now looking at me and not each other, which was a small improvement.

"But . . ." Alan started.

I cut him off. "Dating is supposed to be a fun way to get

to know another person. You and I haven't been doing so well with the fun or the knowing. "I've been expecting the Dear Jocelyn call for the past six weeks—way before I met Colin."

Alan flinched, but I could tell my words came as no surprise. He was smart. He'd known as well as I that we were in trouble.

I continued, "Right now, I'm so confused I don't know what I want. Everything in my life is teetering on the edge. My friends are dead, my job is on the line, and I don't want to make any decisions. I can't. It's possible that I'd like to spend more time with each of you and get to know you better. If you're not okay with that, and I honestly don't know why you would be, I completely understand. But that's all I can do. And either way, you both should leave now. And . . . I don't want to hear from you for two weeks. Let's give ourselves some time to think things over. Then, if you still want to, you can call me."

They didn't like it, they protested, but they were both good men, and finally they left. Grudgingly, it's true, and with a number of daggerlike glares for each other, but go they did. I watched until both cars rolled away in opposite directions, then I quietly closed my front door and carried the glasses back to the kitchen. Without the two men, my little house seemed big and empty and hollow, much like the aching hole that had somehow materialized in the center of my chest. I couldn't decide whether to cry or break things, so I stood motionless until at last I was able to hear the carton of Blue Bell cookie dough ice cream softly call my name.

• • •

A week and a half later, Kyla arrived at my house to pick me up. We were going to Stubb's Bar-B-Que for dinner and then on to the Alamo Drafthouse theater for a Monty Python quote-along. She'd been trying to get me out of the house for days, and this suggestion finally worked. I'd actually found myself looking forward to it. Besides, I'd reached the stage of rearranging furniture and thought it was high time I found another distraction.

Kyla stood in my living room, hands on hips, purse slung over her shoulder, looking around at the new layout. The insurance check had finally arrived, and I'd been able to repay her for the things she had purchased for me, which I felt good about. Now though, I found myself eyeing her purse with great suspicion.

"New purse?" I asked, eyes narrowed.

She gave a wide grin. "Yup. They would have honored my guaranty but I would have needed to send them the old purse, and I decided I'd rather keep it as a souvenir. This one is a different model. Cute, huh?"

"It's a very nice purse," I said stiffly. "What's in it?"

She assumed the innocent expression of a Botticelli angel. "Makeup, wallet, keys. You know, the usual."

I did indeed know, but once again decided not to pursue it. After all, in the end it had saved my neck.

I told her, "Hey, it's finally official. I'm being reinstated. I start back in the classroom on Monday."

"Finally! They took their sweet time about it."

"Yeah, well, I was still on the payroll, so I can't complain too much. But I'll definitely be glad to get back." I picked up my keys from the little hook by the door. "You ready to go?"

"Yeah. So did you really tell those boys not to call you for two weeks?"

"I did."

She shook her head doubtfully. "You might have lost them both, and then I know you'd be sorry. Although I'm still not sure about which one." She gave me a searching look.

I shrugged, trying to look mysterious. She didn't need to know that I wasn't sure either.

Kyla counted on her fingers. "Wednesday, Thursday . . . so what, they've got about three more days? I wonder if they'll call."

We looked around at the dozen vases and bowls of every shape and size filling my counters, each overflowing with flowers in a brilliant mix of scents and colors and each bearing a florist's tag signed with one of two names. Kyla grinned at me, and I couldn't help smiling back.

"I wonder." I said.